PURSUIT IN CY...

The pursuer s... ... ...
vision—a vast pale beast hurtling upward, its
mouth a deep red chasm wide enough to engulf
mountains.

In a moment it would be upon him. Would that
be the end not only of his Matrix existence, but
his real life as well?

Bashir fled with all his strength and still the
leviathan drew nearer. He could feel the coldness
of its negative energy. He could see the rings of
deeper red pulsing through its crimson interior.
Despite his fear, or perhaps because of it, Bashir
couldn't keep from staring into his approaching
doom.

Without warning, a shock ran through his
system. His vision blurred. Had it reached him
already?

No! It was his probes' interface!

Disconnect!

Bashir's thought command created a black wall
between himself and the Forbidden Files defender.
He felt himself fade from computer-awareness...

➤   ➤

THE PLANET BEYOND

uncomplicated. *If only I could be back there,* she thought. In

ALSO BY STEVE MUDD

TANGLED WEBS

Published by
POPULAR LIBRARY

THE PLANET BEYOND

STEVE MUDD

POPULAR LIBRARY

An Imprint of Warner Books, Inc.

A Warner Communications Company

I would like to dedicate this book and,
belatedly, *Tangled Webs*,
to Mom, Carol, and Maureen,
without whom many things
would never have happened,
including my first two books.

Alyssa sat next to her brother on the carved stone bench. She stared north across the smooth surface of Sapphire Lake.

By day its waters were an impossibly vivid blue, justifying the name the Founders had given it. But now, with the sun long set and small silvery Yakimu yet to rise, the lake was an obsidian mirror. It reflected coldly the lights of Home from the far shore, and the greenish Wellglow that spread for some two kilometers to the east of the city.

Maybe the Draths are right after all, she thought bitterly. Since the Founding, the Draths had lived apart from the Wells. Over the centuries, their settlement northeast of Home had grown into the vast empire of Toria—a theocracy governed by the Drath Hierarch.

What had begun as a matter of principle had become in time a matter of faith with the Draths. They shunned the Wells and the advanced technology of Home, and imposed that same restriction on all of Toria.

Maybe the price is too high.

She glanced at Darrin. Dark-skinned, slender, with black eyes and long black hair, he was silhouetted sharply against the white flowers of a nearby sheenwood tree. Darrin could have been her twin, though he was actually ten years older than she. Alyssa blinked back the dampness in her eyes and studied again the dark waters of the lake.

She hated feeling this helpless, especially with so much at stake. The love she and Darrin felt for each other ran deep, but not deep enough to overcome their differences. Not this time. ·

"You don't have to leave Home, Darrin." Alyssa didn't really think she could change her brother's mind. Still, she had to try one last time. She might never see him again.

"Don't I?" His voice was as soft and warm as the still night air.

"That wasn't part of the Assembly's decree." She spoke without looking at him, afraid of what he would say, willing him to say something else.

At last he shifted a little and touched her hand. "Alyssa, what other choice do I have? You've seen what happens to Transgressors who remain."

"I know," she whispered. Barred from the Wells, aging, embittered, Transgressors were eventually shunned even by those who had loved them. Suicide or banishment was the usual end to their lives. But it needn't happen to her older brother! She tried in vain to hold back her tears.

Darrin put his arm around her and held her tightly. The faint sweet aroma of the sheenwood blossoms touched her with memories of summers long past, of childhood games, of Darrin's patience with his little sister, his warm smile.

"It's not fair," she sobbed. "There are plenty of unfilled Welltime slots. You wouldn't have been depriving anybody."

"That's not the point, Lyss. Those places have always been reserved for emergencies. Only the Assembly can grant access to them."

Her childhood name, meant to comfort, only made her sense of loss more poignant.

"Emergencies?" She looked at him fiercely. "Founders' folly! There hasn't been an emergency on Seelzar since the colony ship landed here."

There had been thirteen hundred years of peace and growth. It was only two hundred years ago that the Advisory Panel had suggested, the Executors had requested, and the Assembly had declared that some places at the Wells be reserved for "emergencies."

Alyssa wanted to shout, scream, shatter Darrin's calm acceptance of his fate.

"Now, now, Lyss." He gave her shoulder a squeeze. "They decided openly and each Assembly in turn has concurred. They have their reasons."

Alyssa twisted away from her brother and stared angrily toward the lights of Home. "Reasons? Oldsters' fears and fantasies! We're as secure now as ever. Bribing off-world collaborators with Wellplaces doesn't reduce the risk of exposure to the Interstellar Union—it creates such a risk where none existed."

Darrin sighed. "We've argued this out too often already. It's all beside the point."

"No, it's . . ."

"Please, Alyssa. I've accepted the decision. Why can't you? I wouldn't have stayed in the Wellglow anyway, without Tashiki. Maybe it was stupid trying to forge an entry disk for her, but I knew the consequences. I would have preferred to share our lifespan with her. Failing that, I'm content to live with her people on their terms."

Stupid? It was crazy! Alyssa fought to contain her frustration. He hadn't even *tried* to get Wellstatus for Tashiki, and now he wasn't putting up even a token fight against the Assembly's decree.

Darrin reached over and turned Alyssa's face toward him, gently, firmly. "I love you, little sister. Leaving you hurts already. But we can still keep in touch with one another— that's what the commnet is for." He smiled crookedly. "I don't want you to forget me, but please don't remember me with bitterness and anger."

Alyssa forced a smile of her own. "You know I could never be angry with you, Darrin—even when we were kids. I'm not about to start now."

They both stood, trying to find a graceful way to part.

"Well," Alyssa began, looking up at her slightly taller brother.

His glance fell to the ground. "Well, take care of yourself, Lyss," he said in a hoarse whisper.

A light breeze came up, blowing from the north, from across the lake. It seemed to blow Darrin along as he turned and walked slowly down the path that headed east, then south, away from Home.

"Good-bye," Alyssa said quietly, almost to herself.

A shower of sheenwood blossoms fell from the overhanging branches, drifted across the path, and Darrin was gone.

Alyssa stood there, near the bench by the lake, for a long time. The breeze died down. Yakimu rose in the east and added her silvery crescent to the reflections on the lake's black surface.

On the far shore, the city of Home thrust its towers and domes into the night sky. The first settlement on Seelzar, it was still the planet's largest city. Over ninety percent of the Wellborn lived there continuously, with the rest returning regularly for their stays in the Glow. Alyssa and Darrin had been born in the Glow and had lived in the city for their entire lives, 130 years in Darrin's case. One hundred thirty years he was giving up without a fight. One hundred thirty years erased by the Assembly without a voice being raised in opposition.

It's for the good of all, they had said.

It's the law, Darrin had agreed.

Not just strangers, but friends of over a century had done this to him. And why? Out of fear? Rigidity? Up till now, Alyssa had assumed that the system was good, that the Wellborn's laws were just. Now she wasn't so sure. What price had they paid for their security and their longevity?

Alyssa brushed a white blossom off her shoulder and turned toward the path leading back to the city. Maybe Darrin had accepted the Assembly's decision, but she hadn't. There was someone she had to talk to, discreetly and soon.

If there was anything she could do within the system to bring Darrin back, she was going to do it. If there wasn't, she might have to take matters into her own hands. Maybe the system would have to be changed.

— **2** —

The brown fog was closing in on M'Briti again. Already it was so thick that much of her peripheral vision was gone.

From within the fog, menacing shapes reached for her. She saw them vaguely, just at the limits of her vision. She senses them behind her.

She felt again for the small packet of brownish purple powder. Yes, it was still in her pocket. If she used it now, the fog would retreat, but only for a short while. She forced her hand to leave the packet where it was and to rest beside her on the bench.

She would get her own supply soon.

The shed's single light panel cast a pale blue glow that did nothing to push back the brown fog. It did little more to dispel the natural darkness of her meeting place.

The light had not been recharged in years. That's why she'd chosen this building—it was abandoned, its contents forgotten. The small windowless cube was almost buried under the remains of a larger building that had been partially demolished, then left to rot.

Someone moved outside the shed. It was a cautious step, but in this place at this time of night it sounded loud indeed. M'Briti's nerves sang. She slid her hand over to grip her stunner and pressed herself farther into the shadowed corner.

"M'Briti?" a man's voice whispered. It was Sanders. M'Briti relaxed, but she still held the stunner.

"Yes. Come in. Quickly." She kept her eyes on the door to her right. It was the only entrance. The hinged panel directly behind her only opened from the inside. The panel was a nice touch. She wondered who had put it there.

Sanders slipped in and closed the door behind him. He was a tall, well-proportioned man with smoothly handsome features. He would have been a commanding presence except for his eyes. There was a subtle weakness in them that M'Briti had learned to recognize and play upon.

Now the weakness was masked by simple fear as Sanders stared around the dim, crate-strewn shed, his back to the door. He was wearing a dark, hooded cloak that looked Torian. It didn't hide his plyfab boots, obviously from Home.

M'Briti shook her head. "The latch, please." She put some sting in her voice and was rewarded by Sanders's small jump before he turned and threw the door's heavy bolt. She wondered who'd put that in too.

"This won't keep the security people out for long."

M'Briti eyed him suspiciously. "Are we expecting them?"

Sanders ventured a nervous smile. "No, but a surprise visit would be just as bad."

"Worse. Fortunately, they don't patrol around here." M'Briti stood slowly. She pocketed the stunner, but kept her hand in that pocket. "This is officially Annex territory, and even the Normals don't think it's worth guarding." She beckoned him toward the rear of the shed. "Relax. We're safer here than in our own mods."

"I hope you're right." Sanders sounded half-convinced as he made his way through the scattered wood and plastic crates.

"Of course I am," M'Briti said in her most reassuring manner. She was less than two-thirds his size, but she had no doubt who was the stronger of the two.

They sat down beside each other on the dusty bench. Close, but not too close. She had kept their relationship just short of intimate. She needed his trust, and she'd done the minimum necessary to get it.

Whatever it takes, M'Briti had vowed to herself over a year ago, when it had all begun. *I'll do whatever it takes.* Even so, she would prostitute herself for one of these weaklings only as a last resort.

"You have it?" His voice had still not risen above a whisper.

She nodded and set the small gray packet between them.

Sanders looked at it for a moment. "And is there, uh, I didn't bring . . ."

"Right here," M'Briti interrupted to cover his embarrassment. In her hand she held a short black pipe with a spiral stem and a deep narrow bowl. "It's self-igniting," she explained as she opened the gray packet and poured its contents into the bowl. "Just squeeze here and inhale." She offered him the pipe.

He held the pipe gingerly between his thumb and forefinger. "And you're sure you won't take any creds for this?"

"No, no." She shook her head and smiled. "I'm not in this for the money. I just thought it would do you some good. If you like it, I can put you in touch with my supplier, and the two of you can work out some arrangement."

When he still looked dubious, she gave his hand a gentle nudge. "Go ahead. You'll never know unless you try it." *And then it will be too late,* she added to herself.

"Well," Sanders swallowed nervously. "I suppose that's true enough." He put the pipe to his lips and inhaled, squeezing the bowl tightly. The powder caught in a quick flash, then settled down into a steady smolder.

"You don't have to breathe deeply," M'Briti cautioned when he choked on a lungful of smoke. "Take it in through your mouth and exhale through your nose."

He took another drag, not quite as clumsy as the first. Already the drug was taking effect. M'Briti could tell by Sanders's wide-eyed stare and the startled expression freezing into place on his face. Soon, she knew, his voluntary muscles would be completely paralyzed. He would sit on the bench, black pipe held immovably between his lips, and breathe in the Purple until it was gone. He would be dead to the world, lost in whatever heaven the drug sent him to.

What a waste. She couldn't help breathing some of the smoke Sanders was not drawing in. *Still, he'll probably get better with practice.*

And there would surely be plenty of practice. Few people gave up Purple Heaven once they'd tried it. From what she'd seen and heard, for most the craving just got worse and worse.

M'Briti Ubu did not include herself among those. She was no addict. Sure she smoked Purple, but she didn't have the Wells anymore. Besides, she had reasons entirely her own. What excuse did Sanders have? He was weak, and he needed something to replace the Glow between Welltimes. Just like the others she'd hooked.

Smoke curled thickly around Sanders's head, but he didn't even blink.

M'Briti stood and began wandering around the shed. Her fog seemed to be getting thicker, the movements within it more distinct. The ceiling light only created deeper shadows within the general dimness. It was hard to tell what was stored in the bulky crates lying everywhere. Not that M'Briti cared. She just wanted something to take her mind off that enticing smoke Sanders was letting slip away.

Clutching some of her loose sleeve material, M'Briti rubbed away the thick dust from the top of a crate. Her first swipe revealed a long, meaningless serial number. She rubbed off more of the dust and an item description appeared. It was a nearly antique battery-powered engine.

"These *have* been here a long time," she muttered. When she uncovered the crate's destination, her eyebrows rose in surprise.

"Ebelton? No wonder these were abandoned!" The Draths were adamant about keeping technological innovations out of Toria. M'Briti wondered what fool of a trader or merchant had thought he could ship electrical engines into Ebelton—one of Toria's district capitals. Even old machines like these were far too advanced for the Drath theocrats. At least now the door bolt and rear exit made sense.

Thank the Founders we're not like that, she thought, with only the slightest twinge at the pronoun. The Executors may have barred her from the Wells, but she was still one of the Wellborn. As her parents had been, and her brother.

So she'd tried to tamper with the last Assembly selection—so what? Raising the odds for two applicants wasn't going to bring Home to ruin. Her two might have come up by chance anyway.

M'Briti's transgression had harmed no one personally, but it had struck at the heart of Home's system of government. Her attempt to penetrate the selection program had been unsophisticated, and the Matrix monitors had detected it almost immediately. She had been surprised at how easy it had been to get banned from the Wells.

A *thump* from the back of the shed broke in on M'Briti's thoughts. She turned to see Sanders lying on his side on the bench. The expression on his face had not changed, and he still puffed away on the pipe, which had miraculously not spilled when he'd fallen.

M'Briti shook her head. She'd never seen anyone affected so strongly by the first dose of Purple. It confirmed her theory that the weaker a person's psyche, the more susceptible he was to the drug.

She had a long wait ahead of her before he came back from his drug heaven, but she wasn't about to complain. Sanders was hooked, and she was sure that he would go into the "credits" column with her supplier. That should earn her enough Purple to last two or three months, at least. Soon, she might even merit recognition from someone higher in the distribution chain. She had to hope so. If not, the price she and others had paid would be unbearable.

She sat down on the floor, resting her back against one of the crates of contraband. *Might as well catch a few hours of sleep,* she told herself. She had long since cultivated a third ear that woke her at the slightest unusual sound. One of the tools of her new trade, along with the stunner.

M'Briti shifted her position to take the pressure off her left shoulder. The scar was nearly gone now, but the pain still flared up on occasion, especially when she was tired.

As always, the burning ache brought her back to that dark night almost one year ago. There had been three of them—two Normals and a long-banned Transgressor. M'Briti had just begun dealing Purple, and they had thought to make an easy hit on the new kid.

One of the Normals' half-meter slip blades had sliced deep into M'Briti's shoulder before she'd realized what was happening. But she had just come from her last Welltime. She was quick and strong and she'd adjusted quickly. Her responding kick had crushed the Normal's chest. Her other two attackers had escaped with their lives, barely.

Since then, she had never completely relaxed. No one else had openly challenged her, but she couldn't afford to let down her guard for a second. She pulled out her stunner and set it on the floor, her right hand resting on its grip.

M'Briti set her internal clock for two hours. By then, Sanders ought to be on his way back to reality. She would explain how her supplier would contact him, and they could part company.

She began to feel drowsy, and she let her eyes close, shutting out the blue light from the ceiling. In the blackness behind her eyelids, the brown fog still lurked, spreading, thickening. It would be gone soon enough, she knew. She hoped the threatening shadows would go with it.

— **3** —

Among the throng of Normals, Alyssa stood out like a flameleaf tree on a grassy plain. It wasn't her height, though she was tall for a woman. It wasn't her clothes—the silk-weave blouse, loose-fitting pants, and black jakhide boots were common enough attire in the Annex. It was just that she was Wellborn.

The men might admire her dark beauty, but she was a physical match for any three of them. She lived in the Glow of the Wells, and somehow it showed. People tended to give her room.

At the moment, she was crossing a street, drawn by a particularly appetizing aroma. Its source was a cart tended by a short, bald man whose garish robe did nothing to disguise his rotund body.

"Bozad pies! Hotandspicy bozad pies!" the round street vendor shouted in the sibilant accent of the Draths.

Probably a new arrival from the southern Borderlands of Toria, Alyssa guessed. The Draths controlled Toria, but their religious influence was marginal in the south. A true believer would not have entered Home or the Annex except under the most extreme circumstances. Selling bozad pies hardly qualified, even if they were the specialty of Torian cuisine.

"How much for two?" she asked the sweating fellow as she leaned closer to be heard above the midday din. The Trading Annex was always busy, but its streets resembled a mob scene from late morning to early afternoon.

"Two?" The Torian vendor smiled a wide, gold-capped grin. "For such a lovely lady, a mere seven creds."

"Seven?" Alyssa frowned slightly. "I believe I purchased a pie two days ago for only two creds." She paused as if in thought. "Yes, two creds, from a skinny man with a long red beard." In the Annex, it was bad form not to haggle at least a little.

The vendor's blue eyes opened wide. His smile disappeared. "And you did not succumb to intestinal distress? It is a wonder!" He lowered his voice minutely in a way that suggested but did not achieve confidentiality. "Horkam Jorani's pies are scandalous, an abomination! Dear lady, you should not consider putting yourself at their mercy. I shudder to contemplate the substances enclosed therein."

Alyssa smiled a puzzled smile. "Indeed? Good vendor, they seemed tasty enough to me, and I have clearly survived the experience."

The man spread his pudgy hands palms up and shrugged. "Ah, you are obviously of stronger constitution than most, and more merciful in your judgments." He brought his hands together in a prayerlike pose. "For such a worthy person, Qatar Bulbulian will provide two pies for the minuscule price of six creds."

"Hmmm." Alyssa considered. Not to bargain was considered rude by the populace of the Trading Annex—merchants, craftsmen, beggars, and thieves alike. However, she had already met the minimum expectations with Bulbulian the pie vendor, and she didn't want to be late for her meeting with Bashir.

"Six creds?" She nodded to the round Torian. "Very well, though it makes me a fool and you a thief."

Bulbulian's smile reappeared. "Not at all, not at all." He quickly pulled two stuffed pastries out of his warming cart and wrapped them in insulpaper. "Tastier pies at a better price are not to be found." He pocketed Alyssa's coins and handed her the pies. Before she had turned away, he was calling again, "Bozad pies! Hotandspicy bozad pies!"

"I could have talked him down to five," Alyssa muttered as she hurried down the street. To be fair, she admitted, the meaty pies smelled delicious, much better than the one she'd bought from the red-bearded Jorani. If the taste of

Bulbulian's pies matched their aroma, the man was an artist of Torian cookery.

Cradling the pies close to her in both hands, Alyssa strode quickly through the crowds, moving toward the dingier northern edge of the Annex. The buildings here were lower, the streets narrower and bordering on filthy.

Home was a city of elegant simplicity. Cylindrical towers rose high above steep-sided domes, all predominantly in white and shades of blue. Older, blocky buildings from the time of the Founding huddled in the center of the city, surrounded by a strip of parkland. Wide streets radiated out from that central hub in gentle spiral curves.

Home's boundaries were the Wellfield to the east, Sapphire Lake to the south, the spaceport and industrial plants to the west, and the Trading Annex to the north.

An architectural purist Alyssa once knew had viewed the Annex as a malignant growth on the side of the perfect city. It faced Home across a wide east-west street. On one side, the simple curves and clean blues and whites of the Wellborn. On the other side, the ornately carved stone and multihued glassalloy of the Torians, the Free Staters, and the other Normals on Seelzar.

In general, the Wellborn saw the Annex as a necessary meeting ground between themselves and the rest of Seelzar's inhabitants. It was a place where knowledge, goods, insults, and creds could be freely exchanged with people who would probably never set foot inside Home.

Most of the inhabitants of the Annex, transient or permanent, lived by the law of supply and demand, their primary ethical standard being What You Can Get Away With. To them, the Annex was their chance to take a few creds from each other and to fleece the affluent but gullible Wellborn.

Alyssa thought of the Annex as an excellent place to discuss matters better kept away from the attention of the Assembly and the Executors. The authorities of Home could have controlled the Annex, but they'd decided centuries ago that it would be more bother than it was worth. Alyssa was glad they had seen things that way.

Stepping carefully down narrow alleys and hurrying along the twisting back streets, Alyssa finally reached her destination. It was a small shop indistinguishable from others in the area except perhaps that it was even less imposing. The gray walls were layered with graffiti and faded posters. The lone window was so dusty that nothing but vague shapes could be seen within. The weatherbeaten sign above the door had not seen a coat of paint in at least fifty years. The door itself—a warped rectangle of rockwood on hinges—stood slightly ajar.

Alyssa caught the edge of the door with her foot and pried it open. The dry hinges squealed as she entered the shop.

"Bashir?" Her voice called down swirls of dust from high shelves and rafters, and sent insects scurrying into dark, cluttered corners. The sunlight shining through the open doorway illuminated little—it merely made the shadows darker by contrast.

"Come, come, Bashir! It's Alyssa!" *Really*, she complained to herself. *Just because I'm a few minutes late. He can be so petty*. She balanced both pies in one hand and pulled the door closed with the other. It was not easy. A Normal would have had to strain to move it at all.

Her eyes adapted quickly to the now-uniform gloom. Shelves lined the walls from floor to ceiling, not even stopping for the window. There was little apparent order to the place. The shelves were crammed with thousands of objects, new and old, familiar and mysterious. A cheap solar converter sat next to a priceless sculpture by Dragurahm. A pair of Freelander hiking boots shared a shelf with what looked like a Builders' artifact, a knobby green ellipsoid on a short tripod. One low shelf was filled with obsolete data disks and an antique processing unit.

Larger items covered the shop's floor, leaving barely enough room to walk between them. A two-seater gravcycle minus power pack leaned against the shelves to Alyssa's right. In the middle of the room, a stuffed rakeclaw reared up on its four rear legs and tail, snarling at the window and reaching out with its front pair of legs, ten-centimeter claws unsheathed. Bashir had told her once that its name was Achmar.

Alyssa shook her head. Bashir certainly had an eclectic taste in merchandise, matched only by his apparent lack of interest in attracting customers. Speaking of Bashir, where was the old—?

"My young friend, are you going to stand there the whole day, gaping while those pies become cold?"

She jumped just a little and nearly dropped one of the pastries. The sharp, thin voice came from Alyssa's left. She turned and saw a small man sitting atop a Drath ceremonial altar. He was dark-skinned, bald, with a long gray and black beard. The large semiprecious fleckstone on which he perched was carved in the likeness of the Blessed Victoria herself, and must have been worth a small fortune. Not to mention the life of whoever had removed it from its temple.

Bashir Arak hopped down from the altar and came over to Alyssa. "They smell delicious." He smiled a very white smile and appropriated one of the pies. "Come. Let us go into the back room, where we can enjoy them away from the watchful gaze of Victoria and Achmar."

Alyssa nodded and grinned in acknowledgment of Bashir's little joke. Victoria Knebel Eldrath had been one of the Founders of Seelzar. Achmar Z'areikh was another. As far as she knew, Bashir had not yet acquired a suitable namesake for the third Founder, Masanaru Senyan.

She had seen holos of the Founders, and she'd noticed a remarkable resemblance between Bashir and Z'areikh. With a smile, she wondered at the significance of calling the rakeclaw "Achmar."

Bashir led the way to the back of the dim shop, behind a counter with an abacus and a moneybox on its otherwise clear top. A narrow door slid aside at his approach, and Alyssa followed him into the room beyond. The door closed silently and solidly behind her.

They were in another world. The room was brightly lighted by a pinkish white glow from the ceiling and walls. Adaptapods rose from several places in the floor, waiting to turn into tables, chairs, benches, or whatever else was needed. There were no windows, but four large holoplates, one for each wall, connected the room to various points of Seelzar. At the moment, all four showed mountain forest scenes that Alyssa guessed were from eastern Freeland.

"Here, this will do nicely. A round table and two swivel chairs," said Bashir, walking over to three pods clustered near the middle of the room. As the pods began flowing into the proper configurations, he snapped his fingers at a fourth, larger pod. "And a chilled bottle of Torian brindleberry wine, with two glasses." The pod quivered for a moment, then a slot opened in its side and the desired items slid out.

"Very nice, Bashir." Alyssa smiled as she sat in one of the newly formed chairs. Even the air smelled like the Freeland spicetree forests. "Your hospitality is exceeded only by your good taste."

"Thank you, my dear," Bashir replied, pouring the wine. He sat opposite her and took a sip of the tan liquid, rolling it on his tongue before swallowing. "Eleven hundred twelve. A good year, isn't it?" He unwrapped his pie and took a healthy bite. "Mmm," he mumbled, trying to chew and talk at the same time. "Excellent. Bulbulian's, right?"

Alyssa had just unwrapped her own pie as Bashir was finishing his second mouthful. She looked over at him sharply. "Yes. Bulbulian. How did you know?"

He dismissed the matter with a wave of his hand. "It was nothing. Bulbulian is the only vendor in the Annex who makes pies this authentic and yet wraps them in paper rather than tiano leaves." He took a large drink of wine and cast a shrewd glance at Alyssa. "I've made it my business to know things. For instance, unless I am grossly mistaken, you've come here about Darrin."

When Alyssa didn't deny it, Bashir continued, "What I don't know is, exactly what you want me to do." His dark eyes glittered, holding her gaze as he took another bite from his pie.

"I don't know." Alyssa looked down at her wine glass. "I mean, I don't know what, if anything, can be done." She waved her hand aimlessly. "Oh, Bashir! I just can't see Darrin exiled so pointlessly. There must be some way to bring him back."

"And you want to know if an old reprobate like me has any tricks up his sleeve."

"You make it sound so stupid." If Bashir was going to laugh at her, she would find help elsewhere, somehow.

"Sorry. I didn't mean to." He gestured to Alyssa's pie. "If you don't eat that, I'm going to. So take a bite, then tell me what you've done so far."

"Well, I . . ."

"Eat!"

Alyssa rolled her eyes but did as she was told. Bashir's pie was gone, and hers was disappearing fast, when he spoke again.

"You haven't spoken to anyone yet?"

She shook her head. The spicetrees on the walls around her swayed in a distant gentle breeze.

He nodded. "Smart move. As far as the Assembly is concerned, you've accepted their decision?"

"I think so. Unless Darrin talked to somebody. We had quite an argument about it."

"I can imagine." Bashir sighed. "Will he come back if the Assembly allows it?"

"He will if Tashiki can come with him. Otherwise, no." For the thousandth time, Alyssa wondered why her brother had had to fall in love with a Normal. And so secretly, too. Even a respected authority on Builder artifacts like Tashiki Fotheringham had little chance of being granted Wellstatus. Darrin *must* have realized that.

"I suspected as much. If he felt any other way, this problem would not have arisen in the first place." Bashir refilled his glass and added some to Alyssa's. His dark forehead creased in thought. "I'll have to begin with the Matrix, I suppose. We'll see what turns up."

"The Matrix? How will you get clearance for that?" As far as Alyssa knew, only the Executors were able to grant access to Home's massive quasi-organic computer. All the Matrix's operations were painstakingly monitored, and any unauthorized use was immediately terminated, with such intruders liable to severe sanctions. Bashir Arak had for years opted out of Home's establishment—hardly the sort of person to meet with the Executors' approval.

"I won't exactly get clearance. Let's just say I do have access to it." Bashir's tone discouraged further pursuit of the matter.

"Ah. Well then, is there anything I can do?" It felt like a lame question. This was her problem, not Bashir's.

The old man shook his head. The room's pink light glinted off his shiny scalp. "Not at the moment. I may discover tomorrow what our options are, or it may take me several days." He reached across the table and patted Alyssa's hand. "Don't worry. I'll let you know as soon as I find out how we can help Darrin and Tashiki."

Don't you mean "if," Alyssa had been about to say, but she found Bashir's confidence to be contagious. He wouldn't sound so hopeful if he didn't truly believe there was a chance that they could bring her brother back. "I can't help worrying, Bashir." She gave his hand a squeeze. "But I know you'll come up with something."

"Of course I will." Bashir leaned back in his chair and smiled broadly. "That's what wise old men are for. Now, finish your wine and tell me what you've been up to lately. Besides taking on all the authorities in Home, that is."

Alyssa laughed. Bashir always made her feel good, no matter what problems she burdened him with.

She brought him up-to-date on her work with gravity-field projection and described her much less successful attempts to master the boneharp.

Bashir in turn talked about his latest expedition to search for Builders' sites in the Northern Wastes and passed on some gossip about the Drath Hierarch that he'd heard from a Free States trader who'd picked it up from a Torian merchant whose wife's cousin had a friend who served in the Court at Ebel.

An hour later, Alyssa was leaving the small dusty shop. Outside, the sunlight and shadows seemed more intense. The streets were hot and nearly deserted. Alyssa waved good-bye and headed back toward Home. She walked slowly, feeling the heat soak through her body, savoring the warmth.

For as long as Alyssa could remember, Bashir had lived out here in the Annex, one of the few Wellborn not to reside in Home itself. A friend of her father's, and possibly her grandfather's, he'd been around forever, it seemed.

Bashir Arak was iconoclastic, very private, and unusually well informed about events throughout Seelzar. Alyssa knew little about him, but of one thing she was certain: If anyone would be able and willing to get Darrin readmitted to the Wells, it would be Bashir.

Bashir returned Alyssa's wave. He stood in his doorway, watching her walk away until she disappeared around the corner of a ramshackle building. She looked so strong, so beautiful. *So like her great-grandmother,* he thought. Arak blinked twice and stepped back into his shadowy shop. He pulled the warped door tightly shut. Dust sifted slowly down through the dim light from the window.

He sighed with the weight of old memories and old regrets.

"Enough," he said out loud. "There's work to be done." Entering the Matrix was not going to be easy, and it could be dangerous. He would have to plan carefully and be well-rested for the attempt. He turned, made his way carefully through the clutter of his shop, and reentered his pink-lighted sanctum. The door closed behind him.

One of the adaptapods turned into a couch as he lay back against it. Another produced a second bottle of wine and a glass. The first ones had already been absorbed and recycled, along with the pie wrappers.

Bashir was not nearly as confident of success as he'd led Alyssa to believe. He'd probably have to go deeper into the Matrix than he'd gone before, and even then there was no guarantee of finding a solution to Alyssa's problem.

A breeze rustled the branches of the trees on the walls around him. A brightbeak chirped lustily from somewhere off to his left. He opened the bottle and poured himself a glass of mellow brindleberry wine.

How much are you willing to pay to get him back, Alyssa? Arak wondered. The brightbeak was joined in chorus by another. *And what if he chooses not to return?*

— 4 —

Executor Niala Kirowa sat at the round table in the center of the meeting room, wondering for the hundredth time why she had accepted her nomination as Executor.

Masanaru Senyan, sitting on her left, handed her a sheaf of papers. She glanced through it quickly and saw that it was nothing new—just the agenda for the day's meeting and a few items for future consideration that she'd seen a week ago.

Niala passed the sheaf on to Marguerite Venebles, on her right, who didn't even bother to look at it.

"Let's get on with it, Executor," Venebles said to Senyan.

Sunlight poured through the room's wide eastern archway. A warm breeze ruffled Niala's short dark hair. She wished she could be outside, doing something tangibly useful, rather than sitting at this table, mediating between the other two Executors.

Senyan and Venebles were as dissimilar as two respectable Wellborn could be.

Masanaru Senyan was a powerfully built, stocky man, shorter than the average. His complexion was a dark yellow-brown, his hair black and cut very short. He was 140 years old, average for an Executor, but he was in his seventh consecutive term, a length of service few had ever matched. He traced his lineage directly back to one of Seelzar's three Founders, whose name he bore.

In Niala's opinion, Senyan's lineage plus his unusually long term in office went far toward explaining his conservatism and his arrogance. Even when he seemed to be trying, he had a difficult time understanding new ideas, let alone accepting them.

Marguerite Venebles was a full head taller than Senyan, very thin, with long white hair and piercing blue eyes. At seventy-five years of age, she was one of the youngest Executors ever. Her parents had been Normals—Free Staters who had been granted Wellstatus because of their outstanding work in biosynthetics.

In contrast to Senyan, Venebles was one of the most radical Executors in recent memory. Moreover, in electing Venebles, the Assembly had removed Joshua M'Bato, a long-time friend and confidant of Senyan's.

"Get on with it?" Senyan echoed mockingly. "Very well. Here's a matter we can settle quickly enough." He touched his tabletop control panel and an image appeared before the three Executors. "Darrin Montoya. Charged with attempting to gain Well access for an unauthorized Normal."

Standing in the center of the table was the holo of a tall, handsome, black-haired young man. Floating just beneath the surface of the table in front of each Executor was the man's life story and the description of his crime.

"Executor Venebles." Senyan stared through Montoya's image at the junior Executor. "You placed this item on our agenda, I believe. Is there really anything to discuss?"

Venebles picked up the sheaf of papers Senyan had distributed and slapped them on the table. "The Assembly wants Montoya banned from the Wells, and we haven't even heard Montoya's side of the case."

The truth of this case was not at all obvious to Niala. "Any idea why Montoya refused to speak in his own defense before the Assembly?" She hoped her question would give the other Executors time to calm down a little, to back away from a confrontation. Preserving the peace at these meetings was always a strain.

"Probably," Venebles answered, glaring at Senyan, "because the more conservative members of the Assembly rushed the matter through so quickly he didn't have time to prepare an adequate defense."

Senyan spoke, his voice deep and gravelly. "The case is perfectly clear. Montoya violated the law of his own free will and with full knowledge of the consequences. There is nothing debatable about it.''

"Are you then so perfect?" Venebles asked, stressing the pronoun.

Venebles's words hovered in the room, taunting Senyan.

Niala could hear a small flock of birds outside, flitting about the garden. Inside, the silence lengthened.

"Are you intimating anything in particular?" Senyan's voice was calm, but Niala could see the man's posture straighten minutely, his jaw tighten just so. He controlled his anger well, but to Niala's trained eyes, he hid it not at all.

"Well..." Venebles seemed to consider the possibility, then shook her head. "Of course not. Just that we're all human and we all make mistakes."

"But we don't all break the law."

"Oh, for Founders' sake!" Venebles ran one hand through her hair and looked toward the room's high white ceiling. "It's not as if he did it for himself, is it? Besides, his actions would have harmed no one, even if he had succeeded."

"That is irrelevant!" Senyan's thick hands pressed down on the translucent milk-white tabletop. He looked as if he were about to leap to his feet. "The law is the law. If we make this exception, where will we stop?" He leaned back in his chair and presented his clinching argument. "In any case, there has been no appeal. We have no authority to intervene."

Venebles stared at Senyan, her blue eyes hard, unyielding. "As Executors, we have any authority not expressly forbidden us or delegated elsewhere. As human beings, we have the obligation..."

Niala felt her headache begin. It grew rapidly, seeming to spread out even into her close-cut brown hair. Senyan and Venebles had been at odds ever since Venebles had taken office over four years ago. While the two usually managed to remain civil, they seldom agreed about anything.

"Executors, please!" Niala could see that neither was going to give a centimeter at this stage of the argument. "The Assembly ruled on Darrin Montoya's case only yesterday. Whether we act on it, and how, need not be decided this moment. I suggest we reserve judgment until our next regular meeting. That will give us all an opportunity to consider the case more fully." She kept her voice calm, despite the throbbing ache centered at the base of her skull.

Niala was the smallest of the three Executors, the most soft-spoken, and only in her second term, yet Venebles and Senyan both tended to respect her judgment. Or at least they appeared to. She wanted to believe it was because she was forty years older than Senyan, and the others recognized the wisdom her experience had given her. She suspected, however, that the main reason was that she usually held the deciding vote between Senyan and Venebles.

Senyan inclined his head in a half nod toward Niala. "I agree. This is a matter we can reasonably postpone for the moment. Executor?" he asked, looking at Venebles.

Venebles smiled coolly. "If that is what you wish. We certainly don't want to hasten to a mistake with a man's life at issue."

"And the welfare of all Home's citizens," Senyan replied, mirroring her smile. He waved his hand over the table and Montoya's image disappeared, as did the files displayed before each Executor.

"Excellent." Niala felt some of the tension ease from her. Darrin Montoya's fate was not something she was at all ready to decide. On the one hand, Senyan was right—Wellspace was limited, and there were only a few unassigned places left. Attempts to gain unauthorized access threatened the physical basis of Home's Wellborn population.

On the other hand, Montoya's case was puzzling. Instead of seeking legal Well access for his lover, which might have been granted, he'd tried an illicit technique that had had virtually no chance of success. And he'd made no appeal at all, no plea for leniency. It was almost as if he'd wanted to be caught and banished from the Wells.

Niala wondered whether she should do a little investigating on her own, to see if she could make sense of Montoya's behavior.

"Well, then." Senyan cleared his throat. "The other item of business today is routine—a status review of our operations in Sector Seven of the Interstellar Union." Another wave of his hand brought up a star map in three dimensions. A piece of deep space floated black and cold in the bright warm room. Seelzar's sun was a small green dot at one edge, near the base of a large rough cone of red stars. Only a few pale white stars separated the two.

"Routine?" Venebles raised her eyebrows in an expression of exaggerated surprise. "Please spare us your jokes."

Here we go again, Niala thought with annoyance. *If a rakeclaw were leaping at them they'd argue about which way to run.*

"Routine," Senyan raised his voice, "in the sense that no new developments have arisen. We've all seen the latest reports. Our plans are proceeding as intended."

The tabletop displays filled with coded summaries from each of Home's agents in the Sector. Urtloew, Chou, Rythmun . . . The list scrolled over onto a second page. Each agent's history and reports could be called up in detail, but only by the Executors or with their approval.

"Skulking and hiding hardly constitutes a plan!"

Niala looked up from reading the data display. "Is that truly all you think we've been doing?" Venebles wasn't stupid. She couldn't possibly believe that. "What about Urtloew's success with Selius?" She touched that portion of the coded summaries and Urtloew's report replaced the star chart, scrolling slowly enough so that anyone who wanted to could read it. "A Planetary Overseer is hardly a trivial ally."

"Granted." Venebles turned to Niala, less challenge in her expression. "Agent Urtloew deserves a great deal of credit for his painstaking work in cultivating Overseer Selius as an ally. But it is not individual agents I am referring to. It's Home and, by extension, Seelzar as a whole that is at fault. Instead of acting while there is still time, we cringe out here just beyond the Union's reach, hoping that they'll leave us alone."

"In addition to recruiting disaffected Union officials, we are also supplying some of the planetary resistance movements. Selius's planet, Bekh-Nar, is receiving such aid, I believe." Niala spoke in a conciliatory tone, not wishing to appear to take sides.

"Of course." Venebles nodded her agreement. "But that is still a largely passive role."

"And you would have us do exactly what?" Senyan cut in, though they all knew Venebles's answer.

"Fight, of course," she snapped. "If we can't defeat them, we can at the very least discourage them."

Agent Urtloew's report continued to flow along unheeded in midair, in the midst of the Executors.

Senyan nodded slowly, as if giving Venebles's idea careful consideration. "So. Let's see what that strategy looks like."

He ran his hand over the display in front of him, touching it in three or four places. Urtloew's report vanished, replaced by another star map, similar to the one he'd first called up, but on a larger scale. Now an irregular sphere of over three hundred red star systems dwarfed Seelzar's tiny green dot. A dozen yellow dots among the red indicated planets in the Union where Seelzaran agents were operating.

The sun no longer shone through the room's eastern archway. Even though it was nearly noon, the room seemed dimmer to Niala. Almost, she could feel the chill of deep space flowing from the star map, and from its implications.

"The two million of us Wellborn in Home versus the billions on the Union's hundreds of planets. The numbers do not seem to be on our side, Executor." Senyan said this in a tone of mild surprise, pretending that he had just now learned a disappointing truth.

Niala did not smile.

Venebles slammed her hands down on the tabletop, causing the stars to swirl, blur, and then disappear. "And the numbers are more against us for every day we put off acting. The longer we wait, the stronger and more numerous the Union's forces become. And," she added, frowning at Senyan, "we still won't allow Normals to be an active part of our own defense forces."

"The longer we wait, the better prepared we will be to meet the Union." Senyan tapped his finger on the table to emphasize his points. "Our ships will be faster, our weapons will be more powerful, our forces will be larger, and our understanding of the enemy will be greater."

"I know, I know," Venebles said, looking away impatiently. "We've all heard that argument before. An excellent rationalization for cowardice, I'd say."

"Now wait a ..." Senyan didn't try to disguise his anger this time.

"And in the meantime," Venebles continued, "all it takes is for one of our agents to be captured and the element of surprise is lost."

The comment stung Niala. Twenty years before, she had nearly been captured by Operatives of the Central Council when she and her son, another agent, had contacted Adjudicator Phillips. It had happened on a planet on the fringes of the Union. Her son had died there. Venebles's verbal attack on agents brought the incident back more painfully than Niala would have expected.

"Our agents," Niala said coldly, "have done very well so far. You've read their reports. We have no reason to believe that any of them are in any danger of discovery."

Venebles, apparently realizing the personal relevance of her attack for Niala, reached out tentatively toward the former agent. "Please forgive me. I have only the greatest respect for our agents. But we have given them an impossible task."

"Difficult, yes," Senyan interjected, "but they *are* making progress."

"Oh? I suppose you'd point to agent Urtloew as an example?" Venebles called up a projection of the agents' summaries. "A fine man, to be sure, but recruiting Overseer Selius is unlikely to aid our cause. You did notice that she's being tried before Sector Seven's Triune for treason, didn't you?"

"A charge unrelated to her association with us."

Venebles shook her head and looked scornfully at Senyan. "That's not the point. If she's found guilty, Urtloew's efforts were wasted."

Senyan stood and pounded his fist on the table. "And agent Chou is in an excellent position to defend Selius in that trial. With a cover, I might add, that she has maintained flawlessly for years."

Niala gave no outward sign, but she found herself substantially in agreement with Senyan on this point. After all, she herself had recruited Adjudicator Phillips to Seelzar's side, and he would be sitting in judgment of Selius.

"Even if she's acquitted, her influence is likely to be severely diminished." Venebles held up her hand to forestall interruption. "And in any case, Sector authorities exert little or no influence on the rate and manner of expansion. The Central Council sets that policy, and we can't hope to come close to influencing them."

Senyan sat down again. "That's your interpretation."

"It's obvious. Read their history."

"You're obviously in the minority on this question, Executor." Senyan had his anger back under control. The argument had returned to more secure ground. "Our policy was set well over a century ago, before you were born. It has been reconfirmed by votes of the Assembly, Executors, and Advisors ever since. The facts have not changed over the decades, nor have the strategic considerations. We have always been vastly outnumbered by the Union's forces. Our best hope lies in deflecting their exploration and colonization away from us, and in moderating their militant stance regarding worlds they encounter. Most authorities believe that Sector officials can exert such influence, over time."

"Time we may not have, Executor." Venebles stood up and glared down at Senyan. "You showed us the star charts. You saw how close they are."

Niala reached across the table and touched Venebles's sleeve. "We all share your concern, of course. And yet what alternatives do we have? To launch an all-out attack on as many Union military bases as we can? The only guarantee then is death and destruction on both sides. And if such a strike isn't sufficiently thorough, we'll be at the Union's mercy, with little reason for them to grant us any."

Niala stopped talking. She had just stated the obvious, but it was clear that Venebles wasn't convinced. Niala hadn't expected her to be.

Senyan spoke up with supporting facts from the latest report, calling up a stream of images from the table's holojector. Venebles responded, and the argument wound down to its inevitable conclusion, back where it had started.

It was all very frustrating and very tiring. Senyan and Venebles were intelligent, capable people, but they seemed almost to relish these combative discussions, despite the fact that neither was going to persuade the other.

Not for the first time, Niala wished she could shed her Executor's role and become an agent again. She'd operated in the Union for twenty years. Twenty years during which the risks had been immediate and tangible, as had the rewards. She'd felt alive then. Now, she wasn't sure how she felt.

The meeting adjourned four hours after it had begun, with several administrative matters having been decided, but no significant change in basic policies or positions.

Niala left the meeting room and walked out into the bright early-afternoon sunshine, through the wide garden surrounding the Executors' building. She could hear the honey birds whistling among the flowering shrubs.

Why, she asked herself, *did I ever accept the nomination and election as Executor in the first place, and why did I stay on for a second term?* She'd asked, but she already knew the answers.

Initially she'd seen it as an opportunity to bring her firsthand experience to bear on discussions of policy toward the Union, and to moderate the conservatism of Senyan and M'Bato. Now she saw herself as a necessary mediator between Senyan and Venebles. It was important, as long as those two were Executors, to have a third member who was the ally of neither and who could not be easily swayed to one side or the other.

Unchallenged, Senyan would tend to move Home toward social intolerance and legal inflexibility, just as Venebles would try to push the Assembly into an unreasonably aggressive strategy toward the Interstellar Union.

Niala scuffed her foot in the white sand of the path and shook her head. *And I'm the bulwark of sanity for Home and for Seelzar. Amazing.*

She looked up into the cloudless blue sky, so clear, so uncomplicated. *If only I could be back there,* she thought. In that moment, despite the dangers and despite what being an agent had cost her, she envied agent Chou with all her heart.

— **5** —

Alyssa did not go directly back to her living mod after leaving Bashir Arak's shop. Instead, she wandered through the Trading Annex. She felt a vague reluctance to return home, to reenter the system she was trying to fight. The tenuous confidence she had borrowed from Bashir was melting away in the hot dry streets, the bright sun exposing her doubts.

The Annex, so full of activity and diversion just a few hours ago, now seemed devoid of life. Alyssa made a game of looking for distractions, anything to take her mind off her brother's plight.

What will Bashir find in the Matrix?

Forget that—try to guess what those interesting odors are. Her nose tingled with the herb-rich cooking aromas wafting down from a second-story window.

Why did Darrin have to fall in love with a Normal?

Who knows? Follow this street to see where it leads. She turned down a narrow alley that twisted like a drunken worm between dingy buildings. It deposited her on a street very much like the one she had just left.

What am I going to do if Bashir fails?

Worry about that later—where is that odd music coming from? Around the corner to her right, a young girl was playing a bulbflute, accompanied by an old man on a double lapdrum.

How can I stand by and watch Darrin age and die?

Alyssa was losing the game.

In desperation, she stepped into a nearby shop. Perhaps some human contact would ease her fears, a little haggling halt her spiraling anxieties.

The shop was well lighted but cool, with large awnings shading the open windows and door. Dozens of hand-woven cloaks lined the walls and hung from the ceiling. The cloaks were a rainbow in fabric. Fires burned in them, grasses waved, rivers flowed. Mountain snows sparkled, midnight shadows danced across desert sands.

Alyssa moved in among them, drawn by their beauty. She touched their tight weave, marveled at their colors. Their patterns were primitive, bold, vital.

From the back of the shop, a high-pitched rusty voice called out, "Anybody there?"

Alyssa pushed through the last row of cloaks and stopped short. There, sitting at a low table piled high with the brilliant garments, was a shriveled husk of a woman. Her hair was thin and white, her skin gray. She was sorting the cloaks slowly. Her sticklike arms looked barely up to the task.

The wizened shopkeeper looked up from her stool and grinned. Half her teeth seemed to be missing. "Good day, young miss. Welcome to Jihan's Weavery."

"Uh, thank you." *Young miss? I'm probably over thirty years her senior.*

"Interested in a new cloak?" The woman struggled to her feet, using the table for support. Her spine was so curved that she had to twist sideways to look up at Alyssa.

"No, just looking." *Without the Wells, I'd have been like her decades ago.*

"Genuine herdersweave, missy. All the way from northern Toria." The old woman patted the cloth in front of her. "Keep the heat out in summer and the cold in winter."

Alyssa shook her head. "They are well made, but I don't need one at the moment."

"A girl can always use new clothes. Just let old Jihan show you one." She fumbled through the cloaks lying on her table, finally pulling out an intricately patterned garment in yellow and blue. "Here it is. Looks right good on ye, missy. Dazzle the young men." Jihan's eyes were pleading.

Alyssa looked at the woman's shaking hand, her rheumy eyes. She was old for a Normal, but she probably wouldn't live to see one hundred. How long would Darrin survive apart from the Wells? How long would it take him to reach Jihan's condition?

"Maybe some other time," Alyssa said softly, backing away.

"Just try it on, young miss." Jihan held the cloak out toward Alyssa. "Perhaps we can deal."

"No, really." Alyssa turned toward the doorway, suddenly unable to breathe in the old woman's presence. She ran from the shop.

Jihan's voice followed her. "Best prices in the Annex!" It was a thin voice and faded quickly with distance. "Best prices south of Toria!"

The hot, empty streets echoed with Alyssa's footsteps. Her heart pounded. Her breath came in gasps.

Get a grip on yourself.

She slowed.

Bashir will think of something.

She wiped the sweat from her eyes and looked around to get her bearings. This intersection did look familiar. If she weren't mistaken, just around that corner . . . Yes, there it was: The Wurgle's Retreat.

The sign was in metallic yellow on black. Below it hung a holopict of a wurgle in its characteristic defensive posture, head and upper body buried in the sand, sharp-spined posterior facing the world.

Alyssa shaded her eyes as she squinted at the sign.

Just what I need.

The Retreat was not the most elegant bar in the Annex, but it served the best mixed drink on the planet—the Nosedive. Alyssa took a short flight of steps down to the bar's sunken entrance. The door hissed open at her approach. Sounds of music and conversation trickled out. A cool draft touched her cheek. She went in.

Several hours and several Nosedives later she staggered home.

"Never again," she mumbled, her head already beginning to throb. "Not without a detox pill." The sun had set,

Yakimu had just risen, and the familiar streets of Home had become a dim maze.

The intersections all looked the same—fuzzy yellow glow strips and blurred street signs. The upper levels of many buildings were lighted, where people were still at work or had begun to play. The lower levels of most of the city's towers and domes were dark and silent. They all looked alike.

Alyssa avoided the few people who were out and about, not wishing to embarrass them or herself. It took a *lot* of alcohol to make one of the Wellborn suffer as she was suffering now. It took an equal amount of stupidity to drink so much without a supply of detox pills on hand.

The Nosedives in her stomach rumbled a warning. Alyssa clutched desperately at the admittance post of a nearby dome. A brief but intense battle of wills followed. The Nosedives won. They escaped to the sidewalk, narrowly missing her boots.

Alyssa took a few deep, shaky breaths and straightened slowly. She was mortified, but felt steadier and more clear-headed than before. As unobtrusively as she could, she checked to see if anyone had witnessed her defeat. All she saw were three small sanibots already busily vacuuming up the mess at her feet.

With the crisis past, the world began to make more sense to Alyssa. Streets became straighter, signs became more legible. Her head pounding with each step, she found her way back to her residential tower. Smoothly, silently, its pedramp spiraled her up the wide central shaft toward her living module.

The flowing, unstepped pedramps formed a double helix twisting around the tower's open central shaft. One strand flowed up, one down, with a wide landing at each floor. A low retaining wall topped by a smooth metal railing was all that kept riders from falling over the edge.

Alyssa had never heard of anyone falling from the pedramps. Their surface was not slippery, they moved at a moderate pace, and the Wellborn tended to have good balance and quick reflexes. Still, she stayed away from the edge. It was a long way down.

Most of the tower's eight thousand residents had retired for the night. Alyssa passed the thirtieth floor without seeing or hearing a soul.

She looked across the shaft at the down-flowing ramp. It was empty. She didn't look down.

As far as Alyssa could tell, she was alone in the building's dim core. It began ten stories below ground and rose eighty stories above street level. The walls were of sound-absorbent tiles, which made the place comfortably peaceful during the day. At night, the effect was not so pleasant.

Alyssa had lived in the tower for thirty-five years, but she had never gotten used to its close silence late at night. The air pressed in on her. Her heart pounded in her ears. She was afraid to breathe. Her present drunkenness only exaggerated her fears. It took a conscious effort to maintain her balance on the silently moving pedramp.

Something, her mind whispered. *Something is coming up behind you.* She fought the urge to turn around.

Something is lurking around the bend just ahead of you. She concentrated on the smooth flow of the ramp, let it carry her upward.

What are you afraid of? she demanded of herself. Only residents and approved visitors were allowed in the building.

She heard a muffled sound. Somebody giggling? It was hard to tell. In the stillness, sounds died quickly.

Calm down, Alyssa. You're imagining things. She believed that, but she held her breath and listened even more intently.

She passed the fifty-sixth floor. Only two more to go and she would be home.

There it was again! Louder, closer. Someone giggling. On the ramp ahead? On one of the landings? She strained her eyes and ears, turned her head from side to side, but couldn't be sure where the sound came from.

Alyssa crouched slightly, ready to spring away from who or whatever might be waiting. Her knees were shaking.

She reached the fifty-seventh floor. Nothing here. No one on the landing. Or was there, farther back?

Suddenly a shadow loomed up at the edge of the landing. The giggling rose to a cracked, insane laughter.

"The lights! Oh, lovely lady, the lights!" A skeletal figure rushed out at her, its face a hideous grinning mask.

Alyssa fell backward, jamming her shoulder hard into the retaining wall. A scream caught in her throat.

The figure stumbled past her. A clawlike hand just grazed her cheek as she fell. Was it a man? A woman? Its features were so distorted, its body so wasted, she couldn't tell.

The creature's momentum carried it to the edge of the pedramp and over the retaining wall. Its hand caught briefly on the rail, then it fell. It seemed to fall forever, and its laughter never ceased. That was the one thing Alyssa would never forget—the wild laughter went on and on.

By the time she was able to pull herself to her feet, the ramp had carried her several stories higher. She stepped off at the next landing and hit the security alarm. It was probably unnecessary, she realized. Already the lights had come up to daylight intensity. Residents were stepping out of their mods in curiosity or alarm.

If the manic laughter hadn't alerted security, if some other resident hadn't notified them, surely the impact of the body sixty stories down had done so.

Alyssa shuddered and sank to the floor of the landing.

The investigators arrived in a matter of minutes. They took Alyssa's statement and confirmed her suspicions—the victim had been a resident of the tower, and a Purple Heaven addict. Based on the level of the drug in his tissues, he would have died within a month regardless of what anybody could have done.

If he hadn't had the accident, he would have succumbed to a brain hemorrhage, cardiac arrest, respiratory paralysis, or any of several other major traumas caused by Purple. Alyssa was in no way responsible for the man's death, the investigator insisted.

She knew that, but it didn't make her feel much better. The grotesque grin was no less real, the wild laughter no quieter. She had stared madness and death in the face. It had been *that* close to her, and it might still be nearby. Who else in the building was hooked on Purple? How many others in Home?

Why? she wondered as she returned to the fifty-eighth floor. *Why would anybody, especially one of us, take that stuff?* It was almost instantly addicting and invariably killed its users within a year. *Where did it come from? How did he get it?* No doubt questions the investigators would pursue.

The fear-sparked adrenaline rush was leaving her. She could barely stay on her feet as she got off at her landing. If anything, the evening's shock had exacerbated her hangover.

She stepped through her mod's coded privacy barrier and winced as the message unit began to *honk* for her attention.

"Not tonight," she groaned as loudly as she could stand. The honking stopped.

Whatever it is, it can wait till morning, she decided. *Right now, detox pill, pain spray, and sleep.* She desperately needed to put this night behind her.

Alyssa kept the lights off. There were only a few permanent fixtures in her living space, and she managed to find her way to her sleeping niche without stumbling over any of them. Her bed pod spread out at a whispered command. She sat down on it with a sigh. In a moment she would summon the medibot to dispense various reliefs to her abused system.

Mmm. The bed felt soft, inviting. Safe. Maybe she would lie down for a minute or two before taking those medications. The bot would still be there.

Her eyes slowly shut. Just a short rest.

— 6 —

Farouk Nguyen scowled at the walls. His mod's morning yellow-and-white was insufferable. It mocked him with its artificial cheerfulness.

"Is something wrong, Farouk?" Nina asked quietly.

He jerked around to stare at his wife. How had she appeared so suddenly? Was she spying on him?

"Wrong? No, nothing's wrong!" Assembly delegate Nguyen snarled. "Should there be?" Over the past year Nina had become almost impossible to please. First he shouldn't support the Venebles faction, then he should resign from the Assembly, now he shouldn't go on his jaunts. He was only 210 years old, but she acted as if he were dying.

"Of course not, dear." She laid one plump hand on his arm. "You just look a little tense, that's all."

He pushed her hand away. "Who wouldn't be tense with you after him all the time?" It was unfair, and he knew it. The hurt in her face only added to his guilt.

"I'm sorry, honey," he said, forcing himself to smile. "I guess I am a little tired. That's why I need to get away for a few days." *What I really need is to turn the clock back just over a year*, he thought with all the clarity and frustration of hindsight.

She returned his smile with one that looked genuine. "I understand. Sometimes I do smother you. It's just my..." She paused, then concluded without finishing the sentence. "Have a good time and watch out for the hugglebears."

"Never fear." He gave her a quick hug. "I shall be especially wary of the hugglebears." Then, before she could say anything more, he turned and stepped through their mod's privacy barrier. A short corridor led to one of the dome's lift tubes, which lowered him the ten stories to street level.

An express slidewalk carried Nguyen from his dome to the far northeastern edge of Home. All during the half-hour trip, he willed the walk to go faster. He felt too noticeable in his tan hiking outfit and backpack.

Surely someone would ask him where he was going, or what was in his backpack.

No one did.

At the slidewalk terminus, he rented a gravscooter. He rode it out to the limits of its permitted range, near the edge of the Borderlands. Beyond that, he walked.

Hugglebears. Nguyen shook his head as he hiked up into the Borderlands, the jurisdictional no-man's-land between southern Toria and Home. How like his wife to warn against that childhood bogey. The giant six-armed bears were either extinct or had never existed in the first place, but children were still warned against going where the hugglebears lurked.

Nguyen knew what Nina had been about to say, just before he had left: "It's just my *maternal instinct*." One more source of guilt.

Why had she married him? Why had she stayed with him? Infertility was one defect the Glow did not repair. It was also one that the Wellborn chose not to correct. The Well-space limits required of Home a zero-growth population policy, and not even all the fertile couples had an opportunity to become parents.

"Not my fault," Nguyen muttered, moving farther away from the well-trodden paths, farther into the Borderlands. "But she shouldn't have had to pay for it."

He trudged uphill at an angle, following a hint of a trail through the gnarled, spike-leafed trees. He tried to concentrate on the shaky footing, the low-hanging branches, his backpack heavy on his shoulders. A stubborn part of him held onto the guilt, fondled it, tortured him with it.

All those years she'd stayed with him, and said nothing about her loss. Still, he'd know it was there, and he'd lacked the courage to leave her. First he'd tried to give her more of himself, then he'd urged her to become more involved with her work, her studies, her friends.

She'd pretended not to notice what he was up to, not to mind, but he had seen the pain in her eyes, in unguarded moments. He'd heard it in the congratulations she'd given friends who won the parenting drawings.

Delegate Nguyen shifted his backpack to a more comfortable position. There was no trail here—he was following a series of natural signposts through heavy brush. Here a lightning-split tree, there a boulder with a distinctive knob on top. It was hot, the air still. His shirt clung to him. Sandy soil and loose rock shifted underfoot.

Maybe I am getting old, he thought as he paused to catch his breath. He sat on the not-too-decomposed trunk of a fallen tree. A rivulet of sweat found his eye, stinging and making him blink.

"You know it's not age, you fool," he muttered as he wiped the sweat away.

It was the drug.

Taking the drug made everything wonderful, for a while. Then the euphoria would begin to fade, his mood dim. Before he could get another dose, all the anxieties would come back, all the fear, all the guilt. All the reasons he started smoking Purple in the first place. And each time, the fall came sooner and went deeper. Understanding what was happening didn't help in the least.

"Enough, already!" His shout startled a nearby flock of nocturnal barkorns into confused, hissing flight. It was as if the entire outer layer of bark from one tree rose into the air, swirled around, then settled on another tree farther away.

As startled as the barkorns, Nguyen jumped up and looked around. He laughed with embarrassed relief when he saw the tiny sightless birds regrouping on their new tree.

"Boy, you've really waited too long this time," he told himself, trying for a joking tone and falling far short. "You'll be seeing hugglebears next." He looked around to check his position, then trudged ahead toward his last trail marker.

The large firebush was impossible to miss—it stood out from its field of smaller companions like a torch in a bed of embers.

Nguyen felt uneasy with such a conspicuous destination, but he had no choice. Besides, there couldn't be anyone else out here. No one had any reason to be following him. And who would be this far out on this hot a day just to see a large firebush, or even a hillside full of them?

He kept glancing over his shoulder as he went on.

The smaller firebushes were nearly head high. Only the most acute observer would see a person walking among them. There was no rational cause for alarm, yet Nguyen found himself near panic as he crept forward.

Head down. Avoid open areas.

By the time he reached the tall bush, he was breathless and shaking. He began pacing off the final few meters of his directions.

Step. *It's the heat.*

Step. *It's your age.*

Step. *It's just plain nerves.*

Step.

A small gray box lay under the bush directly in front of him. He stooped and opened it, nearly spilling the contents in his haste.

It's the drug.

He quickly slipped off his backpack and reached inside. He'd packed two sandwiches, one with cumbra honey, the other sliced bozad roast.

The cumbra sandwich contained only honey. The bozad sandwich contained several circuit boards for a fully programmable machine tool factory. They were an old design, nearly obsolete in Home. Still, they were far in advance of anything allowed in Toria. They weren't even allowed in the Borderlands.

Delegate Nguyen thought the Assembly might possibly have shown him some lenience if he were caught using Purple. But violating the Pact to purchase the drug would be inexcusable in their eyes.

He took out the thick bozad sandwich, set it where the gray box had lain, and strapped his backpack on again. Then he walked away as rapidly as he could, still crouching low, still keeping to the cover of the bushes. The gray box he kept firmly gripped in his right hand.

Instead of retracing his path back to Home, he went farther up into the hills. He knew of a small cave up there. It would be shady and cool. It would be safe from prying eyes. It would be a good place to smoke his Purple.

Nguyen resisted the urge to run. The feeling of panic was nearly overwhelming. Someone must be watching, spying on him!

Slow and casual—don't give yourself away. The objective, rational part of his mind was still in charge. He didn't know how long it could hold out.

He left the relative security of the firebush field and crossed a terrifyingly open patch of rocky ground. The hill was steeper here and he scuttled across sideways, using his left hand for additional support. Stones slid out from under his feet. Twice he stumbled and almost dropped the gray box.

Then he was up against a large outcropping of rock, on firmer ground. He edged his way along its base to a narrow fissure and inched through that. The walls were steep, the sky a thin blue band far above.

The fissure became so narrow he could barely press onward. He fought against an attack of claustrophobia.

Where's the cave? he wondered frantically. *Did I choose the wrong fissure?*

Nguyen was about to turn back when the cave mouth appeared. He almost fell into it in his desire to be away from those narrow, crushing walls.

"It's okay, it's okay, it's okay," he whispered to himself as he lay on the cave floor, trying to catch his breath. His words echoed back to him from the depths of the cave.

As desperate as he was, Nguyen knew it was not okay. It hadn't been okay, *he* hadn't been okay, since he'd first smoked Purple a year ago. Instead of relief from his troubles, the drug had brought him more troubles. It had eaten away at his confidence and self-esteem until nothing was left but a rapidly thinning facade of normality.

And he didn't have the strength to end it, to turn himself in, to run away, to kill himself. Such escapes were too definite, too final. So he kept smoking Purple, and kept smuggling prohibited technology to pay for it.

The only thing that would make life okay, for a time, was in the gray box.

Nguyen sat up, his back against the rough cave wall. He ignored the sharp stones prodding his back. Slowly, he opened the box. Carefully, as steadily as he could, he pressed all of the purplish powder tightly into the accompanying spiral pipe.

With his thumb capping the bowl, Nguyen studied the pipe. He knew he would smoke it. But he couldn't dismiss the danger. His highs seemed to getting more manic, less euphoric. Last time, he'd awakened with confused and violent dream fragments rebounding in his skull, and with the knuckles of both hands bruised and bloody.

He no longer came to this dark remote cave just to protect his secret. It was now equally important to protect others. Who knew what he might do in a drug-induced frenzy? Out here, the only person he could possibly harm was himself.

"Cheerful thought, Farouk." He laughed harshly, then said in a flat, hopeless tone, "Let's get to it."

He lit the pipe with a strong inhalation, then held his thumb over the bowl to retain all the smoke. He'd learned to ignore the heat.

His last coherent thoughts, before floating away into Purple Heaven, were of his wife. How much better it would be for her if hugglebears really existed, and if one would leap upon him in this cave and remove him from Nina's life forever.

— **7** —

Honk!

Alyssa stirred groggily.

HONK!

What!? She jerked awake, staring around in confusion.

HonkHonkHonkHonkHONK!

The damn message unit. "I said not tonight!" *Of all the times for the thing to malfunction.*

"It's morning, Alyssa." The unit's voice was a copy of her own. Having someone else deliver her messages day and night would have felt like an intrusion. Besides, she had a pleasant voice—self-possessed yet warm. She couldn't remember why she'd programmed in that annoying *honk* for an alarm.

"Morning? It can't be." She struggled to a sitting position and blinked to clear her eyes. Her mod's walls were still translucent, as she'd set them the day before, but even without clearing any patches from windows, Alyssa could tell that it was indeed morning. Late morning, judging by the degree and elevation of the light.

Too late for a detox pill to do any good.

HONK!

"Okay, okay! Just a minute." Alyssa clutched her head to keep it from exploding. "Medibot! Analgesia spray!"

A half-meter silvery ball popped out of the wall to Alyssa's left, floated over to her, and settled on her outstretched hand. She felt a cool tingle on her palm, then the ball floated back onto the wall.

Her pain evaporated. She could face the world again.

"All right, let's have those messages." Maybe Bashir had already found something useful. More likely, the Seelzar Animal Rights Coalition wanted her to join their campaign to prohibit the hunting of rakeclaws by Free State trophy collectors. *Don't let it be about last night.*

The message unit replayed the messages in its memory. There was only one.

It was not from Bashir, which was disappointing but not surprising, considering she'd left him less than a day ago.

It was not from the investigations unit, which was a huge relief.

It was not from Muryama and Atherton, her collaborators on the gravity project. That came as a surprise, though not a disappointment. The project had run into difficulties of late—no news was good news.

It was not from Lyla, Jem, or Korohoshi, which was mildly surprising and disappointing. Wasn't anyone doing anything?

The sole message was not from any of her friends, relatives, acquaintances, the authorities, or the S.A.R.C. It was from herself. She had recorded it several years earlier. It was replayed every other year at this time, and it was the reason she had received no other messages.

"Alyssa," she heard herself saying in a patronizing voice. "Just a little reminder: It's time for us to take another sip from the fountain."

Oh, no, she thought with mild dismay. *Not again.*

Alyssa always seemed to forget her Welltime, even though it was on an unvarying schedule. She consoled herself with the fact that this time at least she had a good excuse—Darrin's exile had taken precedence over all her other concerns. But even without that excuse she would have forgotten.

She had long ago decided that her memory lapses were a simple avoidance mechanism. Her Welltimes were necessary and, on the whole, enjoyable. But the transition into the Glow was hard on her, actually painful.

Others had similar reactions to the transition, or worse, but her response was far from normal. The fact that no one could explain why some of the Wellborn suffered so upon entering the Glow just added to Alyssa's frustration.

"Perverse, perverse, perverse," she muttered. "First I get drunk, now this."

Alyssa stood up and stretched. Various joints cracked in protest, echoing but not relieving the accumulated tension of the past several days.

If she missed her scheduled two days at the Wells, she would go on a waiting list of others similarly remiss. A place might open up for her quickly, or she might have to wait until her next scheduled Welltime. Such a wait wouldn't kill her, but it would cost her something physically and mentally. She would deteriorate, however little, over those two years, and not all the loss would be made up at her next Welltime.

People missed their Welltimes only for very good reasons. Doing so now would invite questions and speculations that Alyssa would rather avoid.

Damn. Why did this have to come up just after she'd spoken with Bashir?

Alyssa undressed and stepped into her mod's cleaning niche. Eyes closed, she relaxed somewhat in the warm, scented mist. She was probably just overreacting. How much could happen in two days, anyway? Bashir himself had said it might be several days before he could find out anything useful.

Besides, she really had little choice. Skipping her Welltime would only make it harder to help Darrin, not easier.

The scented mist was replaced by a warm drying breeze. A few minutes later, Alyssa spoke into her commnet link, confirming her Welltime.

Less than an hour after her rude awakening, Alyssa was riding the pedramp down from her living mod, heading for the Wells. She had on the sleeveless silver blouse and long pale blue skirt she always swore to the Wells. Her feet were bare.

Under her arm she carried a basket with her provisions for the two days—several cumbra fruits, a loaf of heavy black bread, a small round of yellow Melchor cheese, and a book of poetry by Chatani. It was what she always brought with her. The routine made the transition a little easier, made her Welltime a little less alien.

For two days she would be by herself with the Glow. It would be a time for separation and a time of renewal. A time for putting out of mind the concerns of the world while readying herself to meet them.

Alyssa left the city and walked east along the shore of Sapphire Lake. On her right, sunlight glinted off the water. Small ripples lightly nudged the sandy beach. Far out in the lake, a large fish splashed.

She had made this short trip scores of times, in driving rain and hot sunshine. Still, after all those times, she felt the same anticipation she'd felt on her first trip as an adult, over one hundred years ago.

On her left lay the Wellfield. The Wells filled a roughly circular plain two kilometers in diameter, bordered on the south by Sapphire Lake, the east and north by low hills, and the west by Home. Where Alyssa stood, the Wellfield came within one hundred meters of the shoreline.

Each active Well was the center of a dome-shaped green aura seventy meters wide. At night their combined Glow could be seen for several kilometers. Now it was barely visible, washed out in the bright daylight.

There was little to mark the boundary of the field. Just a watery green tint that set apart everything inside from everything outside. That, and the ten slim black guard towers spaced evenly around the field's circumference.

Ugly.

Alyssa paused. She was standing near the base of one of the towers, looking up at its crown over 150 meters high. A few small blisters and knobs protruded from the dull black metal at about the sixty-meter mark. They became larger and more numerous, like an obscene growth infesting the tower, culminating in a mass of large detectors and powerful weaponry at the bulging top.

Around the tower's base, Alyssa could see the wavering distortion of a high-energy security field. The towers were off-limits to everyone.

She shivered and hugged her basket to her with both arms. There was something about the tower that made her profoundly uneasy, even as it attracted her.

She had long since discounted the childhood stories her teachers had told her—stories of ghostly presences in the towers. The Founders were not there keeping stern watch on wayward boys and girls. Dead Transgressors had not returned to take vengeance on the Wellborn. The spirits of the Builders did not lurk on the fringes of the Wellfield, awaiting their opportunity to evict mankind.

No, Alyssa did not believe those tales. And yet she shivered, standing on the warm sand. Perhaps it was the untarnished condition of the towers that disturbed her, despite their centuries of neglect. Perhaps it was the odd glints of light she'd once seen flickering in their crowns on a heavily overcast day.

Perhaps it's the residue of all those Nosedives, she thought viciously, impatient at her own fancies. *This is a fine way to prepare for your Welltime*.

Alyssa deliberately averted her gaze from the black tower. It was abandoned and empty, like its nine companions. They were only mysterious because they were off-limits. They were only off-limits because their deteriorating weapons were safer left alone, to molder and rust.

Out of the corner of her eye, she saw a quick movement near her right foot. She looked down. Nothing was there but a small flat rock. Curious, she slid her foot under the rock and tilted it over.

A large red and black eye stared up at her. It lay unblinking in the slight depression the rock had formed.

Alyssa almost dropped her basket, but caught herself with an embarrassed laugh. This was not the eye of some dangerous beast or a specter from one of the towers. It was a dodeceye.

She prodded the eye gently with her big toe. It blinked then, transforming instantly into a granular beige circle to match the surrounding sand. She nudged the nearly invisible dodeceye again. It sprouted twelve thin white legs and scuttled away to disappear under a nearby larger rock.

Dodeceyes were startling but harmless. Alyssa remembered catching them as a child and trying to figure out where their front and back ends were. It had been futile—the creatures were omidirectional. Darrin had explained the eyes' odd anatomy to his little sister, patiently repeating himself and drawing diagrams in the sand. She had listened intently and tried hard to understand. He'd been so wise with his ten years' advantage, and so kind to share some of that wisdom with her.

Alyssa shook her head. *Which of us is wiser now?*

On an impulse, she stooped and picked up the flat gray rock. Setting her basket down, she rose and flung the rock as far as she could out over the lake. It described a long pure arc and entered the water edge-on with a barely audible *ploop*.

She stood for a moment, staring out at the spot where the rock had sunk. The breeze ruffled her blue skirt and pushed her long black hair, like a banner, away from the lake, toward the tower and the Wellfield.

I may be wrong, brother, but I have to try, she thought.

"And standing here moping isn't going to get you to the Wells any sooner," she added out loud. She reached down and retrieved her basket.

Ahead, her path followed the shoreline for another few hundred meters, then curved to the left to follow the perimeter of the Wellfield. Alyssa started forward, walking slowly.

With each step, she *felt* the texture of the sand, its graininess, its warmth. She breathed in its tangy aroma. This was why she took the long way into the Wellfield, at the entrance opposite Home. It gave her time to make the transition from civilization to nature, self to world, anxiety to acceptance.

Old habits kicked in. Home and its worries were left behind. Alyssa became the sand, the breeze, part of the dance of life.

A trick, some part of her whispered.

The ground rose slightly. She left the sand and moved among the grasses. The flat shore gave way to a rolling plain. Alyssa flowed with the swells and hollows. Her long light skirt was a breeze through the grass. She was self and other, the droplet and the ocean.

A trick to make the shift into the Glow more bearable.

Her altered perspective seldom lasted long, but it usually gave Alyssa a residue of calm that she carried into the Glow. This time, however, her concerns about Darrin and Bashir remained, quieter but not silent. The start of this Welltime, she feared, was going to be less pleasant than most.

She approached the field's eastern entrance alone, as she'd expected. Most people used the western entrance near the city. Most also arrived or departed much earlier in the day. Alyssa preferred to enter alone. Meeting other people and having to make small talk would have challenged what little calm she'd managed to achieve.

The entrance itself was deceptively simple in appearance. Two identical unornamented archways faced each other at about five meters distance, like the ends of a tunnel leading into the Wellfield. They glowed coppery red in the midday sun.

The two arches might have been the sole relics of a lost civilization, but they were not. They were complex activators for the Wellborn's surgically implanted identidiscs.

They might have bracketed empty space, but they did not. A neuronal barrier ran between them and encircled the entire Wellfield.

Alyssa walked over the hard-packed ground and into the first archway. She waited there, in its thin slice of shade, until she heard a low hum, like an insect flying near her ear. The hum told her that her disc, just behind her left ear, was activated. With that reassurance, she stepped through the arch and toward its companion.

Halfway along the short, heavily worn path, she felt a mild tingle. Without her identidisc, the tingle would have been a painful, paralyzing jolt. She would have suffered a similar shock if she had tried to cross the barrier without going through the entrance arch, or if she'd entered on any but her scheduled day. Wellspace was scarce, and zealously guarded.

Safely beyond the neuronal barrier, Alyssa passed through the second arch, which deactivated her disc. The Glow ruined electrical devices of any sort. Alyssa could have entered the field with an active disc, but she would have had some explaining to do when she tried to leave.

The Glow began ten meters from the second archway. From this close, it was a palpable force, pushing at Alyssa ever so subtly, like a cool, gentle breeze. Against that slight pressure, she walked ahead, and as she did, the resistance quickly grew.

Alyssa's stomach tensed. Already she could tell her fear was becoming reality. This was going to be a punishing transition. She paused for a few deep, calming breaths, then proceeded.

After several steps, the cool breeze had become a cold gale. Alyssa's flowing skirt was not ruffled by the wind, nor were the scattered blades of grass at her feet, but she had to lean forward to make walking easier. The wind was for her alone.

This isn't too bad, she reassured herself. *Maybe this time it won't get any worse.*

A few more steps and she was struggling through an icy river, gasping for air even as she feared her next breath would fill her lungs with frigid water. The cold had seeped beneath her skin, into her muscles and bones. Her head was buzzing and she was beginning to lose her sense of direction.

"Keep going," she muttered through clenched teeth. "You can't stop now."

Two steps away from the Glow, she was trapped in a wall of ice. The cold was burning inside her, twisting her stomach into knots and squeezing her heart in a relentless grip. Her vision was blurred. There was a dull roaring in her ears.

It took all her concentration to remember where she was, and all her will to push forward against the solid cold.

There was a moment of blinding, shrieking ice-blue agony, during which someone pushed one foot ahead, ever so slowly.

There was a moment of black, numb silence, and another slow, halting step.

Alyssa opened her eyes, and the world was quiet and summer-warm and green. Looking around her, she saw green Wells, green huts, green sky, green ground. Green people, too, though most had already settled into their huts for their Welltimes.

Everything in her field of vision wavered and pulsed with the Glow.

She drew a shaky breath as the cold slowly melted away from her bones. Standing just inside the Glow, she blinked a few times and waited for her pounding heart to ease back into its normal rhythm.

Rough—the roughest yet, she thought. *But I made it.* She started forward, into the Wellfield.

The green Wells covered the field. Spaced sixty meters apart, they were twenty meters in diameter and rose five meters above the ground. No one knew for sure how deep they went—some theorized that they reached all the way to Seelzar's molten core.

Each active Well was surrounded by ten small huts, where people spent the majority of their Welltime. One of the few things known about the Wells was that having more than ten people at a time near a single Well diminished its effectiveness.

Without that limitation, Alyssa realized with a pang, Home could have built high-density living domes over each Well. The allowable population of Wellborn would have increased tenfold. They wouldn't have had to be so strict about admitting people to Wellstatus, and her brother...

Alyssa shied away from the thought. Wishful thinking would get her nowhere. She would just have to wait till her two days were up, then check back with Bashir. Besides, even though she was still far from her own Well, she was already being affected by the peripheral Glow of the ones she was passing. It was at once soothing and energizing. She felt as if each cell of her body were being massaged.

Usually, the Glow had a similar effect on her moods and emotions. The world seemed a brighter place and new around the Wells. Negative feelings and depressing trains of thought faded quickly. She did not forget her problems, but she had no doubt that they would all be resolved. Possibilities blossomed in her mind, each more hopeful than the last.

The Glow's euphoria touched every nerve, every molecule of her body. The only way a person could get any higher was to smoke pure Purple. Or so Alyssa had heard. She had never tried it herself. After her horrifying encounter last night, she couldn't imagine ever wanting to try the stuff.

Nobody knew where Purple Heaven came from or how it was made, but it was banned by every governmental authority on Seelzar. Only three or four people were authorized to study the drug, in vanishingly small amounts under the strictest control possible. Any other supplies were destroyed upon discovery.

Still, the resident of her tower had gotten it.

To die that way. Alyssa shook her head. Fits of increasingly manic exhilaration, the brain dissolving into mush in the skull. A final agonizingly intense seizure, then death. It was crazy, it was senseless, it was horrible.

Alyssa scuffed her bare green feet on the green earth as she walked between the Wells. She took a little comfort in the plain gritty sensation. Even the Glow had its limitations. Her mind kept producing one concern, one worry, one fear after another. Darrin, Bashir, Purple addicts, the spooky old guard towers.

Could the Wells renew her when she was so close to the edge? The Wellborn had an average life expectancy of 260 years, but the Glow worked better for some and worse for others. Alyssa wondered if it were possible to worry oneself into that latter category.

For Founders' sake, get control of yourself! She kicked hard at the packed dirt. *Now you're even worrying about being worried!* Perhaps she would find some peace when she settled down in her own hut, she told herself, where she could rest in the full radiance of its Well.

Despite her anxieties, or, rather, because of them, Alyssa took her usual roundabout course from the eastern Field entrance to her Well. She sought calm in the routine, the pattern of curving paths. She met no one else.

The Welltime was a period of quiet, of being alone. Few ventured out of their stone huts until it was time to leave. They read, wrote, ate, rested, meditated. Some played musical instruments, but those kept their huts closed so as not to disturb the peace of their neighbors.

In the midst of some 6000 people, Alyssa heard nothing but the wind sighing amongst the Wells.

Her own hut was on the northern edge of the field, near the Dead Wells. The 74 Dead Wells filled a shallow semicircle, a large bite taken out of the Wellfield. The Glow did not extend into that space.

The Dead Wells were a dull translucent green. Tall bronze-colored field grasses covered the ground around them. Many paths were visible in the waving grass, but the paths were faint. Everyone visited the Dead Wells once; few made a second visit.

The active Wells were extremely difficult to study, since the Glow prevented any electronic devices from functioning near them. Less sophisticated techniques revealed little. The Dead Wells offered no such impediment, but the Wellborn had had only marginally better success analyzing them.

The Wells seemed unaffected by heat or cold. They were opaque to electromagnetic energy of any wavelength and intensity. They were impervious to sheer physical force. One reckless test had created a deep fused crater partially surrounding one of the Dead Wells. The Well itself was unmarred.

The Dead Wells were solid on top, whereas the active Wells had a bright green core. They extended as far into Seelzar as instruments could measure. Little else was known. Serious direct study of the Wells had essentially ceased several centuries ago.

Theories abounded. The Wells were organic crystals, some of which had gone dormant or died. They were alien artifacts, protected by some unseen force field. They were intrusions from another dimension, unaffected by our physical laws. They were God. They were the Devil.

Every theory had its adherents, and most people believed none of them.

Alyssa skirted the Dead Wells' space, staying just within the Glow. Like most of the Wellborn, she was not troubled by the Dead Wells. All the Wells, dead and active, were part of her world. Like the air she breathed, they were essential yet taken for granted. They were a mystery, but one only theoretically knowable, a mild curiosity at most. Unchanged during her lifetime and many lifetimes before that, the Wells would likely remain forever as they were now.

With that thought in mind, she arrived at her hut.

The small semaphore attached to the hut's doorframe was raised, indicating that the hut was no longer occupied.

The man whose Welltime immediately preceded hers must have already departed. Alyssa had met him several times, but only in passing. He was short, heavyset and fairskinned. He was young—in his mid-60s. His name was Thomas something or other. When they'd met before, they'd spoken little, neither eager to intrude into the other's Welltime.

From Alyssa's point of view, the important thing about Thomas was that he was tidy. He always left the hut immaculate.

Alyssa pulled open the rounded wooden door and stepped inside. She glanced around the single room and nodded, satisfied. Everything was as it always was when she first entered.

A small writing table and chair were to her right, next to the larger front window. Farther in on her right was the chemical heater/stove, a small sink, a few cooking utensils and a small supply of nonperishable food.

Set in the hut's rear wall was a large window facing the Well. Below that window, a bed ran parallel to the wall. Along the left wall were the shower/bath/toilet facilities.

On Alyssa's immediate left, a simple rocking chair faced the smaller front window.

There were no lights in the hut. None were needed. This close to the Well, the Glow was as bright as daylight. It passed through the stone walls of the hut undiminished. The rear window was only for those who wanted to look directly at the pulsing, flickering surface of the Well itself.

Alyssa set her basket down on the writing table and closed the hut's door. They were spare accommodations, but reassuring in their familiarity. Besides, she would only be here for two days.

She moved carefully. Everything in the hut had a vague fluidity, the outlines shifting with the rhythm of the Glow. Slowly that rhythm began to work its way into her brain.

That night, Alyssa had a dream. A pack of grinning purple creatures was chasing her and Darrin through the Dead Wells. The creatures had sharp teeth and long claws and ran very fast. Alyssa had to half-carry Darrin, who had somehow injured his legs.

The creatures came closer and closer, forcing her toward the edge of the Wellfield. She could hear their chuckling, throaty barks. She could smell their unwashed bodies. She could feel their hot breath.

The beasts were almost on top of Alyssa and her brother when someone leapt down from one of the field's guard towers to stand beside her. It was Bashir Arak, single-handedly holding the growling pack at bay. In each hand he held a ball of Wellglow.

A feeling of intense relief flooded Alyssa upon seeing the sturdy old man.

Bashir threw the balls into the midst of the creatures, setting off dozens of silent explosions. Green, yellow, and purple starbursts filled the air, blinding Alyssa. When the bursts had faded and she could see again, the creatures were gone. In their place was a stand of swaying sheenwood trees in full bloom.

Alyssa turned to thank Bashir, but he was gone. She turned back to help Darrin to his feet, but he was gone too.

When she awoke the next morning, the dream was a tangle of memory fragments. Lying on her bed, eyes closed, she tried without success to gather them together.

After a while she got up and took a shower. Then, casually and privately nude, she sat in the rocking chair and read some of Chatani's poetry while eating one of her cumbra fruits. The Glow suffused her body and her mind. She was, for a time, at peace. The poems were not profound, but they went well with the honey-sweet cumbra.

— 8 —

M'Briti liked Jaro's Tavern. With Purple in her system, she liked everything, but this was a place she could feel comfortable in even when the Purple was fading. As it was now.

A few orange-yellow globes gave the front room what light they could. They were dim and hung mostly near the bar. The rest of the room lay in shadows. Indistinct figures hunched over drinks at small tables or in the booths along one wall.

Low, mournful music whispered from speakers in each corner of the room. Beneath the music, M'Briti could hear the sounds of hushed conversation and glasses clicking against the hardwood tabletops. She kept her voice low, as did the man sharing her booth.

"They just cast me aside," the man said. He was tall and dark. He looked young. "First the Assembly, then Tashiki."

M'Briti nodded sympathetically, but said nothing. She saw more resolve in him than in most of her marks. *Don't push him*, she told herself.

The man looked down into his drink, his fourth within the hour. He wasn't drunk, yet.

"It's not as if I hurt anyone." His voice was quiet. It held his pain and frustration in soft, sheltering hands.

"Of course you didn't," M'Briti agreed. *Not that it matters*, she thought.

The man's name was Darrin Montoya. She'd seen him come into Jaro's Tavern a short while ago and had recognized him immediately. Transgressors always got some mention on the newscasts. They were unusual and made excellent object lessons. They were also her best customers.

Montoya raised his eyes to look into hers. They were dark, and she saw in them confusion, anger, frustration. Just what she'd expected to see. Just what she'd hoped to see. Still, there was that sense of strength beneath the pain. This one wasn't going to be easy.

"I don't know what I'm going to do," he said.

"Well . . ." She paused, as if seriously considering his options. "There's no chance of getting reinstated, is there?"

His lips twisted in a bitter half grin. "How many of us ever do?"

M'Briti pursed her lips together as if holding back a painful truth. The expression was in part sincere. She reached across the small table and touched his hand.

Montoya sighed. Suddenly his deep brown face seemed to show more of his age, as if anticipating his inevitable decline from Wellborn status. The Wells had kept him young. Without them, he would deteriorate as any Normal would. Well before he reached his two hundredth birthday, he would wrinkle and weaken, turn gray and stoop-shouldered and slow. And die.

M'Briti withdrew her hand and waved one of the servers over. A young man came over to take their order. He was reasonably good-looking but with an air of chronic discontent about him.

"Another one?" the server asked M'Briti, arching one eyebrow and casting a pointed glance at Darrin.

"Two of the same," M'Briti replied, ignoring the server's implication. She might have a talk with him later, in private.

"Very well." The server smiled blandly and went back to the bar.

The tavern was an Annex bar, and not among the more prosperous ones. Here real people did all the work. The robotic technology of Home had not yet trickled this far down the socio-economic ladder. Maybe it never would, M'Briti reflected.

What did the well-off citizens of Home care? What did it matter to the hidebound Drath theocrats? They'd both rather keep Home's scientific knowledge bottled up for use of the Wellborn alone than allow Normals access to it.

The server came back with their drinks. M'Briti handed him three creds. "Keep the change."

"Certainly." His mouth quirked in a faintly derisive expression. His eyes shifted once more to Darrin, then he turned and walked away.

Beneath the table, M'Briti clenched her left hand. She was definitely going to have to talk with that boy. She lifted her glass and took a sip. The liquor tingled sharply on the way down. It helped her relax. She gestured with the glass. "This isn't bad, but it can't substitute for the Glow."

"No," Montoya agreed. He took a large swallow of his own drink and grimaced at it went down. "No, it can't," he repeated with a gasp, sucking in air to put out the fire in his throat. "But what can?"

That was it, M'Briti realized. A deaf man with his fingers in his ears couldn't have missed the invitation. And yet she hesitated. She wasn't used to having matters develop so quickly. Rush someone and you could scare him off. Worse, you could end up under arrest.

M'Briti frowned and shook her head slowly. "I don't know. Maybe nothing can." There was one more hit of Purple left in her personal cache. She wouldn't have to use it for at least three days, and it would keep her going for several days beyond that. Plenty of time to work on Montoya or to find someone weaker or more desperate.

Montoya looked at her searchingly. The effect was weakened by the fact that his eyes were having trouble focusing. The drinks were finally taking their toll.

"What," he began, then stopped. He looked into his nearly empty glass. He raised it and quickly downed the remaining liquor, barely reacting as he swallowed. It seemed to give him the strength to continue. "What keeps you going?"

"Would you believe willpower?"

Montoya smiled at her. "I might. From you I just might." His smile was warm. It was bright. It was a brief flash of life in his dark face. It caused M'Briti to reconsider her intentions toward him, almost.

"You wouldn't be all wrong," M'Briti responded with a smile of her own. Sure she used Purple, some might say needed it. But in her year on the drug, she hadn't become the ruined addict most users became after a few months. She hadn't allowed herself to. Purple was a means to her, not an end.

"What about those of us with weaker characters?"

M'Briti shook her head. "Surely not yourself?" She kept her tone light, but she was beginning to have some doubts. Montoya seemed to be pushing awfully hard for something. Maybe just reassurance. Maybe something more. Could he know that she dealt Purple? Was that what he wanted? Had he found her, rather than she finding him?

Montoya shook his head. "I don't know. After the initial shock, I thought I could adjust. But it's been seven days since the decision, and each has been worse than the one before. After nearly one and a half centuries, I feel like a stranger in the city. I'm afraid to face my Wellborn friends." Montoya waved his hand in a negating gesture. "Not that they've excluded me or anything. It's just that I can't handle their pity and their scorn. They hide it well, but I know that's what they're feeling."

This time when M'Briti reached across toward Montoya, she took his hand in both of hers. "Listen," she said, giving his hand a squeeze. "I know how you feel, but it doesn't have to be like that. Pack up and move to the Annex. I did. People out here won't care what you've done or who you've been."

"You make it sound pretty easy."

"No, hardly that. But it is possible." She stood up and pulled Montoya to his feet. "Come on, I'll show you the neighborhood."

Montoya blinked. "What, now?"

"Why not? The evening's still young and the streets around here are fairly well lighted." M'Briti began heading for the door, dragging Montoya along. He seemed to be having some trouble walking in a straight line, but they made it outside without knocking over any tables.

The street outside was not crowded, but overflow traffic from Founders' Way, two blocks to the east, kept it comfortably busy. The sky was aquamarine in the west, shading to a deep indigo in the east. Streetlights were just beginning to come on—pink and yellow globes at street corners and in the middle of each block. There was a cool tranquillity in the air, and the rough edges seemed to have been removed from all the sounds—a child shouting, a door slamming, electric cars whirring past.

Montoya stopped outside the tavern door and leaned heavily against the wall. "Wait a minute. I've already made one mistake today. I'm not going to make another."

"What?" M'Briti asked with some alarm. Montoya reached into his jacket pocket and she tensed, ready to run or fight.

"I don't usually drink so much," he said, opening a small vial. "Without one of these, I'll be dead in the morning." He dropped a small pill into his hand and popped it into his mouth.

M'Briti laughed with relief. "You did put quite a few down in there. Frankly, I'm a little surprised you made it out without falling over."

Montoya nodded. "I am too." He pushed away from the wall and stood, swaying slightly. "Until the detox pill takes effect, I don't know if I can navigate these streets."

"No problem." M'Briti walked up beside him and set his arm across her shoulders. "Lean on me until you recover. The walk will do you good." With her arm around his waist, she led him down the street. They headed west, their backs to Founders' Way. Ahead of them, the sky was darkening, losing its greenish tint.

M'Briti was more uncertain than ever about Darrin Montoya. What was he—vulnerable Transgressor, agent for Home, or something else? She glanced sideways at his profile, mysterious in the dim light from the widely spaced globes. Whatever, she decided, she would enjoy finding out.

But Founders help him if the answer turned out to be the wrong one.

— 9 —

On the day following his meeting with Alyssa, Bashir tried to enter the Matrix. Wrapped in his probe pod, wired into the computer's circuitry, he scouted its defenses, but found no way in.

On the next day, he found a small opening and entered the system. He stayed long enough to search the material he already knew from his years as an Executor, then the Matrix defense programs began to close in on him and he had to retreat.

Some of the rules and regulations had been modified over the intervening two centuries, but the essential fact remained the same: Formal channels and legal appeals provided little recourse for Alyssa or Darrin. A Transgressor could be reinstated only by making some extraordinary contribution to the welfare of Home.

Shifting from file to file, Bashir mulled the problem over. What could Darrin do that would convince the Assembly to allow him to return to Home, and to bring Tashiki with him? *Easy,* he thought. *Just secure Seelzar against the Interstellar Union or solve the riddle of the Wells.*

As Bashir exited the Matrix, exhausted and discouraged, one further line of inquiry occurred to him, unlikely but intriguing: the Forbidden Files.

Rumor had it that those files had been sealed at the time of the split between Eldrath and the other two Founders. Since then, no one had been able to bypass their security, not even the Executors.

Anything might be stored in the Forbidden Files—vital information about the Builders or the Wells, specifications for synthesizing the organic component of the Matrix, personal scandals made irrelevant by the passage of twelve centuries. Anything. The mystery was irresistible.

Bashir lay still, eyes closed, as his senses adjusted from the pseudo-world of his Matrix probe to the real world of his home in the Annex. It took several minutes—more than enough time to recall the names of the four Executors who had died trying to explore the Forbidden Files. Four experienced, intelligent Wellborn whose brains had been destroyed by the Matrix's defense programs.

However, Bashir mused that evening, *those four used routine Matrix access channels. My probe has some definitely unroutine capabilities.*

He rested in a hammock supported between two adaptapods. The room's normal lighting was extinguished, replaced by the red glow of the setting sun in the Northern Wastes. Dull crimson rays flowed over the sand dunes and set momentary fires in fleckstone outcroppings. Four sunsets in four walls. Bashir was surrounded by their silent burning glory.

"Tomorrow we'll see," he murmured, and the dusk slowly faded into night.

By midmorning of the following day, Bashir was ready to challenge the Forbidden Files. He'd tested every aspect of his probe mechanism, as well as his own physical condition and mental alertness. There was no reason to wait.

As on the previous two days, he lay down on a special adaptapod and relaxed as it slowly enveloped him. The pod was filled with complex microcircuitry—as sophisticated as any in Home. It sent invisibly thin filaments through his skull, some to secrete brain chemistry enhancers, others to attach themselves to key synaptic nodes.

In a few minutes the neural connections were completed. Bashir Arak became the organic element in his own specially designed computer, whose sole purpose was to infiltrate the Matrix. He entered a world where software and hardware blended together, where molecular circuits and data files alike became tangible entities, where programs and electronic impulses took on breadth and depth. It was a world of illusion, yet as real as his dusty shop and the pie he'd eaten there three days before.

His probe switched on and absorbed him. He felt a mild electric shock. His vision blurred for an instant, and then he was floating. Floating aimlessly through a blue-tinged void. No, not aimlessly. He was following a lumpy green vine, rolling along its surface—a dark orange ball with no arms, no legs.

He moved by willpower alone, his probe turning thought into action. He could have gone off in any direction, but that would have taken energy he might need to save for later. It was easier to follow the vine down, down into the blue haze.

Too, there were dangers in the blue emptiness. Pale white *things* swam out there, nearly invisible except when their red pulsing mouths opened wide. From his studies of ancient Earth, Bashir had conjured up a specific shape and a name for those Matrix defenders: sharks.

One of those ghostly sharks could swallow a user's energy globe whole. If the user were mind-linked to the globe at the time, the result might well be death.

Maybe that's what happened to those other four. Bashir pushed the thought away, reminding himself that he was better prepared than they. Still, he pressed more tightly against the rough surface of the vine as he sped down its length.

It was safer to stay with the vine. The sharks would not attack him there. Their purpose was to prevent stray impulses from creating new pathways through the void.

Bashir's probe-altered perceptions made a microsecond seem like hours. He sank for days. It was a struggle to keep his awareness from dissipating into the azure depths. He reviewed his previous trips into the Matrix again and again, trying to anticipate and prepare himself for any contingency. He tried to imagine what might be in the Forbidden Files, and to avoid imagining what had killed the four before him.

Despite Bashir's best efforts, he felt himself tiring. He was heading toward the Matrix at high speed, but the featureless blue world negated any sense of motion. His mind wandered.

His probe-generated vision analog began to play tricks on him. A vague shadow loomed ahead, divided, became hundreds, then thousands of lumpy growths. In shades of green from near black to chartreuse, they hurtled toward Bashir, filling the space around him. They were connected to each other by vines writhing in a network that extended beyond the limits of his electronic vision.

Bashir slowed his forward motion. This was no dream. This was the true beginning of the Matrix. Lulled as he was by the interminable approach, it always caught him by surprise.

This far he had come on his previous entry, and a little farther, exploring the generally accessible regions of the computer's memory. By piggybacking on sanctioned users' inquiries, absorbing a fraction of their energy while hiding in their wakes, Bashir had discovered that ordinary measures and routine channels would not help Darrin.

He'd explored the interiors of hundreds of those bulbous growths—some huge as mountains, others only marginally larger than himself. Each was entered by portals at the bases of the attached vines. Each represented a data file or directory. None had been at all helpful.

Bashir had felt perversely excited by the failure of his previous visit, and that excitement reasserted itself now as he approached his rendezvous with the Matrix proper. The excitement was a heady mixture of curiosity and fear. His earlier explorations had been through relatively familiar territory with predictable dangers, the chief risk carelessness. This time the territory was uncharted, the dangers unknown. People had died seeking the Forbidden Files.

He would have felt guilty taking such a risk just to satisfy his inquisitive nature, since there were people who depended on him, and people he felt near to. But Alyssa had given him an excuse that his conscience couldn't refute, something more compelling than an old man's whim.

Bashir's wife had died well over two centuries ago, a victim of his stubborn curiosity and the unknown. In his own mind, he had failed her, and he'd sworn not to let it happen again. He would protect their descendants as he had been unable to protect her, for as long as he lived.

Now, guilt and curiosity, duty and choice, blended and gave Bashir freedom to do what he wanted to do, despite the risk.

Bashir stopped at the point where his vine intersected another. Now in the Matrix, he could see that the vines were alive with shimmering, rolling yellow globules about his size. Each was the embodiment of an approved user inquiry.

He guessed that a large portion of the traffic was Assembly members making last-minute preparations. The current Session was coming to a close, and final arguments were probably already under way.

They procrastinate more now than they did in my day, and I thought they were bad then. Bashir's critical reaction was tempered by the knowledge that the heavy Matrix activity would make his present task easier. There were before him more than enough legitimate users to follow, to hide behind, to siphon energy from.

He waited at the junction of his vine with the other, waited for a yellow globe to pass in the correct direction. Soon one came by, heading toward his left, and he slipped in behind it. He followed the globe toward a pod perhaps twenty times his size, with a dozen or so vines attached across its surface.

Bashir entered through a portal that opened briefly for his companion. His unwitting host exited from the olive-hued growth, slightly dimmer than when it had entered. He remained behind, waiting for another ride. He was slightly brighter than before, slightly more energetic.

So it went, one step at a time. Each step brought Bashir deeper into the Matrix, each added to his energy.

The pods had no identifying labels, yet Bashir found that he could sense immediately which one best suited his purpose, which path to follow. His own computer read the unique size, shape, and color of each and "pointed" to the one he needed. It felt as if he were endowed with infallible intuition.

He lost track of the pods he passed through, the globes he vampirized. His dark orange hue gradually turned to a yellow nearly as bright as the globes around him. He continued following them along the vines and into the variegated files, channeling his excess energy into the creation of first one trailing globule, then a second.

For a time the pods were close-packed, the vines between them short and thick. Eventually, however, the gaps widened and the vines grew thinner. It became harder to maintain constant contact with them. At the same time, the pale blue spaces darkened from the color of the early morning sky to a twilight indigo.

Even the Matrix defenders were changing. Bashir could swear that the ghostly red-mouthed sharks were more numerous and larger than in the outer reaches of the Matrix.

Quit imagining things. Keep your mind on the job.

The strain was definitely beginning to tell. The clock back in his shop, worlds away, had ticked off perhaps two seconds. In subjective time, he'd been in the Matrix for several days.

Now that Bashir had run out of approved-user impulses to follow, he was forcing his own way through the living portals, trailing three globes of excess energy. One wrong move and he'd be lost—there was no place to hide. If he didn't come upon the Forbidden Files soon, he would have to turn back.

Maybe if my life depends on it, Bashir decided grimly, willing himself to move faster. He wasn't sure how soon he would be able to make it this far again, if ever.

Even so, he was almost at the point of abandoning his search when he came upon the abyss. There was no other word for it. One minute he was traveling on thin green vines among widely scattered pods, the next minute he was staring into nothingness. No pods, no vines, just indigo deepening into near black for as far as he could see.

Nothing. And yet, he sensed that there *was* something out there.

Bashir's probe-born intuition had led him to a spot midway between two small pods, each a part of a near-circular loop of cross-references made obsolete centuries ago. Automatic housekeeping programs should have erased them well before Bashir had even been born, yet here they were.

Something must have been preserving them, something unknown to Home's Matrix monitors.

Bashir scanned the darkness before him intently. There, a little above and to the right, a darker patch. Once detected, it resolved readily into another dark green growth. Bashir guessed it to be of medium size and not very far away, but it was hard to judge with confidence. There were no connecting vines that he could see, nothing to compare it to.

If his judgment were correct, it would not be a long jump. If he were wrong, it might take so much energy to make the jump that he wouldn't be able to return. And in either case, there were the sharks to worry about. Here there was no protecting vine to keep them away. He would be fair game.

Bashir Arak had had a longer life than most, even among the Wellborn. It had been an interesting, eventful life, but it had included few things to match his present opportunity. He considered briefly, then leapt.

His guess had been correct—the isolated pod was reasonably close. But something else was even closer. Bashir felt more than saw the movement below him. When he looked, he could see a large pale shark moving swiftly upward. It was coming fast. Too fast. He would not reach the safety of the pod before the shark reached him.

If Bashir were not towing three extra globes of energy, he might have been able to speed up sufficiently to win the race. Then again, he might not, and to jettison his energy reserves would make his ultimate success much less likely.

The pod was considerably closer now. Bashir could see the entry portal, just like those he'd been passing through in the outer layers of the Matrix. But the shark was closer too. Another few moments and he'd be safe, but he didn't have those moments.

A cold current pushed up at him. He looked down at the shark's gaping red mouth, opened wide.

There was only one chance to survive this and still save some energy for later. All the sanctioned user charges in the Matrix were of a single, fixed size. It seemed probable that the Matrix sharks had been designed to clean up errant charges of the same size. Thought and deed were nearly simultaneous as Bashir dispatched his endmost reserve energy globe toward the shark's gaping maw.

The red mouth stretched wide to engulf the yellow globe. Bashir reached the portal just as the shark swept by to one side. From the relative safety of the pod, he turned to see whether the shark would come back for him. What he saw instead was a swirl of yellow and red fading through green and purple into deep blue. The two forces had canceled each other out, and their energies were dissolving back into the stuff of the Matrix.

He allowed himself a moment of self-congratulation. His system had worked. He had reached the Forbidden Files. Not only that, but he could make the jump back and still have one excess energy globe in reserve for emergencies. Just maybe he *would* succeed.

Bashir pushed into the pod eagerly. He realized that some of his confidence was an emotional spillover from the relief of his narrow escape, but that didn't dampen his enthusiasm in the least.

Inside the pod, there was not the deluge of data he had expected. There was, instead, a stuffy darkness. In the darkness, a woman's voice declared, "This is a security area. Only authorized users may pass the gateway." The voice was quiet but firm. Bashir pressed forward. He had not come this far to be stopped by a mere verbal warning.

As he advanced, the darkness shifted.

He felt a thickening of its substance. His progress slowed. The darkness grew increasingly dense. Now it was clinging to him like black syrup. Soon he would be immobilized, trapped until his power ran out.

Is this what happened to the other four? Wrapped in this suffocating darkness until they lost contact with their probes, until the Matrix traced their access paths and shorted out the interface wires in their brains?

Reluctantly, Bashir drew on his energy reserves, willing himself ahead. The murky barrier yielded grudgingly. He advanced with painful slowness, centimeter by struggling centimeter, each slight gain costing him precious energy.

Then, without warning, he was free. He stood at the exit portal of the gateway pod. The passage had cost him dearly—he had only one energy globe left in reserve. And still he was not in the Forbidden Files.

Where in the besotted bozads are they? It seemed like weeks had gone by since he'd entered his access pod so far away. Bashir was beginning to suspect that he would die of old age before he found the Files.

With a mental sigh, he eased through the portal. The dark indigo of the Matrix seemed bright by comparison to the blackness he'd just escaped. That impression faded quickly, however. In its place was a wholly unfamiliar sensation— vertigo.

He was perched inside the exit portal of the gateway pod. Attached to the pod at the lip of the portal was the thinnest Matrix vine Bashir had ever seen. It was a mere thread. Any smaller and it would have been invisible. The vine ran off into the depths of the abyss until the darkness swallowed it up.

The vine's thinness did not bother Bashir, nor did the immensity through which it passed. What disturbed him, what had him clinging grimly to the exit portal, was the dizzying sensation that he could fall. Until now, gravity had been nonexistent in the Matrix—he had been able to travel with equal ease in any direction, and he had gone nowhere without willing himself to do so. Here, at what he felt was the last stage of his journey, all directions were down, or seemed to be.

The Matrix's final challenge was equal parts physical and psychological: *Maintain contact with this impossibly thin vine or fall. Forever.*

His climbs in the Eastern Mountains had taught Bashir a basic rule in such circumstances: The longer you wait, the longer you are going to wait. A minute leads to an hour leads to a turning away from the edge in defeat.

He focused his attention on the vine and rolled out into the cold blue night.

At first Bashir had to struggle against his fear, against the temptation to clutch the vine so tightly that he wouldn't be able to move, against the siren call of the vast emptiness waiting to claim him.

Rule number two: A ledge is always too narrow if you think of the fall. Think instead of the climb, of the peak.

By slow degrees his tension faded. Eventually, he was able to relax and shift his attention from "down" to "ahead."

With his fear pushed to the background, the rest of Bashir's trip passed with surprising speed. Despite the increasing darkness and cold, he seemed to fly along the tiny vine, and he reached its far end much sooner than he'd expected. What he found there was at first disappointing.

The Forbidden Files, if that's what they were, were housed in a single aquamarine pod. The pod was indistinguishable from the larger growths in the outer sections of the Matrix, as far as Bashir could see.

Except that it's completely alone down here and barely visible in the dark. He hurried toward the entrance, eager to complete his search and leave before any more unpleasant surprises could spring out at him.

The portal offered no resistance. All Bashir felt was a slight tingle as he entered the pod. Inside, he was assaulted by a barrage of multisensory images. The intensity of the input stunned him. He was only on the fringes of the Files, and still the data streams were far more dense than in any other pod he'd ever entered.

Bashir let go of his grip on the portal and began to move with the streams. As he did, their relative speed slowed and he began to pick out discrete images within them. It was as if he were flowing through a random series of incidents from the early history of Seelzar.

Each stream he encountered was dense with information, but most of it bypassed Bashir's conscious awareness to be stored in his probe's memory for later recall and analysis. What he perceived as he whirled through the pod was occasional climactic images from the streams: here, the settlement ship lying damaged next to Sapphire Lake and the darkened Wellfield; there, Victoria Eldrath leading her followers off to the northeast, away from the Wells and the budding city of Home.

Bashir moved toward the center of the pod, meeting with new sequences of images, new information to sort out and analyze later, when there would be more time.

He saw Masanaru Senyan hurrying aboard the settlement ship before its departure with a large crate in tow, a string of official documents flashing past in the background.

Farther in he came upon Achmar Z'areikh walking among the Wells with a Builders artifact in his hands, the Wells glowing behind him.

At the very heart of the Files, he absorbed a composite image of the Matrix, the Wells, and Victoria Eldrath with a series of diagrams and scientific formulae. She seemed to be lecturing Senyan and Z'areikh, or arguing with them.

Bashir was puzzled. None of the perceived images seemed particularly sensitive, offensive, or dangerous. Why had the Files been so well protected? His exploration of the Matrix had been exhausting and terrifying. He'd reached his goal, and yet he wasn't sure he'd accomplished his purpose.

What had he found that could help Darrin? For that matter, what had he found that could appease his own curiosity? He could only hope that his probe-stored details would provide satisfactory answers.

He knew that his conscious impressions reflected only the sketchiest outline of the material in the Forbidden Files. Still, he was strongly tempted to stay, to poke and prod until the Files gave up at least one indisputably worthwhile secret. He didn't want to leave with nothing but historical trivia to show for his efforts.

Bashir rested in the midst of the informational vortex, pondering his next move. As he did, a new image took shape before him. The three Founders appeared, staring at him. He felt again the slight tingle he'd experienced upon entering the Files.

Victoria Eldrath spoke. "You have violated the Matrix's sanctity. Classified information cannot be allowed to leave." It was the same warning voice he'd heard in the small gateway pod.

The Founders' images began to swirl, to merge, to form another shape. It seemed to be drawing energy from the surrounding data streams. The interior of the pod began to dim.

Bashir didn't need further prompting. It was time to leave. He headed for the pod's lone portal as fast as he could. He exited only moments before it snapped shut.

As he started back along the thin vine leading to the outer Matrix, he saw the Forbidden Files' pod swirl as had the Founders' images. He watched its transformation, an awful suspicion growing within him. He rolled along the thin vine as fast as he could through the cold vertiginous depths, looking back as much as ahead.

The aquamarine pod was growing and whitening, expanding into a huge pale shape. It twisted around a few times, sending out currents up and past Bashir, nearly sweeping him off the vine. Then the shape turned in his direction, and he could see its immense mouth. The mouth gaped wide, and pulsed a deep crimson.

If the Matrix defenders were normally sharks, Bashir thought, a more primal word was needed for this monstrosity: leviathan.

The transformed pod came upward with a rush. Bashir realized immediately that there was no hope of neutralizing it with his remaining excess energy globe. The vine he was rolling along would be no protection either—the monster was consuming this guideline as it rose. To survive, he would have to outrun the thing.

The only way to gain sufficient speed was to absorb his reserve energy globe. Such a move was near the theoretical limits of his probe's capabilities. It *might* kill him, but the Forbidden Files' defender almost certainly would.

With a prayer to whatever powers protected crazy old men, Bashir pulled the entire globe into himself.

The world exploded around him. There was a pain as if he were being torn apart from the inside. His perceptions were thrown in all directions at once, his mind drawn simultaneously to the past, present, and future.

He had swallowed a sun.

Bashir fought to control his new energy. Panic would undo him, but the horror below must be very close by now. He clung tenaciously to two things—his own identity and his contact with the vine. Lose either and he would be doomed. With desperate deliberation, he built on those two essential anchors.

Slowly, his consciousness returned fully. He drew his senses back into focus on his immediate surroundings and banked the seething fires within. All the while, he fought the paradoxical battle *not* to think about the enormous thing coming nearer by the second.

Bashir's control over his enhanced energy was not yet complete, but he decided he could wait no longer. He reinforced his contact with the vine, then channeled all the energy he could into flight, up and away.

Behind him, he felt a wave of cold pressure building up. It became intense, freezing. Bashir was certain that the leviathan had him. Still, he pressed on, not daring to look back.

As he fled, Bashir gained control of his new energies as he used them. His speed increased. The cold and pressure behind him eased marginally.

The gateway pod was coming up swiftly. Bashir didn't know whether or not its dark trap would slow him on his departure as it had when he had entered, and he wasn't about to find out. At the last possible moment, he left the vine.

At his speed, the moment of vertigo lasted only a split second, then he was flying across the gap to the outer Matrix, flashing past the large defender shark before it had time to react. He glanced back in time to see the pursuing leviathan engulf gateway pod and shark alike.

He concentrated on looking ahead, taking the shortest route out of the Matrix as fast as he could. He passed through the intervening pods as if they weren't there. He overtook approved users' globules heedlessly, absorbing a small amount of their energy as he whirled past them. He didn't care to think about the damage his huge pale nemesis must be causing.

By the time Bashir reached the long vine that led from the Matrix back to his probe, he felt himself transformed into a blazing white ball with over three times the normal energy of a globule.

Under ordinary circumstances, the Matrix monitors would have had no difficulty detecting and tracing Bashir's movements. He would have been a beacon on their screens. But with the Forbidden Files' defender swallowing everything in its path, he doubted that his small light would even be visible. There was even a chance that the monitor programs themselves had been neutralized.

Bashir's one thought, as he raced up the vine, was that he had to sever the connection to his probe before the leviathan reached it. Otherwise, his probe's circuits would overload and burn out. And since his own brain was an integral part of the probe's circuitry . . .

Just keep moving, Bashir reminded himself fiercely. *Worrying isn't going to get you there any sooner.*

He could see that his lead, which had grown for a while, was beginning to shrink again. Although he had gained considerable energy fleeing through the Matrix, his pursuer had expanded unbelievably. When he looked back, it seemed to fill half his field of vision—a vast pale beast hurtling upward, its mouth a deep red chasm wide enough to engulf mountains.

In a moment it would be upon him. In a moment his brilliant white flame would disappear as if it had never been. Would that be the end not only of his Matrix existence, but his real life as well?

Bashir fled with all his strength, and still the leviathan drew nearer. He could feel the coldness of its negative energy. He could see the rings of deeper red pulsing through its crimson interior. Despite his fear, or perhaps because of it, Bashir couldn't keep from staring into his approaching doom.

Without warning, a shock ran through his system. His vision, so sharp, suddenly blurred. Had it reached him already?

No—it was his probe's interface!

Disconnect! Bashir's thought command created a black wall between himself and the Forbidden Files' defender. He felt himself fading slowly from the computer-awareness and back into his own body.

Through his dimming vision, he saw the black wall buckle under the impact from the other side. Hairline fractures appeared, spreading, leaking dark red light.

Exhausted, unable to move or even to think, Bashir passed out.

— 10 —

Green green green green green.

The world was washed in green. A verdant sheen lay on everything Alyssa looked at. When she closed her eyes, an emerald scintillation danced on the backs of her eyelids.

As she passed through the Wellfield's eastern archway, she was alone. She had the entire expanse of green sky, green earth, and green grass all to herself. Turning, she squinted upward. The early-afternoon sun was a blindingly bright emerald, shining down just for her.

She grinned so wide it almost hurt.

Alyssa twirled once, her skirt billowing around her, then she took off. She flew back to the city, barely touching the ground as she ran and leapt along the field's perimeter.

Ah, marvelous! She was bursting with energy, singing and pulsing with more life than she could contain. It flowed out from her, touched the sand, Sapphire Lake, even the black towers. She could have reached up and pulled the emerald sun down from the sky if she'd wanted to. Nothing was beyond her.

The rapture faded slowly. It carried her along the beach, through the city, and into her reztower. By the time she reached her mod, a few traces of green remained, clinging to its walls.

Alyssa checked her message unit to see what old Bashir had been up to, but its memory was blank. That was fine. Maybe she'd go out to the Annex later and check up on him.

But that could wait. Right now she just wanted to ride along on the lingering vestiges of the Glow. She was in no hurry. She settled back in a reclining chair pod and ordered up her favorite boneharp composition by Halafa. Somehow, the two-hundred-year-old music resonated perfectly with her post-Welltime mood.

Tiny green speckles danced before her eyes, keeping time with the subtle chords. At first a crowd, twirling fast, they wandered away, slowed, dimmed as the music played on, until there was only one lone green point. It drifted slowly toward the edge of her vision, shifting as her eyes shifted to follow it. Then it too was gone and she was alone in the dark with Halafa's music.

Her thoughts flowed along a river of arpeggios in a minor key. Softly, softly. The music gradually faded and only the sense of gentle sad movement remained.

Alyssa rocked slowly in the dark, in the consoling silence. It was a good place, a cool comforting place, and she was pulled out of it with a painful jolt.

She opened her eyes with a start. The music was gone, replaced by a piercing high-pitched wail. The general alarm!

She sat up immediately and looked around.

What was happening?

The siren set her nerves on edge and made it hard to think. She stood up and, her eyes wide, stared out at the city.

Stared at the city?

Suddenly it hit her. Her mod's power had been cut off. Why else had the music stopped? Why else had the walls reverted to their transparent deenergized state?

When she concentrated on the view outside her now-invisible walls, she got a greater shock. All the buildings she could see were likewise clear-walled. Only their flooring, some internal supports, and occasional privacy areas were opaque.

The reztower west of Alyssa's was an architectural skeleton silhouetted black on red against the setting sun.

The entire city must have lost its power.

"No, no, no, no, no," she moaned. It wasn't possible.

Alyssa squeezed her eyes tightly shut, willing this all to be a bad dream. When she opened them again, the same eerie half-visible city stood before her.

Such a failure hadn't happened in her lifetime. As far as she knew, it had *never* happened. Home's essential systems were all maintained by the Matrix, and the Matrix was foolproof. It was too well guarded for sabotage, and had too many built-in redundancies for accidents or errors to slip through.

Then why was the power out?

The general alarm was still blaring away, feeding her anxiety. Alyssa hurried over to the pedestal housing her commnet link. The link connected her with all of Home, and with hundreds of places owned or frequented by the Wellborn. But not now. It remained dead to voice and manual controls.

If the link was down, could anything else be functioning?

With a feeling of approaching panic, she summoned her mod's bots, ordered the lights to come on, called for her message unit. All to no avail. The bots stayed in their niches, the lights remained dark, the message unit continued its silence. Everything was dead. She'd have to look elsewhere if she wanted an explanation.

She stepped closer to the outer edge of her floor. The city's western third spread out before her. She looked out and down, feeling a terrifying vertigo even though she knew her wall was still there.

In the shadowed streets far below, widely spaced emergency lights showed crowds of people milling around in confusion.

Alyssa backed away from the unsettling sight, until she was touching the interior wall of her mod.

The buildings' entrance mechanisms must have locked, she realized. *They don't have anywhere to go.* On the heels of that thought came another: *How was she to get out of her own building?* Alyssa frowned worriedly. There had to be emergency exits somewhere, though she couldn't remember having seen any. She'd never looked for one. There'd never been any need to.

The reztower couldn't be completely sealed off, could it?

Was it her imagination, or was the air already becoming stale?

Alyssa edged toward her mod's doorway.

In chaotic counterpoint to the siren's wailing, she could hear the other residents of her tower shouting to one another across the tower's central shaft. It sounded as if most of them were setting out for the presumed emergency exit, somewhere on the ground floor. Alyssa decided to join them before twilight turned into night.

She stepped out of her mod, through its now-dead privacy barrier, and made her way to the motionless pedramp. As crowded as the streets outside had looked, this was far worse. She hadn't realized how many people lived in her tower. They were like a river pouring down the spiral ramp, carrying her along in their half-panicked flight.

The ramp had never seemed so narrow, the guard rail so low. In all the jostling and shouting and confusion, Alyssa expected to see someone fall over the edge. It didn't happen. They weren't that far gone, thank the Founders.

As she descended the ramp, turn after turn, story after story, she had time to think. Keeping a safe distance from the railing, helping others up as they stumbled, she had time to think about the Matrix.

This was no minor subsystem failure. Something must have gone seriously wrong with Home's quasi-organic central computer.

What could cause such a breakdown? Alyssa was no expert on the Matrix's design, but she knew that nothing predictable could disrupt it to this degree. She considered the possibilities.

A severe earthquake might do it, but in that case the building she was in would have collapsed as well.

Perhaps an attack by armed aliens? No—the orbiting surveillance drones would have given some warning.

No, it had to be something less obvious but just as potent. She began to feel hemmed in by the crowd, impeded rather than rushed along. Couldn't they go any faster?

It had to be something that was selective, affecting only the Matrix. At each floor, more people crowded onto the ramp, slowing her descent.

Something like a clever old man digging deeper into its secrets than he should. She wanted to run, but she could only move at a shuffling pace. The general alarm had not yet been turned off. It filled the tower's central shaft with pulsing waves of sound.

And if Bashir had done this to the Matrix, what might it have done to him? She had to get out of here!

The siren, the crowd, the red sunlight filtering horizontally through the clear buildings—it all took on a personally ominous quality for Alyssa. If Bashir had done this, he'd done it because of her, because she'd asked him to help Darrin.

She began pushing forward, heedless of her fellow citizens' protestations. It gained her little speed, but it was the only thing she could do. And she had to do something.

By the time Alyssa had descended as far as the second floor, she could see the people on the ground floor being directed toward the north side of the tower.

Upon reaching the ground floor, she saw a pair of large sliding doors standing open in a wall she'd always thought was solid. A bright blue EXIT sign glowed above them.

When she reached the doors, she saw the tower's security chief standing to one side of the opening.

"No need to rush," the woman shouted above the crowd noise and siren. "Everything's under control!"

Sure it is, Alyssa thought cynically. *That's why I've just had to fight my way down fifty-eight stories.* She pushed past the large, stern-faced security chief, through the doorway, and out of the tower without a backward glance.

Freed at last, Alyssa ran north along the darkening streets of Home, dodging and weaving her way through the crowds of curious and anxious citizens.

At least they're too preoccupied to notice me. It was the only positive thought she could come up with. How could she have explained her mad dash away from the center of the city?

"See, there's this old guy who lives in the Annex . . . "

No, it wouldn't do at all. *Just keep moving and hope you're wrong.*

* * *

Alyssa crossed the street separating Home from the Annex, and went from darkness into light. The Trading Annex didn't depend on the Matrix to distribute its power, so the blackout stopped on Home's side of the street. On the Annex side, shops were bright and busy, and the sidewalks were filled with people drawn by the spectacle to the south.

Home's dim towers and domes rose into the night sky, glistening transparently in the light from the Annex and from high-riding, full Yakimu.

Home's panic had not yet spread to the Annex. The crowd of spectators seemed to Alyssa to be evenly torn between tension and curiosity. She felt herself become the momentary focus of their curiosity.

The Normals reached out for her, shouted questions at her: What had happened to Home? Where was she going? Would the Annex be affected?

"I don't know! Let me through!" She didn't have to repeat herself. Something in the face of this slim young woman kept the crowd back, something in her dark eyes moved them out of her path. Soon she was beyond them, her long black hair and pale blue skirt flowing behind her.

Away from the boundary street, the lights were dimmer and farther apart. So were the people. The back streets of the Annex were not a pleasant place at night. Mostly they were deserted and quiet, where Alyssa's only company was the echoes of her own footsteps.

Occasional oases of humanity appeared around the widely scattered bars and all-night cafs. The people who gathered on those isolated blocks were for the most part a cross-section of the downside of Annex life—toughs and dealers, pimps and prostitutes, and vacant-eyed losers who'd come to the end of whatever road they'd been traveling.

The respectable citizens were either making or spending money on the boundary strip or along Founders' Way, or they were at home, resting up for tomorrow's labors. The back streets at night were not for them.

Alyssa wasn't worried about traveling this way alone. No Normal, armed or not, would be a threat to her, unless she were taken by surprise, and that was not about to happen.

Not tonight. Her concern for Bashir and her just-completed Welltime would see to that. She'd never been more alert, more on edge.

Now, if somebody'd tried to mug me four nights ago . . .
She imagined the sight she must have been, stumbling home from The Wurgle's Retreat. The image made her grimace, but it didn't slow her down. She maintained what for her was a moderate, energy-saving pace. For the occasional Normals glancing at her from the shadows, it would have been an all-out sprint.

As she neared Bashir's neighborhood, the streets became narrower, darker, ever more devoid of life. Over the final ten irregular, twisting blocks, Alyssa passed three dim street-lights and no human beings. The only living things she saw were two large scrats who eyed her suspiciously from atop a garbage can.

When Alyssa came within sight of Bashir's shop, she paused. The shop fronted on a small square that had at one time been a marketplace. Over the decades, the life, the light, and the business had moved on.

Now, standing in the mouth of an alley across from the shop, Alyssa saw nothing but cracked paving, a dried-up fountain, and drifts of litter blown up against the buildings.

No lights showed anywhere. Under Yakimu's silvery glow, the scene was devoid of color: shuttered windows and recessed doorways nearly black, the smooth-worn stones of the fountain nearly white, all else shades of gray. The front of Bashir's shop was in deep shadow.

Alyssa stared at the shop for several minutes. The Wells had sharpened her vision, but she still couldn't see through Bashir's stone walls.

Is he all right? Am I going to look like a fool if I barge in there?

She couldn't even see through the thick shadow of the doorway.

Maybe I'm too late. Why am I standing here like a quivet startled by a shade hawk?

She could see, hear, feel, taste, and smell nothing amiss. This was a tired, decaying section of the Annex and the hour was late. It was perfectly natural for the streets to be dark and deserted, the buildings closed up, the people asleep. What was she waiting for?

When she could come up with no good answer to her own question, Alyssa stepped out of the alley's shadows and walked directly across the square to Bashir's shop. All the short interminable way she kept her eyes straight ahead, fighting the urge to glance back to see who or what might be sneaking up on her.

Alyssa reached Bashir's heavy wooden door without incident. As usual, it was not locked, and as usual, it took more than a Normal's strength to open it.

The hinges' squeal echoed around the silent square. Alyssa slipped through the opening and stepped to one side of the doorway. Nothing happened. She took a deep breath to calm herself and nearly choked on the acrid smoke that hung heavy in the air.

Fire?!

"Bashir!" she called in a loud whisper. The sound was swallowed by the thick, dark air. There was no answer.

She kept the door partly open for the little additional light it admitted and began to work her way toward the back of the shop. She moved cautiously, step by sliding step.

Except for the smoke, everything seemed to be in order, or in the disorder she'd come to expect in the outer room. The dim shapes she could see and the shelves she touched in passing were all in their familiar places.

The odor of burning became stronger as she crept farther into the shop. The smoke itself did not get any thicker, however, and her eyes adjusted somewhat to the difficult conditions.

By the time Alyssa came to the desk at the back of the shop, she could see well enough not to bump into it. She could also see that the door behind the desk, the door that led to Bashir's living quarters, was half retracted into its slot, and that it was twisted and warped out of shape. Beyond it, the darkness was impenetrable.

The harsh stench and the smoke were oozing out of that black opening. The air was barely breathable.

"Bashir!" This time it was a shout of anger and despair. There was again no answer. Not a word, not a sound, not a hint that anything was alive in there.

He was dead. She felt that truth like a lead weight in her stomach. He'd challenged the Matrix and lost. Because of her and Darrin, Bashir had died in there. Somehow the Matrix had reached out and destroyed that dear, clever, wiry old man.

Alyssa rushed around the desk and yanked the drawers open. Bashir must have kept a light in there someplace. She began frantically searching through the drawers with her fingers, squinting against the stinging smoke. Where in the Founders' damned eyes was a light?

She wasn't going to leave his body in that horrible room. She had to get him out of there, to give him a decent funeral. She owed him so much more, but now that was all she could do for him.

Alyssa threw a drawer across the shop, shattering one of the front windows. She'd come too late to save Bashir, and now she wasn't even going to be able to find him.

She pounded on the desktop so hard it cracked. Why why why why why hadn't she even had sense enough to bring a light with her? She could have gotten a portalamp in one of the Annex shops. If only she'd been thinking!

Sobbing and cursing, Alyssa turned toward the back doorway. If she couldn't see in there, she'd feel her way to Bashir. The air would be hard to breathe, but not impossible. She squared her shoulders, took as deep a breath as she could stand, and stepped forward.

"He is not there, lovely lady."

Alyssa whirled around. The voice had come from somewhere behind her, in the shop.

"Who's there?" she demanded, angry rather than frightened. If this was someone responsible for Bashir's death . . .

One hit left.

The thought gnawed at M'Briti. She shifted nervously on her chair of hide and polished wood. She was sitting on the flat rooftop of her two-story house, watching the sun melt down into an orange-red smear. At this time of day, as sunset faded into twilight, the western hills became an irregular black silhouette stretching across the horizon.

Out here, on the northwest edge of the Annex, nothing stood between M'Briti and the distant hills but a few low buildings and a broad expanse of virgin prairie. Her view was usually unobstructed. On clear days, she could count the few stands of trees dotting the prairie and watch their shadows lengthen as the sun went down. But not this evening.

This evening, a brown fog swirled within M'Briti's eyes, obscuring the scene. It dampened the sky's colors and dulled the edges of the hills' shadows. It made the scattered trees invisible. She blinked her eyes several times and rubbed them vigorously, to no avail.

M'Briti shivered and pulled her jacket more tightly around her. The fog brought with it a chill that overrode the summer evening's warmth. It even impinged on her hearing, with a sharp but faint wailing sound, like a distant siren.

You don't have to take it yet, she declared silently.

It shouldn't have come to this, she realized. She should have followed up on some contacts by now, hooked another customer, earned a new supply of Purple. But she'd become preoccupied with Darrin Montoya.

In some ways, Darrin was the perfect mark for her—a Transgressor, newly banned from the Wells, deserted by his lover, and sounding very much like a man without hope. And yet there were things that didn't fit, such as his failure to appeal his banishment and the underlying strength of character she'd sensed in him. Not to mention the crime he'd attempted—certain of detection and just as certain to fail.

Darrin's crime was, in that respect, not that dissimilar to the one she'd attempted a year ago.

The brown fog in M'Briti's eyes thickened, and her chill grew deeper. She got up to walk around the rooftop, stepping carefully to avoid tripping over obstacles or walking off the edge. The low railing enclosing the roof was more decorative than practical.

M'Briti stopped by the square chimney in the center of the roof. She slapped her leg hard in frustration. *If only he didn't look so much like M'Taba!*

The withdrawal symptoms were the price everybody paid for the glorious highs Purple gave. M'Briti was not immune, though she'd held off the drug's worst effects longer than anyone she'd heard of. In that sense, she had not lied to Darrin—willpower could make a difference. She was using the drug, not being used by it. How long she could maintain that distinction was another question altogether.

Shaking, she leaned against the chimney. Its rough stone surface still retained much of the heat of the day. M'Briti pressed against it, seeking to absorb some of its warmth and solidity.

Had her brother, M'Taba, gone through this struggle before he'd died? That question had become increasingly important to her as Purple's grip on her had tightened. Had he fought the drug, or had he given in, perhaps welcomed it as it had slowly and surely killed him?

"That will not happen to me." M'Briti spoke the words through clenched teeth, in angry determination. She had truly loved her brother, but she admitted to herself that M'Taba had been a weak person, as had most of those whom she herself had hooked on Purple. They were at least partly responsible for their own fates. Nobody had forced them to give in.

M'Briti jammed her fist against the chimney. It wasn't her fault that they fell so easily for the apparent escape Purple offered. She didn't notice the blood dripping from her knuckles. If she had not provided them with the drug, someone else would have. Someone whose motives would be solely mercenary.

Is Darrin one of them—one of the weak ones? she wondered. Despite her need for more Purple, and therefore another customer, she hoped he was different. At their first meeting, only two days ago, she'd felt something sympathetic develop between them. They'd spent much of the following evening together.

M'Briti hadn't been close to anyone for over a year. She found her attraction to Darrin hard to understand and just as hard to deny.

She shoved away from the chimney. The roof was all shadows and drug fog, alive with vague shapes. M'Briti felt her pulse pounding. Suddenly the tension she'd felt all day was heightened. It became difficult to catch her breath.

A face began to coalesce from the darkness. She backed away, but the face moved with her. It was almost recognizable. Dark shadow eyes, brown skin, black hair. Was it M'Taba or Darrin Montoya? Her brother, or her next possible victim?

The face came closer. It smiled, and its teeth gleamed white in the night.

"No!" M'Briti's anguished cry was swallowed by the darkness. She turned to run, caught her foot and fell. In slow motion, she saw the low railing rising to meet her. Beyond it, two stories above the street, the smiling, accusing face floated, taunting her.

When she came to, she was lying facedown on the rooftop. She felt cold and numb. Her head throbbed from where she'd struck it against the railing. Her hands were scrapped raw from the rough gravel of the roof.

She pushed painfully to her knees, then stood slowly. A small bomb seemed to explode inside her skull, causing her to stumble against the railing. She caught herself before going over the edge, and immediately vomited onto the sidewalk two floors below.

"Founders' damn," she gasped once her stomach had settled down. She straightened up and stepped back from the railing. She looked around slowly, puzzled. Something had changed.

The neighborhood was dark, with no streetlights. A dim glow crept out through a few partially shaded windows. And yet she could see the low dark buildings around her clearly. Their outlines were distinct, their chimneys blacker silhouettes against the night sky.

What . . . ? She shook her head and winced as the throbbing in her skull flared up. Then she realized what had happened. The brown fog was gone.

M'Briti had experienced at other times some ebbing of Purple's effects, but never a complete cessation. This time, as she stood in the still night, breathing in the warm air, her symptoms were nearly all gone. Her vision had cleared. She no longer felt chilled. The unfocused anxiety that had been gnawing at her for most of the day had vanished. Only the odd ringing in her ears remained.

Gingerly, she walked around the roof, barely breathing, not wanting to disturb the magic. It couldn't last, she knew that. But while it did, she wanted to savor it.

To the west, a faint afterglow of the sunset still outlined the far hills. To the north, stars were beginning to gleam in the darker sky. To the east, the lights from the heart of the Annex pushed back the night—the business along Founders' Way was no respecter of nature's rhythms. And to the south, of course . . .

M'Briti stopped her casual survey. To the south, Home was supposed to be a glow of towers and domes above the lower buildings of the Annex. But it was not.

Instead, M'Briti saw faint outlines of buildings, spidery shadows where the bright skyline should have been. And, as she stared southward, it seemed to her that the ringing in her ears came from that direction too, rising and falling like a siren or alarm.

She frowned. Had her Purple symptoms been replaced by a new, localized hallucination? She touched the aching lump above her temple. The stab of pain made her eyes water, but

Home remained strangely dark, and the siren sound continued.

Real, then, she concluded. *Not an hallucination.*

A breeze came up from the west, whispering across the roof, bringing with it the scent of open prairie. That, and a faint taste of electricity, a hint of weather change in the air.

M'Briti turned away from the darkened city to the south and went back to sit in her west-facing chair. Whatever was happening in Home was none of her business. She was still a Wellborn, but the Annex was now her home, and those who used and dealt Purple were her concern.

As she watched, the sky above the western hills darkened by almost perceptible degrees from aqua to indigo. The stars began to shine with crystal sharpness. The hills became merely a darker line where the stars stopped.

One hit left. The thought returned, mockingly. Her withdrawal symptoms were gone, but she knew the respite was temporary. Had she become, gradually over the past year, one of them? One of the users and dealers? Had means and ends melded indistinguishably?

M'Briti hunched down in her chair, drawing her knees up to her chin. Was she willing to pull Darriŋ Montoya into this morass, in the faint hope that sacrificing him would move her closer to her brother's killers?

She shivered and hugged her legs tightly against her chest. The evening breeze seemed to be getting cooler, with a promise of rain.

— 12 —

"Sabotage! That's the only explanation." Senyan's deep voice conveyed both outrage and fear.

"We don't know that yet, Executor." Niala was inclined to agree that the Matrix failure was more than an accident or a malfunction, but she refused to rush to a judgment.

Venebles nodded in satisfaction, as if Niala were now on her side.

"Bah!" Senyan settled back into his chair, glowering at the dim milky tabletop.

The table, like the rest of Home's links to the Matrix, was essentially dead. Occasional images flashed across its screen, or from its holojector, but they were random and uncontrollable. A small emergency radio transceiver was the Executors' only remote link to the rest of Home.

As soon as the power had failed, Niala and the other two had converged on their regular meeting room, each assuming the others would do likewise. They had found the place dark, like the rest of Home. Its solid stone walls had suddenly taken on a menacing quality, enclosing a blackness unrelieved even by starlight.

Since their arrival, their emergency staff had installed four portable light panels on the room's walls. The long multiple shadows cast the Executors' features into eerie relief and heightened Niala's sense of foreboding.

As she reviewed with Senyan and Venebles what little information they currently had, she had the fleeting impression that the others had been transformed into caricatures of themselves. Senyan became a dark, shadowy boulder on her left. Venebles was a tall stick figure, crowned with silvery fire.

A cool breeze blew through the room, jiggling one of the light panels and making the shadows dance.

In the midst of their discussion, the milky table's holojector sprang suddenly to life, flashing a string of numbers, several full-body shots from personnel files, and a star chart. Then it went blank.

"Damn it, how much longer is this going to go on?" Senyan grabbed the radio and switched it on. "Hello, Matrix Control?" The radio sputtered some static at him. He banged it on the table and raised his voice. "Matrix Control! This is Executor Senyan!"

"Yes, sir?" a voice responded, thin but clear. "Chief Monitor Aspinal here."

"How much longer before the Matrix is fully operational, Aspinal?"

"That's hard to tell, sir. The comm links should be up shortly, but some of the more intricate functions are giving us problems." Aspinal paused for a moment. "It's almost as if the Matrix were alive, and resisting our efforts at repair."

Senyan glanced at the other two Executors. He looked as puzzled as Niala felt. *The Matrix alive?*

"What kind of nonsense is that?" he demanded.

"That's the best way I can describe it, sir." Aspinal sounded apologetic. "We're running into safeguards where none were ever programmed in. And our attempts to access deeper levels of the system are being blocked in ways we don't understand. We're slowly restoring the peripheral functions, but the more basic ones, we just can't say."

"Very well, Chief." Senyan did not sound pleased. "Let us know if anything changes."

"Certainly, sir."

Senyan scowled as he turned the transmit switch off. His swarthy complexion looked a shade or two darker than normal.

"As I was saying," Niala raised her voice slightly to compensate for the interruption. "The prudent assumption is that this is more than an accident and more than a malfunction. Whatever has caused the Matrix to break down affected some basic operating system elements, and something seems to be resisting the monitors' efforts to analyze and correct the problem."

Venebles nodded. "Granted, those are all facts, based on the preliminary reports. But we all know those reports are incomplete and hurried and possibly in error. More to the point, why do those reports rule out accident or malfunction?"

"Oh, please," Senyan growled. "It's obvious that this required deliberate tampering. No conceivable programming error could have gotten past the safeguards, and just about *everything* would have had to malfunction at the same time to cause a breakdown this extensive."

"Exactly." Niala was relieved that Senyan agreed on that point. But then, that interpretation had been his from the beginning. "And only a very sophisticated intrusion could have gotten into the Matrix deeply enough to cause such widespread disruption."

Senyan pounded his fist on the table, which lit up in brief flashes before going dark again. "Just the sort of thing the Draths have been hoping for for years."

"That's crazy," Venebles said scornfully. "What do you know about the Draths, anyway?"

"Listen," Senyan replied coldly, "I've been around long enough . . ."

"Too long," Venebles muttered.

" . . . to know that the Draths resent our technology and the Wells. We're almost devils according to their religion."

"Listen," Niala began, but was ignored.

"Amazing." Venebles leaned far forward, toward Senyan. "Listen to me." She spoke with exaggerated slowness. "You are paranoid. The Draths accept us just as do the rest of the Torians and the Free States." Her voice began to rise. "Talk to them. Read the treaties. Look at the trade agreements. Open your eyes!" She ended with a near shout.

Senyan smiled condescendingly. "So now you're an expert on the Draths. And yet you've never heard of the Red Hand?"

"Purely a fringe sect," Venebles snapped.

"But they do portray the Wellborn as evil, don't they, and the Wells as a device of the devil?"

Venebles rolled her eyes upward, as if looking for divine intervention. "Yes, yes, yes. That small, minority fringe sect hates us. They would like to see us wiped off the face of Seelzar. But that doesn't mean all Draths feel that way, and it certainly doesn't mean they sabotaged the Matrix. Next, I suppose you'll be blaming them for the spread of Purple addiction as well."

"Now that you mention it, maybe they *are* to blame!"

"Do you suppose we could get back to the issue of the Matrix?" Niala asked pointedly, her patience wearing thin.

She knew that Purple Heaven was yet another point of unending contention between Senyan and Venebles.

The older Executor viewed Purple as a legal problem to be solved by enforcement. He advocated punishing the users and dealers, and was especially concerned with tracing the drug to its source and putting that source out of business in any way necessary.

To Venebles, Purple was more a social problem. She wanted to determine why the Wellborn would take such a drug in the first place, and thought rehabilitation of the victims should be Home's first priority. She was bluntly skeptical of Senyan's view that some group outside Home was using the drug as a weapon to attack the Wellborn.

Venebles turned to Niala. "That is a very serious accusation the Executor just made. I don't believe we can let it go unanswered."

"What accusation?" Senyan asked with mock innocence. "I just think we have to consider all the possibilities."

"You know very well . . ." Venebles began.

"Enough!" Niala called on her military training to make the word a command. She continued in a voice that was quiet but intense. "With all due respect, Executors, this wrangling is accomplishing nothing. We cannot decide here and now who caused the Matrix breakdown, and we certainly cannot solve the Purple epidemic."

She leaned forward, tapping on the table for emphasis. "What we can do is to give direction to the Matrix monitors. Does either of you have a good reason why we should not have them start with the provisional assumption that this was an act of sabotage by a Wellborn?"

Niala looked hard at Venebles, then at Senyan. They both shifted uncomfortably under her steady gaze, making their stretched-out shadows jerk along the floor.

"It does make sense as a starting place, I suppose," Venebles agreed after a moment. "As long as that assumption does not automatically become the conclusion."

"Of course not," Niala said. "The Matrix monitors and security have no reason to make of this more than it is. And you, Executor?" she asked Senyan.

The stocky Executor took a deep breath, then let it slowly out. "That does leave open the question of outside backing for such a person, which could be pursued after we've caught the agent, Wellborn or otherwise. Let's do it." He looked down at the tabletop and pressed some of the contact points. A jumble of disconnected images flickered across the display screens. Blurred multicolored shapes swirled in the holojector's field.

"Better, but still not functional," Senyan growled. "We'll have to use this thing." He picked up the small radio unit and roughly flicked its transmit switch on.

"Matrix Control? This is Executor Senyan."

"Yes, sir?" someone other than Aspinal answered.

"I'd like to speak with Chief Monitor Aspinal, please."

"Just a moment, sir."

Senyan drummed his fingers while he waited. Venebles leaned back to stare at the dim white ceiling. Niala crossed her fingers and hoped that the other two wouldn't be too upset by what they were likely to hear.

"Aspinal here."

"I'm getting tired of this radio, Aspinal. Any progress?"

"Definitely, sir. We shouldn't have to rely on the radio much longer. Communications within Home are nearly restored. The whole commnet will take at least another day. The deeper systems could take a long time."

"And your investigation as to the cause of this disaster?"

"We are proceeding as Executor Kirowa ordered, sir. We've eliminated most of the legitimate access channels, but some of our people think they've found an unregistered line. They're trying to trace it through the areas of heaviest disruption."

"As Exec . . . " Senyan caught himself. "Very well, Chief. Let us know immediately of any new developments."

"Certainly, Executor."

Senyan flicked the transmit switch off. He and Venebles both stared accusingly at Niala. She felt herself beginning to blush.

"It was more a suggestion than an order," she said, trying to keep her voice from sounding too apologetic. After all, she knew she was right, and Senyan and Venebles had just agreed to her approach.

"That's not what Aspinal seems to think." Senyan was still clutching the radio unit. He held it out to Niala. "Why don't we just give you this and go on home? Clearly Executor Venebles and myself are no longer needed."

"Oh, put that thing down." Why did Senyan have to overreact to every perceived slight or offense? "When the power failed, I knew it had to involve a Matrix malfunction. On my way here, I visited Matrix Control. It was only a few blocks out of my way, so I stopped by there first to find out what the situation was."

Niala spread her hands. "They were coping as well as they could at the time, but they seemed to need some direction." She smiled at the other two Executors. "No harm was done, and I've saved them a couple of hours. If this was deliberate sabotage, every minute is crucial."

Senyan and Venebles still didn't look very happy about the situation. An uncomfortable silence settled around the table, broken only by the low moan of the wind blowing through the doorways.

Finally, Venebles cleared her throat and said, "Well, Executor Kirowa, at least you seem to have come up with a way to keep Executor Senyan and myself away from each other's throats." Her lips were curved in a way that might have been a smile.

Senyan sighed and looked down at the tabletop again. "It does appear that, as you say, no harm was done. And I suppose that in circumstances such as these some deviations from standard procedure are excusable."

"Thank you for your understanding, Executors." Niala knew that she was right, but she also knew that two votes to one could get her actions investigated by the Assembly after this crisis was over. That grief she could do without.

"But," said Senyan, slamming his palm down on the table, "I would feel a lot better about this if *your* investigation were to turn up something!"

As if in answer to his demand, the displays in front of Senyan and the other two began to glow. In a moment, a man's face appeared on the screens. He was thin and tan, with gray-flecked brown hair. He looked tired but excited.

"Aspinal here, Executors. Are you receiving my signal?"

Niala was the first to react. "Yes, indeed, Chief. And you, ours?"

Aspinal smiled. "Loud and clear. It looks as if we've got the comm systems in Home back on line."

"At last, some good news," Senyan declared, brushing the radio unit off the table with a sweep of his arm. The action may have been accidental, but Niala doubted that. The radio had been for Senyan the symbol of the crisis.

"That's not the real news, Executor Senyan." Aspinal lowered his voice. "This is a secured line. May I speak confidentially?"

The three Executors exchanged puzzled glances before Senyan replied. "Of course, Chief Aspinal. There's no one but the three of us at this end."

"Good." Aspinal's face grew larger as he leaned closer to the pickup at his end of the link. "One of my techs came up with the idea that all the Matrix disruption is coming from the Matrix itself, in response to a deep illegal probe. If somebody went in as far as the Forbidden Files and tried to pull something out, we don't know what safeguards might be activated."

Niala felt a cold satisfaction. The possibility was one she herself had been considering. The Forbidden Files had been created during the lifetime of the Founders, and no documentation existed of their nature, nor of the protections surrounding them. What was known was that the only way anyone had even come close to accessing the Files was by using a total interface probe. It was a risky procedure, and the four who had tried it had been killed by a Matrix-directed system overload.

"So we assumed," Aspinal continued, "that the intruder's path into and out of the Matrix would also be the path of greatest damage. It's been hard work, with the Matrix itself fighting us, but we've located what looks like the remains of an illegitimate access line in one of the lower levels of the main housing."

"Remains?" Venebles asked.

Aspinal nodded. "A burned-out junction in the back of one of the subunit cabinets. Right against the wall. The system must have sent a huge power surge back along that line. Part of the cabinet was melted. There's a charred hole where the intruder's cable came out of the wall."

Senyan leaned closer to his display screen. "Can you trace it further?"

"We've already started, Executor. We have a microprobe following the path left by the burned cable. There've been a few blockages, but we're making good progress . . . What was that?" Aspinal turned to look at somebody off-screen. All Niala could hear was indistinct mumbling. The sound pickup at Aspinal's end had a narrow focus.

When he turned back to the Executors, the Chief Monitor looked as if he were unsure about how to take the news he'd just received.

"Executors, I've just gotten word that our probe has reached the end of the trail. The readings we're getting suggest that it's in a room full of burned-out wires, none of which lead beyond that room."

"And can you locate that room?" Senyan asked eagerly.

"Umm, it's somewhere . . . It did what?! I see." Aspinal was trying to carry on simultaneous conversations with someone at his end and with the Executors. He turned back to face the Executors. "I'm sorry. Things are a little frantic around here at the moment. The probe itself just overloaded. Must have hit a bare wire. The reading we got came from the older part of the Annex."

"The Trading Annex?" Senyan asked sharply.

"Yes, sir," Aspinal replied. Someone handed him a slip of paper. "According to our information, the location coincides with a small antique shop . . . "

"A perfect base for Drath spies," Senyan said, looking triumphantly at Venebles.

". . . owned by a possible Wellborn named Bashir Arak," Aspinal concluded.

A moment of silence greeted that announcement.

Venebles rubbed one finger across her forehead, as if trying to remember something. "Arak. Arak. Wasn't there once an Executor named Bashir Arak?"

"Yes, but he held office more than one hundred fifty years ago," Senyan said, dismissing the possibility. "He'd have to be well over three hundred years old by now. This can't be the same man. Executor Arak must be dead."

"If he was on the other end of that Matrix probe, you're probably right," Niala said grimly.

The Executors' many shadows spread throughout the room. Aspinal looked out expectantly from the three tabletop displays, awaiting further instructions.

— 13 —

Alyssa tensed as a short round bulk emerged from behind the large Drath altarpiece in Bashir's shop.

"Please do not be afraid. I am a friend of Bashir's."

The voice had a sibilant Torian accent. It sounded vaguely familiar. She stared hard at the shadowy figure, but it remained shadowy. What Torians did she know who might know Bashir?

"It was not my intention to upset you, dear lady." The short shape moved closer. "But Bashir said to be sure you weren't followed."

Wait a minute. Something clicked in Alyssa's mind. "Bulbulian!"

"At your service." The lump bobbed once.

"And Bashir?"

"I am to take you to him."

"Then he's all right?" Alyssa hardly dared to hope.

There was the slightest of pauses.

"We must not stay here any longer than is necessary. Here, you will need to wear this."

Bulbulian pressed something into her hands—a full-face mask with a hard faceplate and a rubbery flange and headstrap.

"Bulbulian, what about . . . ?"

"Come, there is no time to waste." His voice became muffled as he put his own mask on. "Follow me, quickly." He stepped around the desk toward the half-opened doorway in the back of the shop.

Alyssa frowned. What was this all about? Bashir couldn't possibly be waiting for them back there in the charred living quarters. What was Bulbulian up to?

The round pie vendor stopped in the doorway and turned to face Alyssa. "Please." The dim light glinted off the faceplate of his mask. "It is not far."

"What choice do I have?" Alyssa mumbled as she pulled on her mask.

The mask's faceplate was a high-power lumalens. The sudden brightening of the shop was almost painful. Alyssa squinted at Bulbulian and saw him squeeze through the now clearly visible doorway. She took a deep breath (*air filters too!*) and followed.

The room beyond was a smoke-filled ruin. Melted adaptapods covered the floor like a growth of plastic and metal fungi. Tangles of wire trailed out of recesses in each wall where the holoscreens had been. Of the screens themselves there was no sign. The ceiling was cracked and sagging.

Some of the acrid smoke crept in beneath Alyssa's mask, making her eyes water.

Bulbulian was busy in a far corner of the room, working on one of the lumps of adaptapod. Wires ran from the pod to a battery pack by his feet. Other wires connected the pod and a microphone he held in his right hand.

Alyssa walked over to where Bulbulian stood. She followed carefully the path he had made in the ashes and debris. The floor looked weak in some places, where cracks and depressions were evident beneath the rubble. But where Bulbulian had trod, she was certain that the floor would support her too.

"What are you doing? The machinery can't still be functional."

"A pile of useless slag, isn't it?" Bulbulian replied as he attached another wire to the pod. "When Bashir does something, he does it right."

"You mean he did all this to his own home?"

"Not the mess." The pie vendor turned to Alyssa. "But this." He raised the microphone and spoke into it. To Alyssa it sounded like gibberish. It was certainly no language she'd ever heard.

"What . . . ?"

The answer came before she finished her question. Just behind Bulbulian, a small section of the floor sank about half a meter.

"Our lift." Bulbulian gestured toward the irregular two-meter circle. "Please step over there, Alyssa, while I disconnect these wires."

Alyssa stepped onto the recessed slab gingerly, but it felt as solid as the stone streets outside. It didn't even budge when Bulbulian hopped down onto it. He studied the circle for a moment, then carefully stamped on it in several places.

With no warning, the slab began to descend rapidly. The drop was so sudden that Alyssa nearly lost her balance. Her stomach tried to bob up into her throat.

The lumalens masks were extremely efficient, but even they needed some light to work with. Soon Alyssa could see virtually nothing of her surroundings. Bulbulian was the merest suggestion of a shape next to her, and she suspected her imagination was more responsible than her eyes for that faint partial outline.

"Bulbulian, where are we going?" Alyssa struggled to keep her voice calm. She knew they must be hundreds of meters below ground by now. Bashir had always had a good selection of wines, but Alyssa didn't think his cellar was this deep.

They could have been dropping down a mine shaft from Home's pre-Annex days, though she doubted that. A thick layer of very hard and largely useless igneous rock underlay the entire basin around Sapphire Lake. Where could this shaft lead?

"Why, to Bashir, of course." From the sound of Bulbulian's voice, he'd taken off his mask.

"Yes, but where *is* he?" Alyssa pulled off her own mask. The air rushing past her was cool and dry. She could smell only a trace of the stench from above.

"I know it is not easy, but please be patient, Alyssa."

She imagined an apologetic smile on his round face, and gritted her teeth.

"We shall be there shortly. Bashir will answer your questions better than I could."

Better, maybe, Alyssa thought, *but definitely not soon enough.*

Their platform's deceleration was so gradual, Alyssa wasn't aware of it slowing down until it had nearly stopped. It settled with a muffled *chunk* and Bulbulian said something in the same unintelligible language he'd used on the adaptapod above.

What now? Alyssa looked around for some clue to her surroundings. Nothing. Just black and more black.

The moment Bulbulian stopped speaking, a slow, heavy vibration began. It shook the platform beneath Alyssa's feet and pressed against her ears. It felt as if a stone giant were grinding his teeth while she was standing in his mouth. To her right, a thin vertical line of light appeared. It widened in time with the vibration shaking her bones.

The light showed Alyssa the shaft they'd come down— green-streaked black rock polished to a high shine. It showed Bulbulian next to her, shielding his eyes against the growing brightness. It showed a thick stone slab pulling back farther and farther, and a long tunnel of the same green-black stone as the shaft, equally shiny.

Then the vibration stopped. In the stillness that followed, Alyssa could hear Bulbulian's breathing.

"Ah. Alyssa, Bulbulian. Come in." The voice came from just inside the doorway. There was a hollow metallic quality to it. Alyssa frowned.

"Bashir? Is that you?" She stepped from the platform into the doorway, but saw no one there or along the tunnel.

A chuckle echoed from the tunnel. "No, it's the big bad hugglebear. Of course it's me. I apologize for not greeting you in person, but Bulbulian knows the way."

Alyssa followed the round pie vendor down the tunnel. She was accumulating questions faster than she could keep track of them. What had destroyed Bashir's shop? Who was Bulbulian? Had Bashir found anything in the Matrix?

"What is this place?" The question popped out of its own accord.

Bashir's voice answered. "My lair. My workshop. My retreat."

Alyssa looked carefully at the smooth walls and floor. The audio pickups and speakers were well hidden. All she could see was micro-thin light panels and shiny green-black stone.

Retreat from what? she wondered. Aloud, she asked, "How did you dig all this out?"

"I didn't. I found it."

Bulbulian rounded a turn in the tunnel and stopped. "Here we are." He gestured to a floor-to-ceiling circular opening in the wall. "After you, Alyssa." His voice was subdued.

Alyssa walked through the odd doorway into a large dome-shaped chamber. On the far side of the chamber, twenty meters away, was a gleaming silver medunit. A man lay on its cushioned surface, his upper body encased in a milky white rehab cylinder. Only his lower legs showed.

"Bashir?" Alyssa asked in a whisper. She took a hesitant step toward the medunit. There was a sickly grayish cast to the old man's brown skin.

"Hah!" An amused snort came from speakers somewhere in the walls. "If you think this is bad, you should see the other guy!"

— **14** —

Alyssa paced back and forth along one side of the medunit. Her sandals slapping the floor sent little tapping echoes bouncing around the large dome-shaped room. She was not happy.

She was worried about Bashir. He was completely hidden from view. His lower legs were covered by a thin woven blanket. The rest of his body was encased in the medunit's opaque milky white rehab cylinder. The old man had assured her that he would be fine in a day or two, and Bulbulian had concurred, but she needed to see for herself.

Along with her worry, she felt a terrible responsibility for having caused the disaster. If she hadn't come to Bashir, seeking his help, he'd never have entered the Matrix, and it would never have struck back at him in so deadly a fashion.

Bulbulian, seated in a stout chair at the foot of the medunit, spoke up. "I am not as incapable as you might think, Alyssa." He said it lightly, almost flippantly, but Alyssa could see no trace of humor in his eyes.

"That's not the point!" she snapped, punctuating each word with a slap of her sandals. She was also angry. Bashir had just explained that in a day or two, as soon as he was able, he and Bulbulian were going to journey to the Torian capital of Ebel. Never mind that the Drath theocrats were notoriously hostile toward the Wellborn, or that travel between Home and Toria was strongly discouraged by both parties.

No, Bashir couldn't tell her what he expected to find there.

No, he couldn't tell her how long he expected to be gone.

No, she couldn't come along.

She glared down at the head of the rehab cylinder. "It's my fault you're doing all this, and Founders be damned if I'll let you take all the risks alone." Maybe Bashir really didn't know what he would find in Ebel, or maybe he was just being mysterious. It didn't matter. Alyssa wasn't going to let him travel all that way with Qatar Bulbulian as his sole companion. The round pie vendor seemed competent enough, but he was just a Normal. Until Bashir had recovered completely from his burns, Alyssa was determined to stay with him.

"Be reasonable, Alyssa." Microphones inside the rehab cylinder transmitted Bashir's voice to speakers on the room's walls. "There's no reason for you to make this trip."

Alyssa fought down the urge to scream or pound on the rehab cylinder. "Of course I'm going with you. Don't be stupid! You might very well need me, and anyway, where else can I go?"

Bashir sighed with resignation. The sound, amplified through several speakers, echoed around the room. "All right. I don't like it, but I'm in no position to stop you. Besides, I can't very well send you back the way you came."

Alyssa nodded. "The fire must have damaged your lift mechanism pretty severely."

"No, no, no." Bashir chuckled, though Alyssa thought she heard more pain than amusement in his voice. "Everything is perfectly functional. But I've shut down all the power between this room and my shop. Less chance of detection."

"You really think they'll be able to trace your Matrix probe that far?"

"If that damn computer didn't set itself on fire when it tried to fry me, the monitors will probably find my access point. Once they find that, it's just a matter of following the trail of melted wire." Bashir growled with disgust. "I should have anticipated this possibility, constructed a less obvious link."

"How could you know?" Alyssa rested her hand on the cool white surface of the rehab cylinder. *Why does he have to be so hard on himself?*

Bashir's voice was suddenly fainter. "I should have considered the possibility." There was a pause. "And planned accordingly."

Bulbulian spoke up then, his sibilant voice firm though scarcely above a whisper. "Alyssa, please." He raised his voice slightly. "Bashir, you must rest now. It is necessary to conserve your strength."

"Nonsense. I'm not dying here, Qatar."

Alyssa could hear the weakness in the old man's voice. "He's right, Bashir. It's very late. I think we could all use some rest."

Even with the room's speakers, Bashir's reply was difficult to hear. "If there's one thing I hate," he began haltingly, "it's being," his voice was fading rapidly, "patronized."

The last word was barely a whisper. Alyssa wondered whether or not she had imagined it. She looked over at Bulbulian, who shrugged but who seemed to be trying for a reassuring smile.

"He will be fine, Alyssa. Bashir has an extremely strong constitution. He just needs time to rest."

Alyssa nodded, but stayed where she was, one hand still resting on the milky rehab cylinder. What was Bashir's condition, really? She had Bulbulian's and Bashir's word for it that her old friend would be fine, but she had seen, only a few hours ago, the burned ruin of Bashir's living quarters above. It was hard to believe he could have survived that at all, let alone in reasonably good health.

"Come, Alyssa." Bulbulian touched her arm. "We should rest too. If he needs anything, he will let us know."

Alyssa smiled wanly. "I'm not so sure about that, Qatar. He is one stubborn old man."

"That he is," Bulbulian agreed. "And he will probably outlive us both. Come, I'll show you to your room."

"Very well." Alyssa allowed herself to be led away. At the high open doorway, she paused and looked back at the medunit. She could see nothing of Bashir. The light blanket covered his lower legs, the rehab cylinder covered the rest of him. But she could hear his breathing, coming through the room's speakers. It was easy and regular. It filled the room with a reassuring ebb and flow of sound.

Alyssa felt some of her tension ease. Bulbulian was right. Bashir was going to recover. He had to.

— 15 —

Bashir was running, harder than he'd ever run before. But he was barely moving, and the thing chasing him was getting closer and closer. He could feel its hot breath.

He didn't dare look back. That's what his monstrous pursuer was waiting for, for him to look back into its gaping jaws, into its heart of flame, to falter, to stumble ever so slightly. Then it would be on him, and he would be consumed in its fiery clutches.

Bashir awoke sweating and feverish and chilled. The pump of the medunit whirred loudly, filling the rehab cylinder with an analgesic, antiseptic mist. The mist swirled before his eyes, lightly soothed his skin. He breathed it in deeply.

On the display screen above his head, a pair of indicators glowed orange-red. His pulse rate and blood pressure were approaching the danger zone.

Slowly he calmed from his nightmare panic. Slowly the lights shifted down the spectrum toward green.

The display screen also showed him the time—one hour to go before dawn. As if the sun's progress across the sky could have any effect on his world inside the milk-white rehab cylinder. Even less could it touch the maze of green-black tunnels and rooms he and Alyssa and Qatar were now hiding in.

It was little comfort to Bashir that his nightmare was more memory than fantasy.

He actually had been chased, in a very real sense, by some beast spawned in the depths of Home's Matrix. It had come within nanoseconds of catching him before he'd severed his connection with the quasi-organic computer.

Even then, its pent-up charge had overwhelmed his probe's circuits, and the resulting fire had destroyed his living quarters.

He'd escaped, though barely and with severe injuries.

Now all he had was a confusing jumble of memories and impressions of what he'd seen in the Forbidden Files. He was certain of only two things: The Files had contained information from Seelzar's Founding and even earlier times, and something he'd seen there pointed him toward Ebel, the Torian capital and seat of power for the Drath Hierarch.

The medunit's pump slowed as its medicines began to take effect. Bashir felt some of his pain easing and allowed himself to relax. With time, he knew, his memories were likely to sort themselves out and become clear. Trying to force them would only drive them farther away.

Bashir couldn't help feeling troubled, however. He didn't like lying to Alyssa, even by omission. Yet revealing the gaps in his memory could have led to lengthy arguments and objections, perhaps more active opposition to his plan.

Alyssa was a headstrong woman. Bashir knew he needed to go to Ebel to solve the mystery of the Forbidden Files, but he had no proof to give Alyssa or anyone else.

To wait for his memory to return completely might take too long. He and Qatar might be discovered down here in the meantime. That, he definitely couldn't afford.

If only he'd been quicker, or planned better! He and Qatar could have been on their way already, instead of waiting for him to recover sufficiently to travel. Alyssa would be back in Home, giving whatever support she could to Darrin. She didn't need to be risking herself on this trip to Ebel, but try to tell her that!

Bashir heard the medunit pump speed up. The indicator lights were heading toward red again.

This won't do, old man, he scolded himself. If he and Qatar were going to get safely to Ebel, with or without Alyssa, he'd have to be in better control of himself. *You've done the best you could, Bashir.* That thought was his only comfort.

The cool white mist began to thicken in the rehab cylinder. Gradually, it obscured the display screen. Bashir squinted, but he could no longer see the clock. Its regularly shifting numbers had disappeared.

What did it matter? He settled back into the cushioned pad of the medunit. All he needed to do now was to rest and recover his strength. In a few days, he'd be able to travel. He and Qatar could make their way into Toria and Alyssa could wait safely back in Home.

Bashir closed his eyes. His thoughts wandered from Qatar to Alyssa to the Matrix, from the Annex to Home to Ebel, aimlessly yet with a vague sense of urgency.

The white mist continued to swirl, blotting out the red lights in the cylinder's display panel.

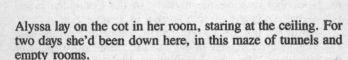

Alyssa lay on the cot in her room, staring at the ceiling. For two days she'd been down here, in this maze of tunnels and empty rooms.

At first she'd hoped Bashir might recover quickly, that perhaps his injuries had been superficial burns, bruises, and strains. But she was beginning to have serious doubts about his condition. He was still in the rehab cylinder, and from what she could tell from its status display, he was a long way from full recovery.

She'd tried to talk to Bashir during those times when he was awake, but he either didn't know or didn't want to tell her anything more about why he needed to go to Ebel.

Her only satisfaction came from her own refusal to leave without him. She wouldn't allow Bulbulian to escort her out of the tunnels, she wouldn't leave on her own with a map, and she wouldn't promise to separate from Bashir once they did leave the tunnels. She'd stay with him until she decided otherwise.

She ran her hand along the smooth stone of the wall. The surface looked and felt flawless. There were no rough spots, no ridges or indentations where the green veins ran into one another or where they met the black surrounding rock.

Bashir had said that he'd found this underground complex, and Alyssa had learned no more from him than that. She'd tried to work off some of her frustration over the past two days by exploring the tunnels and rooms, at least the lighted areas. Her only conclusion was that the humans who'd settled Seelzar had probably had nothing to do with carving out this maze.

For one thing, the carving or cutting was too good. Home's best technology couldn't have achieved such a finish, and Home was technologically far ahead of the rest of Seelzar.

For another, the shapes and proportions weren't quite right. Doorways were too broad, benches were uncomfortably high or low, the floors were slightly concave. And the rooms were all hemispheres. They varied in size from two meters across to over thirty, but they were all the same shape.

Finally, there was absolutely nothing down here that Bashir had not brought.

Alyssa had pressed Bulbulian on this, searching for clues to the tunnels' origins, but he had been unable to show her so much as a splinter of wood, a bit of metal, or a fragment of cloth. And as diligently as she had looked herself, Alyssa had found nothing either.

The tunnel builders had left nothing behind or had never had anything down here to begin with. Neither possibility was consistent with human behavior as she knew it.

It was an interesting puzzle, intriguing and even a little frightening. Who had done this thing, and why?

As she'd wandered through the tunnels at the edge of Bashir's lighted region, her imagination had occasionally asserted itself, and she'd thought she'd heard strange noises, slitherings and whisperings in the darkness beyond, in the black tunnels and unseen rooms.

She shivered a little at the memory of those fancied sounds. "Grow up, Alyssa. There's nothing down here," she chided herself.

"Hssst!"

At the sound from her doorway, she jumped up so fast she nearly cracked her head on the sloping ceiling above her cot.

"Who's there?" she demanded in a voice she hoped was more forceful than frightened.

"It is just I, Alyssa. Qatar. Who else could it be?" The pie vendor's face was peering around the edge of her doorway. He was smiling apologetically. "I'm sorry if I startled you."

"No, no," Alyssa said quickly, catching her breath. "That's quite all right."

"May I come in?" His voice was low, secretive.

"Please do." She gestured him in, and he stepped over to within an arm's length of her. "What can I do for you, Qatar?"

"Bashir does not know that I am here." Bulbulian glanced toward the doorway and Alyssa waited for him to elaborate. "I wanted to tell you before he did, so things would be easier."

"Tell me what?" Alyssa asked sharply. This didn't sound good.

"Please, not so loud, I don't want to disturb him." Bulbulian again glanced at the doorway.

"Okay, okay," she said, keeping her voice quiet despite her impatience. Why didn't he get to the point?

Bulbulian stepped closer. "Bashir wants to leave for Ebel tomorrow," he whispered. His voice slid around the smooth walls of Alyssa's room. The not-quite echoes set her nerves on edge.

"What?" she hissed, grabbing Bulbulian's shoulders with both hands. "He's still in the rehab cylinder!"

"I know," Bulbulian agreed, trying to pull away. "But his condition is improving, Alyssa."

"He can't even walk yet!" Alyssa kept her voice low, but her fingers dug into Bulbulian's shoulders for emphasis. He winced.

"Please, Alyssa! This is his idea, not mine."

"I'm sorry, Qatar." Alyssa released her grip on the pie vendor. "It's just so frustrating. I can't get him to listen to reason."

Bulbulian rubbed his shoulder and nodded. "I know what you mean. But I can tell you this. I have never known Bashir to take foolish chances. Either he is closer to recovery than we think, or he believes we can't afford to wait any longer."

Alyssa dropped into a chair and looked toward the open doorway. A hallway light panel glowed back at her, cool and steady, its light reflecting off the polished green-black stone of the walls, floor, and ceiling.

"What if he's wrong, Qatar? Doesn't he ever make mistakes?"

Bulbulian walked over to a low bench of marbled stone protruding into the room from the wall. He sat down with a grunt. "Of course he does, Alyssa. Fewer than most of us, I'd say, but he's still human, if Wellborn." He rested his hands on his knees and leaned forward slightly. "Still, he clearly knows something we don't. We'll just have to trust him."

"I'd like to," Alyssa said quietly. "And yet..."

Her thoughts shifted to her brother. Darrin had always seemed to know more than she did. He had been someone she could always trust to make the right decision, to give her sound advice, to teach by example. And yet now he was a Transgressor, banned from the Wells, and Bashir was in his current condition because he'd tried to help Alyssa clear Darrin's name.

Nobody is perfect. Everyone makes mistakes. And yet, if she didn't trust Bashir now, what were her alternatives?

"Okay," she said, smiling tiredly at Bulbulian. "This may be the biggest mistake of our lives, but let's follow Bashir's lead for now. What else can we do?"

— 17 —

Home was dark and wet. The sky was overcast, the air filled with a heavy mist. The park circling Home's central district, Oldtown, was sodden and cheerless, all the color washed out by three days of cold rain.

Niala strode along a winding path, through a stand of cumbra trees, stepping heedlessly through puddles. Her mood matched the weather. She was getting worn down by meetings, discussions, and consultations.

In addition to their usual governing duties, each Executor had nominal responsibility for some area vital to Home's well-being. Normally that responsibility was delegated to an assistant approved by the Assembly. Under the current emergency, however, the Executors had been forced to become actively involved in their areas of expertise. There was too much to do to allow for much delegation.

As a consequence, Senyan was overseeing the work on the Matrix and the commnet; Venebles was directing the restoration of basic services to the citizens of Home, and Niala was in charge of security.

The path left the relative shelter of the trees and a gust of wind whipped around Niala. She clutched her broad-brimmed rain hat as it tried to fly away.

If ever Home would be vulnerable to hostile forces, now was the time. Not that Niala expected any large-scale attack. She didn't believe that the Draths were seriously plotting to overthrow Home, and the most recent reports from Home's off-planet agents gave no indication that the Interstellar Union had located Seelzar yet. Still, those possibilities couldn't be absolutely ruled out. And in the meantime . . .

Water splashed up on Niala's pants leg, above the tops of her boots. She stopped and looked down to see a group of mudspringers hopping across her path. Each in turn landed heavily in the puddle directly in front of her, then bounded away on its three squat legs. Eyestalks pointing in all directions, the springers disappeared beneath the sheltering branches of a cluster of bushes.

In the meantime, Niala thought, resuming her walk, *I have enough security problems to keep me busy*. The blackout had brought on a rash of criminal activity by Normals and Wellborn alike. Though mostly small-scale theft and vandalism, some of the crimes were more serious, including several violent assaults and two murders.

Especially disturbing was the fact that some of the assaults and at least one of the murders had almost certainly been committed by Wellborn. Normals would have lacked access to the crime scenes or lacked the strength needed to have carried out the crimes. Niala suspected a connection between Purple and some of those crimes, but she hadn't been able to confirm it.

All in all, she had been so busy that she hadn't had time to check up on Darrin Montoya or Bashir Arak. Very frustrating.

Niala pulled her cloak tightly about her as she marched out of the park and into Oldtown. The winding path ended abruptly, replaced by a wide expanse of large, flat paving stones. Heavy, primitive-looking buildings rose here and there, gray hulks in the mist. A few large, ancient trees still grew in Oldtown, but none were close enough for Niala to see them.

The buildings in Oldtown, survivors from Seelzar's Founding, were a jumble of shapes and sizes, from small flattened domes barely three meters high to a slit-windowed cube more than thirty meters tall. They had in common their sturdy design and the white stone from which they'd been built. The native stone was extremely hard and showed very little wear after thirteen centuries.

On a sunny day, Oldtown made a bright and impressive display. Now, the mist and wind and gloom aged the buildings as the years had not been able to. Everything was gray and indistinct. The clean lines and sharp angles were blurred.

In keeping with her security duties, Niala knew every street and building in Home, including those in Oldtown. Almost without looking, she knew where each building was and what it was.

Some of Oldtown's buildings were museum pieces or monuments to Seelzar's Founders and Home's early inhabitants. Niala had no interest now in those. The building she was looking for was old on the outside, but modern on the inside, and served a very useful function.

She made her way between the darkened buildings, following paths worn just noticeably into the stones through centuries of use, until she came to a truncated pyramid some twenty meters tall. There were no windows in the slanting sides and only two doorways. In the front, a double set of shining metal doors was recessed slightly into the building. On an adjacent side, a single door, also metal, lay flush with the inclined outer wall.

The pyramid was, to all appearances, as dead as the other Oldtown buildings, but Niala knew better. This was where Senyan had asked her to meet him. One of the few fully functioning facilities among so many relics, the building housed the Permanent Archives of Home, and had since the city's earliest days. It was where Senyan had spent much of his time since the Matrix had crashed.

She walked up to the front door and felt a faint tingle behind her left ear. Or imagined that she did. The thick metal doors retracted silently to either side, revealing a second set of doors just beyond.

Niala stepped into the unlighted alcove between doors. The first set closed behind her. In the ensuing darkness, she felt the tingle again, and the second set of doors opened. The room beyond was large and well lighted. It occupied most of the building's interior.

"Executor Kirowa!" Senyan's deep voice echoed from somewhere high up in the middle of the room.

Squinting against the brightness, Niala saw the stocky Executor standing on a small platform near the ceiling, surrounded by projection terminals. As far as she could tell, he was the only person in the room other than herself.

"Come on up!" Senyan pointed straight down, where a thin staircase spiraled from the floor up to his platform.

"Right!" Niala called in return. Her boots clicked loudly as she crossed over to the stairs. All around her, the floor was covered with low cubes of translucent white. In the cubes, minute points of light flickered and danced.

This was the Archives, or the upper floor of the Archives. The remaining floors extended fourteen stories below ground. They housed complete information on Home and its citizens. From the Founding on, any information that had been recorded about the city and its inhabitants had found its way into the Archives. Over time, the files had grown downward, a new floor every century or so.

Niala reached the stairs and began climbing. As she did, she looked around the room from her ever-higher vantage point. The Archives had a large permanent staff, with eight or ten people on duty at any one time. Senyan must have sent everyone away or to the lower floors. Whatever his reason for meeting her here, it was apparently something he wanted no one else to know.

She looked up, but could see nothing through the opening in the platform at the top of the stairs. When she stepped up onto the platform itself, she found herself facing a dozen images, some moving and some still. They all had the peculiar quality of narrow-field projections—each image was only clear when she looked directly at its projector. They had virtually no peripheral visibility.

Again the secrecy, Niala thought, looking quizzically at Senyan.

"Arak," he replied to her unspoken question, nodding at the evanescent images.

Niala withheld her other questions while she studied the projected Archive information more carefully.

Her attention was drawn immediately to one projector that was flashing a series of still images of people, mostly in public settings. Each image stayed for perhaps two seconds before being replaced.

A group posing in front of the Assembly Hall, two people standing at a speaker's platform, a solitary figure walking along the shore of Sapphire Lake, five people sitting at a conference table—the images came and went, came and went. The only thing Niala could see that they had in common was their poor quality. All of the scenes were slightly blurred, especially the faces. No one in any of the scenes was identifiable.

Niala turned to Senyan. "Can the computer enhance these at all?"

"No." Senyan seemed sourly amused. "Nothing I've tried improves them in the slightest. And I've tried everything the computer is capable of."

"So what you're telling me—"

"They're all like that. As far as the computer can tell, the distortion is real, not a flaw in the imaging."

"And which Bashir Arak are these supposed to show us?"

"The Executor who served one hundred sixty-four years ago. Our Annex shopkeeper had no image listings in the Archives."

"How many other Bashir Araks are there?"

"None, according to the Archives. At least among the Wellborn. The files are far from complete beyond the confines of Home."

"Do we know that the shopkeeper was one of us?"

"No. In fact, there's nothing to suggest he was. The only information we have on him is in the Title Transfers file." Senyan indicated a projection on Niala's right.

Her eyes narrowed as she read the document. "This is just like the visual scenes. Previous owner's name—indecipherable. Date of transfer—illegible. Buyer—Bashir Arak, no previous address. Sale price—five thousand creds." Without turning, she asked, "What are we dealing with, anyway?"

Senyan's deep voice rumbled. "There's more. Look at the others—they're everything I was able to find."

For all his closed-mindedness on some questions, Niala respected her fellow Executor's ability and tenacity. If these projections held everything he had found, they probably held everything that was available. With a curious mixture of unease and anticipation, Niala studied the other images, one by one.

Bashir Arak the shopkeeper was a nonentity except for the single listing as property owner. Bashir Arak the Executor was listed many times, but there was no useful information in any of the files.

His birthdate was indecipherable. It could have been three digits or four. His parents were Jusilla Arak and David Tentabo. Neither parent was included in the Archives, except for that one entry. Yet, Arak's parents must have been Wellborn for him to be one, unless he'd earned a Wellspace on his own. He was not listed among Normals who'd earned that privilege.

There was a gap that must have covered at least several decades in Arak's life. His next appearance was as a member of the Assembly. No details of his activities were included—bills sponsored, committees served on, positions taken, votes cast—nothing.

After his Assembly term expired, he disappeared from the files again, for another undetermined length of time. Then he appeared as a successful candidate for Executor. Again, no details of his career. After three terms as Executor, he disappeared from the files for good—no further mention of him appeared anywhere.

There was no spousal agreement with anyone, there were no children, there was no note regarding a career after his Executorship. There was no obituary, not even a date of death, let alone a cause and a listing of relatives.

For all practical purposes, Bashir Arak the Executor had simply vanished.

Niala shook her head in disbelief. "It isn't possible to leave such a faint impression, is it?" She looked at Senyan, who'd been standing by silently all this time.

Senyan grinned as if he were an illusionist with one more trick up his sleeve. "It's even fainter than that, Executor Kirowa. Take a look at that final list over there."

She turned to where he'd pointed, and a previously blank space filled with a list of names and numbers. It was the comprehensive index of all the Wellborn's names and identi-disc codes, available only to Executors currently in office.

Niala quickly scanned the list of names. Araito . . . Araj . . . Arajani . . . Aram . . . No Arak.

"So." Niala leaned against one of the projector consoles and smiled at Senyan. "We're looking for a figment of someone's imagination?"

Senyan frowned. "This is not a joking matter, Executor."

"I wasn't joking." Niala swept her arm to indicate the surrounding projections. "Does Bashir Arak really exist?"

"I'm inclined to say yes," Senyan replied. He began to pace back and forth across the platform. "There are several possibilities, none of them comforting. One is that there are two Bashir Araks who've lived normal, blameless lives, both of whom the Archives have recorded very inadequately. And if the Archives have failed here, how much else have they missed?"

"That ignores the Matrix intrusion we traced to Arak's shop in the Annex," Niala objected.

"Indeed." Senyan kept pacing. "A second possibility is that someone who owned that shop, perhaps named Bashir Arak, wanted to cover his tracks. If he could infiltrate the Matrix, he could probably alter the Archives' files as well and make himself virtually untraceable."

"But then he'd just erase his own records and leave everything else intact. This business with Executor Arak's file would be pointless."

Senyan stopped near the edge of the platform. He looked down at the Archive interface cubes below. "There is," he began softly, "another explanation, harder to believe but better suited to the facts at hand."

Niala waited, suspecting what Senyan had in mind, but waiting to hear him say it.

He turned slowly to look at her. When he spoke, it was as if he were daring her to laugh. "The two Araks might be the same person."

She nodded. "Not a comforting thought, is it? Not even the Wellborn are supposed to live that long. If he's found a way to do that, and to infiltrate the Matrix and the Archives, what else might he be able to do?" Despite the worrisome possibilities, or perhaps because of them, Niala found herself perversely enjoying the situation.

"Moreover," she continued, "if he's capable of doing all of that, why should we assume that he actually died when his shop was destroyed?"

Senyan shook his head slowly. "Of course, we can't. And if he's alive, he might be up to anything."

Niala looked at Senyan's sober expression. The man was worried, and he was also exhausted. It was clear he'd done everything he could to pin down the elusive Bashir Arak.

"We can't do any more about this now, can we?"

"Not without a lot of people and a lot of time," Senyan agreed. "Neither of which we have at the moment." He stepped over to the central console and shut the projectors down. He looked sideways at Niala. "Oh, by the way, I'd appreciate it if this stayed between the two of us for now."

She nodded. "Of course." She paused before descending the twisting stairway. "If you don't mind my saying so, I think you should get some sleep."

His head still bent over the console, Senyan smiled thinly. "You may be right. I'll see what I can do."

After a moment's wait, Niala walked down the narrow stairway. It was unusual to find Senyan in such a noncombative mood. He was obviously frustrated about not being able to find out more about Arak, let alone finding the man himself. Senyan needed to be in control, and in this instance there was nothing he could do.

As she reached the main floor and began walking slowly back to the exit, she frowned. How would this affect Senyan's ability to deal with his other responsibilities? If he put this Arak puzzle aside for the time being, fine. But if he couldn't do that, if it kept gnawing away at him . . .

The mist had turned to rain by the time Niala left the Archives building. That did nothing to brighten her mood.

Bashir Arak, whoever you are, she thought savagely, *I hope to Builders' hell you're satisfied with what you've done.*

— 18 —

The wooden cart made little noise as Alyssa pushed it through the dim tunnels, following Bulbulian's lead. It was a well-made vehicle, rough-looking but sturdy, with enough room for Bashir, a portable medunit, and some supplies. The medunit was hidden in the cart's false bottom.

The occasional squeak of a wheel bearing or scrape of a shoe on the floor was all the sound that the small procession made. The other sounds Alyssa heard may have been faint echoes, but she had her doubts. She was glad of the electric lamps they'd attached to the cart.

"How much farther, Bulbulian?" she asked in a voice little more than a whisper.

"Not far," he replied in an equally subdued voice. "A kilometer or so."

The black-green tunnels were much more extensive than Alyssa had guessed. She'd thought at first that Bashir's lighted and furnished section was the center of a small complex of connected rooms, but her sense of the underground maze had slowly expanded.

They'd been walking steadily for hours already in a fairly straight line. Intersections with cross-tunnels were as common now as when they'd begun their trip, and she had no reason to believe that the one they were traveling was longer than any of the others.

"I hope Bashir knows what he's doing," she said, more than a little worried about her old friend's slow recovery.

A raspy voice answered from the cart. "Of course I do. I got us this far, didn't I?" A sound that may have been a hoarse chuckle punctuated the remark.

"You certainly did," Alyssa replied. "Let's hope our luck holds out."

"Bah. Just keep pushing."

A smile quirked the corners of Alyssa's mouth. "Yes, sir."

They continued without speaking further, but Alyssa felt comforted by Bashir's feistiness. The tunnels, with their small sounds and echoes, seemed less threatening. After all, this walk wasn't new territory to Bashir or to Bulbulian— how else could they know where the tunnels led?

Just keep pushing, she told herself. *And pray you don't have to push this cart all the way to Ebel.*

Suddenly Alyssa found herself pushing the cart over a floor covered with loose rock and gravel, between rough stone walls. Sooner than she'd expected, the trio had emerged from the tunnel.

The smooth-sided tunnel had opened into what looked like a natural cave. From the tunnel's mouth, the stone floor rose and the walls converged to a narrow opening. She and Bulbulian walked up to that point and peered through the barrier of brush and stones piled high where the walls came closest together.

From the makeshift barrier, she could see that the floor sloped gently downward and the walls spread apart. About forty meters downslope, the cave turned abruptly to the right. From the cave's entrance, somewhere around that bend, the tunnel would not be visible. Even from well within the cave, it would be hard to spot.

"Would you assist me with this, Alyssa?" Bulbulian asked.

"What?"

Bulbulian gestured at the crude barricade. "I need to go out and scout around a little."

"Oh, of course, Qatar," Alyssa replied, reaching for some of the obstructing material. The barrier was tightly packed, but the two of them managed to clear it quickly.

When a path was opened, Bulbulian turned to Alyssa. "This may take some time," he said. "Please stay with Bashir until I return."

"Certainly." Alyssa knew she was better qualified physically to wander through what was probably rough terrain, but she was just as certain that Bulbulian knew the territory and that she didn't.

She went back to the tunnel mouth and pushed Bashir's cart into the cave, staying on the tunnel side of the spot where the walls narrowed.

Even though a mere trickle of light made it all the way to the back of the cave, it seemed almost light compared to the utter darkness of the tunnels. Alyssa wondered what the weather was like outside. After being so long below ground, it didn't really matter to her—she was anxious to be out under the open sky again, rain or shine.

She looked down at Bashir, resting in the cart. He was asleep, a calm expression on his face. He showed few outward signs of his injuries, except for a grayish cast to his skin and a slightly shrunken look. That was to be expected, she supposed, given the accelerated healing he'd just gone through.

The rehab cylinder had done its job, according to the medunit's monitors, but it had drained Bashir's body of most of its energy reserves. He still needed complete rest and large amounts of nutrients. The portable medunit was along in part to provide the latter. Alyssa and Bulbulian would have to do what they could to guarantee the former.

It was three hours before Bulbulian returned, hours during which Alyssa worried and kept checking on Bashir and tried unsuccessfully to get some rest. When he did come back, he moved so quietly that she didn't realize he was there until he had nearly reached the gap where the barricade had been.

"I've had some luck," he announced with a smile. "There's a village not far from here, and one of the tradesmen in the market put a very reasonable price on these." He handed a large bundle to Alyssa. She opened it to find three heavy cloaks of Torian wool, dyed in dark colors. There was also a pair of jakhide boots in her size.

"It has apparently been raining for most of the past two days, and more seems likely. We'll need these when we set out tonight."

"Tonight?" Alyssa asked, thinking of pushing Bashir's cart through unknown terrain in the dark and the rain.

Bulbulian nodded. "But of course, Alyssa. We cannot risk being seen coming out of the cave. I was able to slip out unobtrusively, even with my girth, but the three of us plus the cart would be too conspicuous by far."

"And how will we explain ourselves when daylight comes again?"

"Oh, let it not concern you," Bulbulian said casually. "By then we will be far from here, and may even have acquired a better form of transportation."

He seemed so assured of himself that Alyssa couldn't help asking, "Bulbulian, was it really a matter of luck that you got these cloaks?"

The round pie vendor merely smiled broadly. "Of course, Alyssa. What else? But that is to be expected—luck is a part of every successful venture. Come, now. We should use the time we have left to rest up. We shall have a long night ahead of us."

With that, he began pulling the brush back in front of the narrow spot in the cave. Alyssa helped him silently, wondering just how much Bashir and Bulbulian had planned ahead for this journey. She wondered, too, how a Normal, especially one as apparently unfit as Bulbulian, could move so quietly and could lift some of the larger concealing stones with such apparent ease.

Bashir was standing in front of a heavy wooden door. He was pressed up against the door's rough planks to peer through a small slot cut into it at eye level. The door was the only exit from a huge underground maze he'd become trapped in. The door was locked.

Behind him, Bashir could faintly hear the beast approaching. Still distant, it was nevertheless on his trail. Slithering through the lightless corridors, fire in its belly and death in its jaws, it would find him and devour him, unless he could escape.

Through the slot in the door, Bashir could see a vast plain of Wells, glowing bright green under a blue sky. Among the Wells wandered a dark-skinned man. The man carried something in his right hand, but he was too distant for Bashir to make out what it was. Where the man walked, the Wells' green glow died.

The beast in the corridors was getting closer.

Bashir yelled for the dark man to come and open the door. Perhaps what he held was a key.

The man seemed to hear Bashir. He paused, looked around, then turned toward the door. His pace was unhurried, deliberate. The thing in his hand was not a key, but a rod of some sort, with a knob on one end.

From the darkness behind him, Bashir could hear the beast's scales rasping across the stone floor. It was loud now, perhaps just a turn or two away. Bashir wanted to look back, to see how close it was, but he had to concentrate on the window and the Wells and the man outside.

The man was walking faster and heading straight for the door. As he approached, he began to seem familiar to Bashir, someone he recognized but whose name he'd forgotten. The rod in his hand was glowing a bright green.

Hot air swirled around Bashir, and he knew the beast was nearly upon him. He called frantically to the dark man to hurry. In a moment it would be too late.

The man was close now, barely an arm's length from the door. He looked directly at Bashir and smiled, and Bashir knew him. The man raised the glowing rod, and it was not a rod, but a scepter. It was a scepter Bashir had seen somewhere before.

The man swung the scepter down at the wooden door, and in that instant Bashir felt the beast's huge jaws close around him.

He awoke with a start. It was dark and cool and silent. As his nerves slowly quieted, he hoped he hadn't called out in his sleep. Embarrassing.

Raising himself up on his elbows, he looked around. He was still in the wooden cart he'd taken from his tunnel hideaway. He was underground, but not in the tunnels. He blinked a couple of times and sat up straighter.

Bulbulian was sitting to one side against a pile of rocks, his legs pulled up, head resting on knees, eyes closed.

Alyssa lay on the other side of the cart, curled up on a dark heavy cloak.

That's it. I fell asleep before we left the tunnels, and now . . . Judging by how dark it was, Bashir guessed it must be nearly nighttime. Time to begin their journey in earnest.

Bashir lay back down. He was feeling much stronger than he had, even this morning, but he was far from fully recovered. The trip to Ebel would take about two days if everything went as planned. It would be a tiring two days.

It galled him to have to rely so much on Alyssa and Bulbulian. He was accustomed to looking out for himself, even to having others rely on him. The reversal of roles made him feel guilty and angry and helpless.

Still, he had to go on, whatever it took. More than ever, he knew he had to get to Ebel. The dream from which he'd just awakened was fresh in his mind, and he recognized it for more than just a fantasy. There was a connection between the Matrix's Forbidden Files and the dream and Ebel, and the whisperings in his head told him that the connection was not something he could ignore.

He heard Bulbulian beginning to stir, coming slowly awake, and decided to hasten the process.

"Time to get up, Qatar, Alyssa! We have a long way to go before morning." He forced his voice to be clear and strong, just to let the others know who was still in charge.

Shortly after Bulbulian led the way out of the cave, it started to rain again, as predicted. Alyssa pulled up the hood of her cloak and let it fall forward as far as she could while still being able to see.

As Bashir had explained, the cave was in the Borderlands north-northeast of the Annex, very close to Toria. The terrain was rugged. Excellent for hiding in, miserable for traveling through.

Bulbulian unfolded the cart's canvas top and fastened it over three metal hoops, one at each end and one in the middle of the cart. The covering kept most of the rain off Bashir and their supplies.

The going was anything but easy. Sometimes Bulbulian helped with the cart, but more often he scouted ahead, looking for the least difficult path and trying to avoid encounters with anyone else crazy enough to be wandering in such weather. He seemed to know where he was going, though Alyssa only recognized that they were maintaining a generally northeasterly heading.

After a few hours of struggling to push and pull Bashir's cart through thick brush, around and between rocky outcroppings, and over a series of increasingly slippery hills, Alyssa was thinking longingly of the close darkness of the cave they'd left behind. At least it had been dry.

Even though their progress was slow, she was convinced that they'd gone much farther than the village Bulbulian had visited earlier, where the cloaks had come from. It made sense that the trio not wander into the village nearest the tunnel entrance and invite speculation. Still, Alyssa hoped Bulbulian and Bashir didn't plan to go all the way to Ebel without stopping for more supplies. At their current rate, that would be four or five days at the least.

She was about to raise the issue with Bulbulian when the pie vendor-turned-scout raised his arm to call a halt to the small procession. He came back to stand next to her. He spoke quietly, his voice not much louder than the rain drumming steadily on the cart's canvas top.

"There is a village not far beyond the next hill. I know a man there who owns an inn and stable. I should be able to get one or perhaps even two hexoxen from him." He paused and looked off into the rainy darkness. "He can be trusted not to talk, but the less he knows, the more he can be trusted. If you will wait here to guard Bashir, I will go try my luck with him."

Alyssa nodded.

"And remember the stunner hidden in the cart."

"Of course." Alyssa looked down at the end of the cart, to make sure she could locate the small sliding door in the dark. When she looked up, Bulbulian had already turned and begun working his way around the hill before them. She'd had no chance to ask him what she was to guard Bashir against.

Fine, Alyssa complained to herself. *First in the cave, and now out here. Wait, wait, wait.*

She pushed the cart over to where a large boulder leaned outward, providing partial shelter from the chill rain. Looking back over the terrain they'd just covered, she could see no signs of life except for a few widely scattered trees, their thin, twisted shapes rising above the surrounding rocks. No living thing crept or bounded or flew across the wet, rough landscape. So far, they'd come across nothing more dangerous than some dense clumps of thorny bushes.

"Guard against a cold, perhaps." Alyssa snorted as she blinked away some water that had avoided the boulder and found her eye. She pulled her hood down farther over her face.

"You shouldn't be too hard on Qatar. He means well."

Bashir's voice startled Alyssa. She'd found herself falling into the habit of assuming he was asleep. She leaned in under the canvas top and saw Bashir looking quite alert.

"How are you feeling?"

"Better by the minute," he replied. His voice did sound stronger to Alyssa than it had even as recently as in the cave. "But don't change the subject. You really don't think there's anything out here to worry about, do you?"

She shook her head. "Except perhaps the possibility of succumbing to hypothermia while we wait for Bulbulian to come back."

Bashir smiled ruefully. "Ah, the wisdom of youth."

Alyssa frowned. "Youth? I'm over one hundred—"

"Yes, yes, my dear. Well over one hundred years old." Bashir's eyes narrowed, suddenly all business. "But what do you know of Toria, of the land we're traveling through now?"

"What everybody knows," she answered with a shrug. "Population thirty million, low-level technology, ruled by the Draths, capital is Ebel, in western Toria, founded by Victoria Eldrath and her followers... Should I go on?"

Bashir shook his head. "You know what the rest of the lawful citizens of Home know. That is far from all there is to know. Did you know that the most accurate map of Toria in all of Home is over seven hundred years old, or that the population figures we have could be off by as much as one hundred percent?"

"Well, I—"

"No, you didn't. Hardly anyone does, and those who do don't want to make a point of the fact that Home knows very little about Toria." He rapped on the side of the cart for emphasis. "Everyone knows we have a treaty of mutual respect and noninterference, but few know what that means, how deep our ignorance runs. Satellite surveillance of Toria is prohibited, and the Wellborn are forbidden to enter Toria unless they are official representatives of Home invited by the Hierarch and escorted by Drath guards."

Alyssa nodded. "Of course, I know that. They want to maintain their spiritual purity or some such. But we don't need to know all about Toria. Even if they're actually hostile, their technology is too far behind us to be much of a threat."

"Harrummph," Bashir grunted in response. "Tell me, Alyssa. Do you know why Torians, even educated ones, will not travel alone at night except in well-settled areas?"

She chuckled. "Afraid of the dark? Worried about hugglebears?"

Bashir sighed. "Even though you are over a century old, Alyssa, I feel compelled to tell you a story."

"What?"

"Now, now." Bashir made a patting motion with his hand. "Bear with me. I'm an old man, and old men are supposed to tell stories."

She smiled briefly and nodded. *All this talking is probably part of the recovery process.*

"A long time ago," he began, "long before you were born, there was a young couple who were Wellborn. The man was nothing to look at, but the woman was tall and dark and beautiful." Bashir looked up and his eyes twinkled. "Very much like you, my dear." He paused, then continued.

"They were among the lucky few who had been allowed to have a child, and they had a baby girl. Fortunately, she took after her mother.

"Now, this couple were both archaeologists, and their project was to search for Builder sites. Being good at their profession, they were given free rein to search wherever they wanted, within the law.''

The wind began to pick up, and Alyssa moved to where her body would shelter Bashir from the brunt of it. He thanked her and went on.

"One day, when their daughter was three years old, the couple decided to search in the Borderlands north of Home. It was the man's idea, but the woman agreed, reluctantly.

"They left their daughter with friends, as they'd done before, and departed. Naturally, they told no one where they were going, it being strictly forbidden, then as now, to travel in the Borderlands.''

Alyssa thought she heard a catch in Bashir's voice, and wondered if he was tiring himself too much.

"The couple were gone for six days without finding anything significant. Still, there were tantalizing hints that a Builder site was somewhere in the area. The man was caught up in the search and wanted to continue, but the woman felt they should quit before they were caught, and return to their daughter.

"They argued all of day seven and well into the night, and on the morning of the eighth day, they parted company. He went on, following what he thought was a trail that would lead to a Builder site. She turned back, retracing their route to Home. It was not a difficult path and should have taken perhaps two days for someone not stopping to look for artifacts.''

Bashir paused, and the pause went on long enough for Alyssa to look in on him, to see if he'd fallen asleep. He had not. His eyes were closed as if in thought, and he seemed to be wiping away a couple of raindrops that had somehow gotten through to hit him in the face.

He opened his eyes then and smiled weakly. "Yes, it was an easy path and she was an experienced hiker and camper. No reason to worry. But as the day wore on, the man did begin to worry. His mind wandered from his search. What if something happened to her? She was Wellborn. She was young and strong and smart. She had plenty of supplies. Still, as sunset approached, he worried.''

Bashir nodded to himself, as if confirming his claim. "Yes, as he set up his tent, he thought of her doing the same several kilometers behind him. Nothing could happen, but he had a sleepless night, with dark dreams interrupted by eerie cries in the distance, as of some alien creature."

"Bashir," Alyssa asked in a firm voice, "is this a ghost story?" She couldn't help thinking of the black guard towers around the Wellfield and the stories told about them. She also couldn't overlook Bashir's odd sense of humor.

Bashir sighed deeply. "No, though I wish it were." He shifted around in his cloak, seeming to sink deeper beneath it.

"In the morning," he continued, "the young man could stand it no more. Calling himself foolish every step of the way, he packed up his supplies and went back along the trail the young woman had taken the day before. It was a hot, clear day, a day on which everything stood out in sharp relief from everything else. Each stone, each gnarled branch of each twisted tree, each small white wispy cloud in the faded blue sky.

"He had no trouble following the tracks the woman had made—she'd not tried to hide them. Everything was so clear and sharp, and everything was as he'd expected it to be."

A brief pause.

"When he came upon her campsite, he was for a moment unable to take it in. It wasn't supposed to be there at all. The tent, the portastove, the small recycler—they were all supposed to be gone, kilometers farther along the trail, along with the young woman. That much closer to Home, that much closer to their daughter."

"Where was she?" Alyssa broke in, as Bashir seemed reluctant to go on.

"Not there," he replied in a voice dulled of emotion. "And not anywhere else that he could see. All he found were several footprints, widely spaced as if she had been running, that headed away from the campsite and away from the path she had been following. They ended at the base of a large rock, a rock with enough knobs and crevices in it to make it climbable.

"There was nowhere else to go," Bashir stated flatly. "He climbed. The top of that rock was smooth and flat and shadowless under the burning sun. He could see everything: her shoe; her hunting knife, the blade broken; a smear of rust-red blood. The flies surrounding the blood were the only things moving in the entire world. They made the only sound."

The rain continued to fall, though the wind had died down.

"How do you know this, Bashir? Who were those people?"

He spoke as if he hadn't heard Alyssa. "He never found her, though he spent every waking moment searching. The days ran together for him, and his nights were haunted by half-heard cries from the darkness. Sometimes it was the woman calling for him, sometimes their daughter crying for her mother, sometimes it was an inhuman ululation echoing among the barren rocks. He ran out of food and water, lost his equipment, and in the end stumbled along unseeing, unable to give up the search.

"He was found at last by some Torians who were illegally prospecting the Borderlands for deposits of fleckstone. They took him, half delirious, back to their camp and nursed him back to health. In response to his story, they nodded knowingly but were unable or unwilling to explain what had taken the woman. Something that was faster and stronger than a Wellborn. Something on which an alloy knife blade would break. Something that left no tracks, no trace of its presence."

"Bashir . . ." Alyssa wanted to say something, but wasn't sure what. His story was unsettling, as he'd obviously intended it to be. How much of it was true, and how much embellishment? How much outright fiction? She jerked violently as something grabbed her arm.

"Alyssa," Bashir said, his grip tight above her wrist. "That was not a bedtime story for children—it was a warning." His voice sounded urgent but very tired. "This land is not settled and familiar. It is wild and unknown, and after thirteen hundred years, humans are still the aliens here."

He swallowed audibly. "I didn't want you along on this trip, not because you're incapable of handling yourself, but because there are things out here that no one may be able to handle."

His voice was weaker, urgency giving way to exhaustion. "But as long as you're with us, please be watchful."

His last words faded into the rain sounds.

"Of course, Bashir, of course," Alyssa said reassuringly as he released her arm. His hand fell slackly, resting on the edge of the cart. "Bashir?" Alyssa whispered. The only response was a light snoring. She lifted his hand and gently tucked it back under his cloak. He shifted slightly in his sleep.

Alyssa straightened, then reached down and opened the compartment hidden in the back of the cart. Her fingers curled around the handle of the stunner. She pulled it out and closed the compartment. The stunner was a heavy-duty military model, with a range of two hundred meters on its narrow-beam setting. The weight was a comfort to her as she looked out into the rainy wilderness.

"Bashir," she whispered to herself, "did you know those two people?"

In the darkness before her, she could see no glimmer of lights from Home or the Annex, no trace of the Wellfield's Glow. The wind picked up again, swirling some rain into the shelter of the rock at her back. Somewhere in the distance, she thought she heard a high, thin keening sound. The wind? Some animal in distress or calling to its mate?

She huddled closer to the rock and the cart, her cloak tight about her. *Damn Bashir and his stories, anyway*, she thought viciously. Staring out at the half-seen trees and rocks, hills and ravines, Alyssa shivered, but not from the cold.

— 19 —

M'Briti lay, half asleep, eyes closed, listening, listening. The sound of rain on her roof was somehow homey, comforting. It closed out the rest of the world with its muffled pattering. She snuggled deeper under her covers, seeking to recapture the pleasant, barely remembered dream she'd awakened from. The covers were soft and warm on her bare skin.

Next to her, Darrin's breathing was soft and slow, a deep relaxing sound. Close. Human.

Earlier that evening, their lovemaking had been slow and tender. It was as if he'd really cared for her. And for a while she'd almost believed it. During those too-fleeting moments when their bodies had moved as one, she'd sought refuge from the world in that physical sensation that could signify so much more.

She turned onto one side, then the other, her thoughts making her restless, pushing the dream farther away. The rain, she knew, was cold, and the refuge had been illusion.

The rhythm of Darrin's breathing changed, became less regular. He smacked his lips two or three times and twisted so that he was half facing M'Briti. His eyelids fluttered and then popped open. He looked surprised and pleased.

"Then it wasn't a dream?" he mumbled in a deep, sleep-blurred voice.

M'Briti forced a smile. "No, it wasn't." *Now is as good a time as any,* she thought with a trace of sadness. "You were very good."

His smile widened, white teeth and dark brown face. So like and unlike her brother. "I could be again," he said, reaching for her.

She pushed his hand away. "Not that," she snapped. "I followed you yesterday."

"Oh."

She leaned toward him. "It wasn't easy."

"No, I suppose it wasn't," he replied. He closed his eyes and let his head fall back onto his pillow.

M'Briti waited for a moment, but Darrin said nothing more. He just lay there, eyes shut, lips pressed tightly together.

"That's all you're going to say?"

"What would you like me to say?" He opened his eyes but did not look at her.

M'Briti held back an angry response. During her year in the Annex, she'd learned that control was everything. In as calm a voice as she could manage, she answered, "How about starting with an apology? Something along the lines of, 'I'm sorry, dear, for playing fast and loose with your emotions, for spinning a tale of lost love and lost hopes just so I could get into bed with you. But I promise it won't happen again.' How would that be?"

Now he did look at her, raising himself up on one elbow and turning to face her. "Is that what you think? That this has all been a game to trick you into having sex with me?"

Not exactly, M'Briti thought to herself, *but I can't afford to raise the other possibility.* Aloud, she said, "What else? It's pretty obvious you're not the lost soul that you claimed to be, alone in the universe. That was definitely a woman who greeted you in that reztower mod in Home yesterday afternoon. She didn't seem a bit surprised to see you, either."

"Listen," he began. He started to reach for her. Something in her eyes made him pull back. "I haven't been completely honest with you, but this, tonight, was real."

"You'd have to say that anyway, wouldn't you?" She was not going to lose her advantage that easily, no matter how much she wanted to believe him.

"No, damn it, I wouldn't!" He jumped out of bed and went to stand by one of the windows. M'Briti's Purple withdrawal symptoms had begun asserting themselves again, but just barely. Despite the dark, she could still see quite clearly Darrin's well-shaped legs, his firm buttocks, the slender but well-muscled upper body. She felt her body starting to respond even as she told herself she couldn't trust him.

He stared out the window for a time. M'Briti could see the tension in him. What was he hiding? He was agonizing too long for it to be the simple peccadillo she'd accused him of. Rather than give him anything new to respond to, she just lay in bed and watched him, waiting.

The rain continued to fall, tapping on the roof, emphasizing the silence in the room.

Finally, he said, "I did lead you on, back at Jaro's Tavern. There I was, the complete hard-luck story, and making no secret of it. Sooner or later, I was certain, someone would approach me with an offer of salvation. And"—he turned his head so that she could see his profile against the dim gray of the window—"there you were. You sat down with me for no particular reason and listened to all my woes and sympathized and drank with me and escorted me around the Annex and, no matter how hard I pushed, offered me no easy answers."

He turned to face M'Briti, apparently at ease with his nakedness. "At first I thought you might be dealing drugs, maybe even Purple, but you never even suggested I try any. I had to ask myself why?"

M'Briti sat up in bed. "Did you find the answer?" She left unasked the question, *What were you looking for in the first place?*

Darrin shook his head. "I didn't find the answer, but I did find out about your brother."

The room suddenly felt chilly, as if the rain were falling inside. M'Briti shivered and pulled the blankets up around her.

"Or, rather, I refreshed my memory and filled in some details." He looked down at her from across the room, his eyes unreadable in the darkness. "M'Taba was his name, and he was a Purple Heaven addict. It killed him. From what background I could learn, you seemed to be close to each other." He paused.

"That seemed to rule you out as a dealer, especially of Purple. So why the interest in me?" Another pause, longer. "I've seen holos of him, M'Briti. Is it because I look so much like him?" His voice had taken on a sharp tone, but more of hurt than of anger. "Am I helping you revive the brother you lost?"

"No." M'Briti's reply was so soft, she wasn't sure Darrin could hear it. She swallowed and repeated, louder, "No."

Darrin walked over to sit on the edge of the bed. "Not at all?"

"That's ridiculous!" M'Briti pounded her fist into the bed's yielding surface. "You're an attractive man. That you bear some vague resemblance to my brother is coincidental and irrelevant. The truth of the matter is, he was a weak man. Yes, I loved him dearly, but he was weak, and that's what killed him." She was dangerously close to crying. "Nothing I do can change that."

She leaned toward Darrin. "You're not weak. I sense a confidence and determination in you that he never had." Her voice dropped into a fierce whisper. "But M'Taba never lied to me, even about his addiction. He lied to himself, but never to me. And now, finding myself wanting to love you, I discover that everything you've told me is a lie."

Darrin started to say something but M'Briti cut him off.

"If you weren't lying, why did you check up on me? What were you looking for? Why did you try to hide your visit to Home? What were you really doing in Jaro's Tavern? Who in the names of the Founders are you, anyway?" Her voice rose until she nearly shouted the last question, and when she finished, she sat back, breathing heavily, her eyes burning into Darrin's, daring him to lie again.

Darrin squeezed his eyes shut and rubbed his hand across his face in a gesture of frustration. "We're back to that, aren't we?" He sighed. It was a deep, heartfelt breathing out, as if he were releasing more than just air from his lungs. "Very well," he said in an almost-brisk tone. "This may get me banned for real, but here's the story."

"For real? Then—"

"Please, dear. You asked, so let me tell you."

M'Briti merely nodded.

"It began over a year ago. The increasing use of Purple Heaven had become a serious concern for the authorities of Home. I was approached by one of them who thought the conventional investigation was proceeding too slowly. This person wanted someone to become the equivalent of a spy, to infiltrate the drug network."

M'Briti suppressed a shiver. "Why you?" she asked before she could stop herself.

Darrin shrugged. "For five years, I've had my name in to become an off-planet agent. Not many people want to do it, but there are even fewer openings. I suppose they wanted someone with the interest and aptitude, and who wasn't already part of Home's security. For my part, it was an opportunity to gain some valuable experience while possibly helping to end the Purple trafficking.

"So, with a year to build up a cover story and very little actual training and virtually no experience, I got myself banned from the Wells in hopes that a Purple dealer would contact me. Instead, I got approached by a beautiful woman who sees some of her brother in me and who's as far from dealing Purple as you can get."

He flopped backward and clasped his hands behind his head. "And now she hates me because I wasn't good enough to fool her." He gave a short, harsh laugh. "Falling in love with my very first suspect! I wonder what that will do for my chances to become an off-planet agent?"

M'Briti couldn't help but smile. Her suspicions had been correct—Darrin was more than he'd appeared to be. So her ability to read people hadn't failed her, and no harm had been done. More than that, keeping her secret might still allow her to keep Darrin. All she had to do was to continue to hide her dealing, at least until she could identify the persons controlling the Purple trade. The smile faltered for a moment. *Yes, that's all,* she thought with more than a trace of self-mockery.

In the meantime . . . She lay down on her side next to Darrin. "Hey, buddy, anyone can make a mistake." She reached over to him. "And as long as you're still on Seelzar, would you care to fraternize some more with one of the natives?''

He turned his head to look at her, and she saw his frown slowly soften and disappear. ''If I can find a native who'll have me.'' His voice was husky, his breath warm against her cheek.

M'Briti pulled his body tightly to hers. ''Here's one who's had you once and would be glad to have you again.'' She began to move slowly against him and felt the double pleasure of her own arousal and his.

Darrin rolled over on top of her without breaking their mutual rhythm. Between shallow breaths, he asked, ''What'll I tell my superiors?''

''Mmm.'' M'Briti shifted languidly under him. ''Don't tell them anything.'' A part of her mind wanted to ask a question or lodge a protest, but it was pushed back and back and back until it was shut away and silent. *Later,* she thought hazily. *Just for now, lets...and let's...and let's...*

— 20 —

For a summer morning, it was cold. Despite her warm clothing, Niala was several degrees shy of comfortable. Pale blue thermoweave curtains were pulled across the two entrance archways, but the Executors' meeting room was still chilly. Tendrils of the cold wind outside crept under, around, and through the curtains.

Marguerite Venebles smiled, as if enjoying the cool temperatures. A draft nudged at her long, fine hair. ''As you can see, Executors, power has still not been fully restored.'' She made a broad gesture that included the room, the archways, and possibly the weather outside.

"We can't afford to divert energy to the heating units yet." Her insulated suit gave added meaning to the words. "But this odd cold spell won't last, and we will soon have bypassed the remaining Matrix junctions. Once the power grid is operating again, the other work should proceed much more rapidly."

Her smile shifted to a look of puzzlement. "One problem our techs have encountered is that the junction circuitry doesn't seem to correspond to the specs on file in the Archives. One of our people said that the organic components in particular look like they've been altered." She turned an appraising eye on Senyan. "You're the Matrix expert. Any ideas?"

Niala waited for the stocky Executor's reply. To her relief, he did not glance covertly at her, did not try to signal her in any way that she could see. Perhaps he was going to play this straight, and not try to enlist her in yet another attack on Venebles.

Senyan cleared his throat, then answered, "Frankly, no. It should be impossible for anyone to alter the Matrix's components, organic or otherwise, without our knowing of the attempt." Now he did look at Niala, but quite openly. "We have no knowledge of such an attempt, have we?"

Niala shook her head. "Of course not. We would all have been notified immediately in such an event. An intrusion such as the one by Arak is another matter entirely. Its effect, regardless of its intent, seems to have been destruction. Alteration would require much more subtlety and control."

"And the Archives, we know," Senyan added to Venebles, "are at least as secure." This time he did not turn to Niala.

Aha! So he's going to hold that back. Niala had wondered how much of the Archives problem Senyan would reveal. For the moment, she decided to go along with him. She could always tell Venebles later if it seemed appropriate to do so. Besides, what Senyan had said was true. It just invited an incorrect inference. It looked as if the Archives and the Matrix had *both* been altered.

Venebles started to speak, stopped, then shrugged. "A puzzle, then. Something to be dealt with later. In the meantime, the essential services of Home are functioning adequately. Complete restoration in most areas should take several more days, perhaps ten.'' She looked pointedly at Senyan. ''That is, if nothing else inexplicable crops up along the way.''

Senyan appeared not to notice Venebles's gibe. ''Of course, we cannot definitely rule anything out, but the damage seems to have been contained.'' He set his broad hands palms down on the tabletop and looked solemnly at Venebles and Niala.

''Let us make no mistake. The Matrix has been severely damaged. Some files may be lost forever, and some of its processing and integrating capabilities may not be fully restored for a very long time. Years, perhaps. I . . .''

He paused for a moment, staring at the table between his hands. ''Frankly, we've come upon some of the same phenomena that you have, Executor.'' This was directed at Venebles. ''There are configurations in some of the Matrix units that do not correspond to anything in the technical specifications. Oddly, our initial search of the performance records indicates that the altered units have performed better than expected, at least in the recent past.''

''That seems to rule out sabotage as a motive,'' Niala commented, ''unless something extremely devious is going on.''

''Unlikely or impossible for anyone outside of Home to do such a thing.'' Venebles didn't try to hide her satisfaction. Niala could almost hear the unspoken addendum, *So the Draths can hardly be blamed for this, can they?*

Senyan nodded. ''Agreed. Moreover, the nature and pattern of these alterations argue against any outside agency, by which I mean anything outside the Matrix itself.''

''Huh?'' Venebles snorted. ''You're telling us that the Matrix is sabotaging itself?''

''Please.'' Senyan spoke distinctly and deliberately. ''Do not miscontrue my words. These changes are, as far as we know, all improvements. What I am suggesting is that there may have been from its inception capabilities built into the Matrix for self-adaptation, capabilities that for some reason no one was told about.''

"Or which we have long since forgotten about," Niala added, seeking to tone down Senyan's suspicions.

"Yes," Senyan agreed in a grudging voice.

"And you're worried about that?" Venebles asked. "It seems like an advantage to me."

"Only if we know the programmed directives, and the constraints," the stocky Executor explained impatiently. "The Matrix is nothing more than a complex, sophisticated tool. The less we understand it, and the less we control it, the less useful it becomes." He paused. "It could even become dangerous."

"Come now, Executor Senyan." Venebles's voice was heavy with skepticism. "That seems a trifle melodramatic."

Senyan frowned, reminding Niala of nothing so much as an angry boulder. "Look around you, Executor. The Matrix is responsible for all the repair work your crews are doing. Is that trivial? Home was completely without power for two days. Was that trivial?"

Venebles was shaking her head while Senyan talked. When he paused for a moment, she replied, "All of this happened because we've become too dependent on the Matrix, perhaps. The fault may well be ours. What happened," she raised her voice over Senyan's attempt to respond. "What happened was simply that the Matrix deactivated a large portion of its circuits and cut us off temporarily. A purely defensive response to someone's tampering."

"Oh, is that all?" Senyan stood and leaned over the table, looking directly into Venebles's eyes. "What about the fire that destroyed that Annex shop? That was a little more than deactivation of circuits, I'd say."

"Not really. Arak apparently tapped into some of the Matrix's circuitry, and the Matrix just burned that part out. Why make more of it than that? Does it really help us to see enemies and threats behind everything?"

Senyan pounded his fist on the tabletop. "When they exist, yes! By the Founders, I swear if the Interstellar Union had a fleet overhead, you'd say they were a trade delegation!"

"Aha, so you admit the Union is an immediate threat, that perhaps we should do something about it?" Venebles gloated.

"Bah!" Senyan pushed back from the table and strode over to the western archway. He parted the curtains slightly and stood, back to the room, staring out into the cool gray morning.

Venebles leaned toward Niala and whispered, "Speaking of which, how secure are we without the Matrix running out defense shield?"

The invitation to confide surprised Niala. That was not Venebles's usual style. She thought briefly of lying to Venebles to avoid further arguments. *Tell her everything's fine, that human monitors can detect intruders as well as the Matrix would have, that human tacticians can analyze and direct as well as the Matrix programs could have.*

"We'd be in serious trouble if that hypothetical fleet were to appear soon. At even strength we'd have the advantage, from what we know of Union technology. That was true twenty years ago, and they haven't advanced much since then."

"But, of course, if they do locate us, they'll come in large numbers."

Niala nodded. "That's what we have to assume."

Senyan turned and started walking back to the table.

"If only we weren't so dependent on the matrix," Venebles muttered, her right hand clenched in a fist.

"Ah, strategizing, are we?" Senyan had adopted an outwardly jovial attitude. "Our current crisis does tend to make moot the debate about adventurous off-planet policies, doesn't it?"

Venebles stared coldly at him for a moment. Then a sly smile slowly spread across her face. "So that's why you sabotaged the Matrix—to keep us from being able to launch a preemptive strike against the union!"

Niala braced herself for another round between the two, but Senyan declined the opportunity.

"No, I thought we'd settled that matter even before the Matrix crashed." He looked toward Niala. "What is our security status?"

Niala ran her hands over the tabletop sensors. A holojection appeared, showing Home and its immediate environs. A ring of red dots appeared around Home.

"I believe there is virtually no chance of hostile action from anywhere on Seelzar. In the unlikely event that such an attack did occur, we may depend on the Borderland sensor array to give us sufficient warning. It's a system of independent units that broadcast back to our security offices. The Matrix failure doesn't affect them at all."

"As regards possible threats from the Interstellar Union, the picture is less optimistic." She moved her hands again and the scene changed to a view of Seelzar as a blue-green ball floating in blackness, accompanied by a tiny white ball.

"We are able to maintain radio and hyperwave contact with Yakimu Base and with our automated defense platforms, and they are all fully functional." Several green dots appeared, one on the small white ball, the others surrounding the larger ball at various distances.

"However, we have lost our hyperspace monitors. Without the Matrix, we cannot track them through the h-flux. So if the Union does locate us, we'll have virtually no warning of their approach. And once they arrive, we won't have the Matrix to coordinate the platforms' responses with our own ships." The green lights blinked out, then the entire projection disappeared.

Niala smiled grimly at Venebles. "It appears that you may be right, Executor. We have perhaps come to rely too heavily on the Matrix. I have formed a working group of our best military planners to devise strategies in the unlikely event that the Union should come upon us in the near future. That's the best we can do, in my opinion." She glanced at Senyan, who looked more displeased than ever.

"We're going to place some monitoring stations far beyond Seelzar's orbit, something we should have done all along." She brought up another holojection. It showed Seelzar's sun and its five planets. The orbits were illuminated yellow lines. Six red dots appeared on the edges of the system.

"As you can see, all six will be the same distance from the sun, approximately eight billion kilometers, four in the system's plane, and one at each of the poles."

"How soon can they be up?" Senyan asked.

"It will take ten days, maybe twenty."

"And in the meantime?" Senyan pressed.

"In the meantime, we get on to other matters," Venebles interjected irritably. "If this were all a Union plot, they would have brought in their fleet by now, and we'd probably be cinders or slaves. Since we are neither, we can assume that they don't yet know where we are, and there's no reason to believe they'll find out in the near future."

She looked at Senyan. "So I would like to thank Executor Kirowa for doing a fine job under trying circumstances, and move on to the next item on the agenda. Or is there no next item?"

Niala erased the holojection of the planned monitoring stations. "That's all I have to report." She glanced at Senyan. "Beyond congratulating you for getting *this* terminal fully on line, is there any other business?"

Senyan nodded to Niala. "Thank you. The major commnet links have been restored, and most terminals now have access to the basic data files. So progress is being made."

Glancing at Venebles, he continued, "There is always other business, as we all know, but some items are more pressing than others." Senyan leaned back in his chair, elbows on the armrests, and steepled his fingers. It was a relaxed, thoughtful pose. Niala sensed repressed excitement underneath it.

"Up to now, we've had no choice but to focus on the Matrix failure and its ramifications. Soon, however, we shall have to turn our attention to other matters. One that comes to mind is the Purple Heaven epidemic."

"That again?" Venebles asked in a disgusted tone.

Senyan nodded. "Indeed. All the reports I've seen indicate that Purple use is rising quite rapidly, even over the past half year. Nothing we've done so far has had much effect on stopping the trade, but that may be about to change."

To Niala, he sounded smug, self-satisfied.

"You've uncovered new information?" she prompted. She didn't want to encourage Senyan, but she wanted even less to give Venebles time to start arguing with him.

"You might say that. Within a few days I should have something to show you."

Niala glanced over to Venebles, expecting a cutting remark. Indeed, the white-haired woman did seem tense, but when she spoke, she sounded more anxious than angry.

"Why the big secret? We are all basically on the same side here, aren't we?"

"Are we?" Senyan smiled without any pleasantness. "I'm only certain of what side I'm on."

"And what's *that* supposed to mean?" Venebles's hands twitched ever so slightly.

Senyan's smile broadened. "Nothing. I didn't mean to offend anyone. I just want to be sure of my information before I pass it on."

Niala noticed that Venebles's hands were now out of sight beneath the table. The thin Executor pressed Senyan further. "Do you feel you'll be able to identify the suppliers?"

"Patience, please." The stocky Executor stood up. "All in good time. For now, I can say no more. I take it there is no further business?" He looked at Niala, then Venebles. Neither said anything. "Very well. I'm sure we all have other matters to attend to. Good day." With that, he turned and strode from the room.

Niala watched Senyan part the curtains he had earlier brooded at, then pass through them. The sound of his boots clicking against the stone walk receded quickly, leaving only the faint whistling of the cool breeze to disturb the room's silence.

Niala turned to look at Venebles. "What do you make of that?"

The other jerked slightly, as if startled out of some reverie. "What? Oh, I don't know." She smiled shakily. "You know how he is—he has to be in control. He's probably making a rakeclaw out of a wurgle, and hoping we'll be impressed."

Niala frowned. "I don't know. It's not like Senyan to be so mysterious. Maybe he really is onto something."

"Hah!" Venebles's smile turned abruptly into a snarl. "He wouldn't know valuable information if it bit him in the ass!" With that, she swiveled her chair around, stood, and stalked off through the eastern archway, the one Senyan had not used.

Niala remained sitting at the round table, staring at its milky surface. Before her, described by thin silver lines, were a number of shapes, seemingly just beneath the table's surface. Squares, circles, ovals, triangles. In themselves, they meant nothing. But knowing their code, she could tap into all the information of Home, and a great deal of information from the rest of Seelzar. Excluding Toria, of course. And information in the Matrix's Forbidden Files. And information never officially recorded. And information locked away in people's hearts and minds, sometimes unknown even to themselves.

What is going on? Niala asked herself in frustration. Senyan was behaving in an uncharacteristically coy manner, and Venebles's response had been completely out of proportion. Niala would very much have liked to put the senior Executor under surveillance, to find out what he was up to. Once again, she chafed at the limitations of her position, and the ambiguities.

The silvery lines seemed to dance beneath the tabletop, inviting, enticing, taunting her.

What is going on?

Niala knew of no code that would reveal the answer.

— **21** —

M'Briti lay back in her lounge chair and gazed through half-closed eyes at her glowball. The night was cool, but warmer than the previous three had been, and the glowball was radiating at minimum power. Small red tracks of incandescence wandered across its surface, shedding just enough heat to let her leave the windows open.

This won't be easy, she thought for the hundredth time that day. Becoming involved with Darrin Montoya would be bad enough if he were just another Purple user. His being an agent for Home, albeit a novice, complicated things immeasurably.

She couldn't take him to her usual hangouts without risking exposure as a dealer. She couldn't approach new customers or contact her own supplier while Darrin was around. And she couldn't smoke her last hit of Purple until she could be away from him for nearly a day to let the most obvious effects pass.

And if she didn't smoke Purple again within a few days, the withdrawal symptoms would probably give her away.

She'd actually taken her pipe out of its hiding place a half hour ago, well after Darrin had left. It had been a close thing. She'd nearly smoked her last hit. Only with some effort had she convinced herself the risk was too great.

From atop its meter-high pillar in the center of her living room, the glowball cast faint shadows. They wavered and shifted as the red sparks crept around the ball, scattering, gathering, weaving their patterns silently.

Outside, night had fallen, quieting the Annex. People were either at home or on Founders' Way, enjoying the bright lights and the safety of numbers. That's where Darrin had gone, had said he was going, an hour ago. To get a special wine to celebrate their being together and the end of the rainy weather. Or so he'd said.

M'Briti listened for the sound of his returning footsteps. She heard distant sounds of construction work from Home, where they were hastily making repairs all over the place in the wake of the Matrix failure. Closer, she heard a night bird calling from a rooftop, and a fainter answering cry from the plains to the west.

She wasn't actually worried about Darrin. He could take care of himself, and she could trust him. Still, she listened.

Her withdrawal from Purple was in its early stages. She could feel the tension building inside her, and the faintest dullness had crept into the edges of her vision.

She was a long way from the full-blown hallucinations and panic she'd suffered just four nights ago, but she knew that such a crisis would come again, unless she smoked more Purple.

That knowledge gnawed at her, made her more sensitive to possible signs of trouble. Was her anxiety normal, or drug-induced? Was there really a fog returning to her peripheral vision, or was she just imagining things? Were all those sounds she was hearing real or not?

As if in response to her unspoken questions, the regular beat of footsteps coalesced from the night's background noises.

Darrin? No, there were two sets of them, and they were slower, more subdued than his would be. Cautious. No—furtive. The harder she listened, the fainter and softer they became. They seemed almost to be hiding from her attention, shying away, very much like the shadowy figures she remembered in her drug-withdrawal fog.

Maybe that's all these these footsteps were. They were paradoxically closer yet fainter, sneaking up on her while fading away. Any minute they would cease altogether and she'd never know the truth of them. With a sigh, she turned her attention back to the glowball, seeking a measure of peace in the stately dance of its red sparks.

The footsteps, barely audible, were right outside her door. M'Briti watched flowing red embers define the surface of a hollow sphere. The footsteps stopped. Only the night bird's cry broke the late-evening silence.

M'Briti willed herself beneath the glowball's surface, imagining herself surrounded by its fiery sparks. Protected. Safe from the drug and her personal quest and her doubts about Darrin.

Crash.

The front door splintered open and M'Briti instinctively rolled off her lounge chair toward the back of the room, not sure whether she was in a nightmare or reality.

With another *crash* the back door flew open. Two dark-clothed figures faced her, one in each doorway. Their black bodysuits absorbed the feeble red light. Their matte face masks were dull orange-gray ovals. Bright glints shone from their right hands, speaking of weapons leveled at her.

She stood slowly, studying the intruders. Too sophisticated for Annex thugs, their equipment suggested something worse to her—security agents from Home. And that in turn meant that she'd been wrong about Darrin after all. Who else could have turned her in, and why else had he not returned with the wine he'd gone to get?

The figure in the front doorway took one step into the room. When he spoke, his voice was firm but not hostile.

"M'Briti Ubu?" It wasn't really a question.

"Come with us, please." It wasn't really a request.

M'Briti knew she couldn't afford to be taken into custody and returned to Home. If the authorities had gone this far, they must be sure of their case against her, and if she were convicted of dealing Purple, she'd never escape from Home's detention center. With her arrest, her freedom would be gone forever, along with her chance to avenge her brother's death. She'd worked too hard to let that happen.

She would have to take the first chance that came along. The smallest mistake, the slightest distraction, anything to improve her odds.

"It would be easier if we didn't have to carry you." That was the one by the back door. A woman. The voice a little more tense, a little more aggressive than the man's. From her stance, her voice, the way she held her gun, M'Briti decided that she'd be the one to watch, the one more likely to overreact if something unexpected came up.

In response to the woman's threat, M'Briti walked toward the front door. The man backed through it, keeping his weapon aimed at M'Briti but swiveling his head to survey the area outside. He gestured that all was clear and stepped back farther. M'Briti came out, followed by the woman.

The party turned left, away from the heart of the Annex, toward the open plain not many blocks from M'Briti's house.

With the two agents, one on either side and slightly behind her, she went slowly down the empty street. Her heart sank. The way they were taking would offer much less opportunity for her to escape.

Damn Montoya anyway, she cursed savagely to herself. *And damn me for trusting him.*

She had to make her move while they were still in the Annex. Here, among the crowded buildings and twisting alleys, if she could disable one of her captors and get a few steps head start, she had a chance to get away. Out in the open, her chances were next to none.

From one of the side streets ahead, she heard the off-key singing of a drunk, or perhaps a Purple addict coming down. The voice sounded vaguely familiar, but she knew so many Annex dwellers of that type that it was pointless to try to remember this one's name. Even more pointless to call for help.

The trio was nearly at the intersection when the drunk—he was carrying a bottle in one hand—stumbled out in front of them. He seemed barely able to keep his balance and his face was grimy. He had a tattered old cloth draped over his head like a hood, a pitiful attempt to keep out the night's chill.

The male agent, on M'Briti's right, stepped forward and reached out his hand in a peremptory gesture. "Stand back, please. You're blocking our way."

"Wha . . . ?" The drunk squinted up at the agent in a confused way.

M'Briti saw the only opportunity she might get. With the speed only a Wellborn could summon, she spun and kicked at the other agent's gun hand.

Behind her, she heard the sound of breaking glass.

In front of her, as if everything were in slow motion, she saw her leg straightening, snapping her right foot into the woman agent's forearm. It should have smashed the bone and left the woman open to a follow-up kick, but M'Briti had been away from the Wells for a year.

The woman was leaning back, swinging her arm up and out of the way. M'Briti had also been on Purple for most of that year, and it had taken its toll. Her follow-through pulled her off-balance.

As she twisted to roll with her fall, she saw the woman's gun coming down to center on her. M'Briti tucked her arms in tight and swiveled her shoulders to turn faster, hoping to throw off the woman's aim.

Out of the corner of her eye, she saw a dark figure standing in a half crouch where the drunk and the other guard had been. She felt the sting of the woman's stunner across her back and heard the weapon's faint *snap*.

Pain rushed outward from her spine, setting all her muscles on fire.

Founders' damn, she cursed to herself. *If I live to see that bastard Montoya again, I'll kill him.*

As she began to lose consciousness, she thought she heard, far away, another *snap*.

There was a sound. *Huhuhuhuhu.*

A watery echoing sound. *Ellellellellell.*

It came from everywhere and beat against M'Briti's brain. *Owowowowoww.*

It hurt her head. *Hellellellellell.*

She moaned and tried to wave it away. *Lowowowowow.*

The sound came from somewhere in front of her. She opened her eyes. Everything was dim and blurred. *Hellellellell. Lowowowow.*

Her head was pounding. Every nerve in her body was being prodded by a hot needle. She blinked a few times and her vision began to clear. There was a shadowy face before her. *Hellellell. Lowowow.*

Her bones were lead weights. Her stomach was a knot cinched tight. The face was talking to her. *Hellell. Lowow.*

Her mouth was filled with sand. Her throat was a rakeclaw's scratching post. The face leaned closer. Its voice sounded familiar. *Hell. Low.*

She blinked the remaining grit out of her eyes. Suddenly the face and the voice were clear.

"Hello," said Darrin Montoya.

M'Briti struggled to sit up. "You bast—" She coughed, choking on her words.

"Please, M'Briti, relax." She felt hands on her shoulders, pushing her back down. She hurt everywhere and had no strength.

"What are—" Her throat seized up on her. It felt as if the rakeclaw had shredded it. She tried to hit Darrin, but her arms flopped helplessly at her sides.

"Take it easy." His hands were gentle but firm, as was his voice. "You're safe now."

Safe? She didn't say the word—her throat wouldn't let her.

"Don't worry," Darrin said, as if reading her mind. "You'll be fine. Here," he reached to the side and pulled over a bundled-up blanket or cloak. "If you promise not to attack me, I'll give you some broth." He looked into her eyes. "Promise?"

M'Briti nodded, and a broad smile lit Darrin's face. "Fine." He raised her head and placed the bundle under it for a pillow. Then he picked up a thermal squeeze bulb and held it to her lips. "Just a small sip at a time—no choking allowed."

By the time the bulb was empty, M'Briti was beginning to feel nearly alive. The pain had dropped a notch or two. She could move a little.

From what she'd been able to see while drinking the broth, she had a general idea of where she was.

The place was musty, lighted by a few dim glow panels in the ceiling, and half filled with barrels and tarp-covered machinery. It looked like one of the many deserted storage sheds and small warehouses in the Annex—places whose owners had died or gone out of business and which no one else had bothered to locate or reopen.

This was the sort of place she would use for meeting her customers, her Purple addicts. It was not at all where she thought Home's security agents would conduct an interrogation. How had she gotten here?

She was lying on a blanket on the floor in an open space at one end of the building. There were several small windows high up along the side walls. They were dust-covered and dingy, and just clear enough to tell her that it was night outside.

The broth had soothed her throat enough for talking, at least a little. She suspected there'd been more than broth in that bulb.

"Darrin?" she asked quietly, gingerly. She felt only a small twinge.

"Hmm?" He was sitting a few meters away on the floor with his back against an old polyplast barrel, watching her.

"What's going on?"

He smiled wryly. "That's what I'd like to know."

"Don't"—she swallowed—"make me draw it out. It hurts too much."

His smile disappeared. "I'm sorry." He scooted over to her and sat, cross-legged, elbows on knees, his chin resting on his palms. "Some of it I can tell you, some I can only guess at along with you. For starters, I was and am investigating the Purple traffic for Executor Senyan—everything I told you about that is true."

He paused, sighed once, and added, "And I really did want to believe you weren't dealing. I had nearly convinced myself you weren't involved."

"Then why . . . ?"

"Why did I send those agents for you? I didn't, but I think Senyan did. I'm guessing that he traced my inquiries about you and decided to take a chance on quick success with a covert arrest and interrogation.

"And why did I rescue you from them?" He nodded at her look of surprise. "Yes, that drunk was me.

"I stopped in at Jaro's Tavern on my way to get the wine, just for old times' sake. The server on duty was the same one who'd been there when we first met. I asked him about his black eye." Here Darrin raised an eyebrow at M'Briti, who half grinned in embarrassment.

"He told me this and that, just enough to get me to see several things in a new light. I got the wine and headed back to your place with a lot of questions in mind. I arrived in time to see the one agent break down your front door and hear the other coming in the back."

He stopped and looked at her intently. "At that moment, with all my suspicions and questions, all I could think of was losing you to Senyan. He's not a bad man, but he is a stubborn one. If you were innocent, you'd probably go free, but if not, I'd never see you again. So I followed you, bottle in hand, found some props in an alley, and came to the rescue.''

He raised his head and spread his hands apart, palms up. ''What else could I do?''

She wanted to believe him, but it was the stuff of fantasy. People didn't do things like this. ''Where are the agents, then?''

''In an alley far from here. When they come to, they'll need some time to untie themselves.'' He gestured vaguely behind himself. ''I have their guns wrapped up back there.''

He sat before her with an expression that invited comment. M'Briti didn't know what to say. Could she now trust him, or was this a subtler tack he was taking? She closed her eyes and asked tiredly, ''And what do you think—am I guilty or innocent?''

She heard him stand up and walk back toward where he'd been sitting. ''From what I know of you, I'd guess that there's more to it than guilt or innocence.'' He rustled around in the pack he'd had on the floor beside him, by the barrel. ''But I can say for certain that you're becoming a little careless, unless those two agents caught you in the act of hiding these.''

She knew Darrin wanted her to look, and when she opened her eyes, her fears were confirmed. There he stood, her black spiral pipe in one hand, a small packet of brownish purple powder in the other. His expression was neutral.

M'Briti closed her eyes again and tried to make sense out of the situation. In rescuing her, Darrin had gone against his duty to Home and his arrangement with Senyan. If she'd been innocent, he just might have been able to defend his actions, but now that he knew she was on Purple, honest excuses would be hard for him to come by.

Darrin broke the uneasy silence. ''I think I know what you're doing, but I need to have you tell me. Are you dealing Purple as well as using it?''

''Yes,'' M'Briti said. The word came out louder than she'd intended. It seemed to echo from the bare walls and dusty barrels of the warehouse.

"This has to do with your brother, doesn't it?" His voice was quiet, gentle. He wasn't accusing, wasn't blaming.

Suddenly the long year since M'Taba's death came crashing down on M'Briti. The year of furtive dealings and secret meetings, of playing friend of the weak and lost and frustrated users, of playing ally to the corrupt and greedy suppliers. The year of fighting her own growing addiction while feeding the addictions of others. The year of loneliness and fear.

It all came down on her, crushing her, squeezing the truth out of her.

The words poured forth with no premeditation and no holding back. For the first time in a year, she no longer cared what effect her words had. She told Darrin about her brother and his addiction and his death, about her resolve to find those responsible, about her clumsy crime designed to get her banned from the Wells. She told him of her first contact with a dealer of Purple, of the first time she'd smoked the drug.

She told him, between sobs, of the unmatched high Purple offered, and of the unquenchable thirst it created. She told him of how she'd become a dealer, and of when and where she contacted her supplier. She told him of what she knew and what she'd guessed about the Purple traffic.

She told him everything, and when she was finished, squeezed dry and empty, he knelt down and held her in his arms, and she, with returning strength, held him.

In the deserted, dust-filled warehouse somewhere in the nether reaches of the Trading Annex, they held each other for a minute or an hour. And then they lay back and fell asleep, still in each other's arms. And the last thing M'Briti remembered, before she slipped into vague and chaotic dreams, was Darrin's voice, softly in her ear, whispering something about plans to be made.

— 22 —

No air moved in the small courtyard. The weather had turned warm again, and heat was collecting in the enclosed space. The man standing before M'Briti was large and angry. Sweat was beginning to drip from his beard.

"Why'd you bring me to this place?" he growled. "If we get caught, I swear I'll..." He fingered his long-bladed knife.

Sandor was over a head taller than M'Briti, broadly built. But he was a Normal and M'Briti, though weakened, was a Wellborn. She grabbed the front of his jacket in both hands and smiled. With one twist of her body, she slammed him against the rough stone wall. As he gasped and tried to regain his breath, she snatched the knife out of his hand.

"Sandor, you're a fool," she hissed, pressing him against the wall with one hand, holding the knife in front of his face with the other. "I know it's dangerous to meet in the daytime, but if you try threatening me again, I'll make you eat this thing. Understand?"

He glared hatred, but he said nothing, merely nodding his agreement.

"Good." She let go of him and stepped back. There was, she knew, only a small chance that they would be overheard. The courtyard was walled in on all four sides by the windowless backs of abandoned two- and three-story buildings. No doors opened onto the five-meter-square space. The only entrance was a hole someone had knocked in one of the walls.

The courtyard seemed more an accident than anything else—a space that was unused because no one realized it was there for the taking. And now the vagaries of growth

and decay had left it in the middle of a small urban desert—
a few blocks of the Annex where no one chose to live or do
business, and hadn't for several years.

"Now listen closely. I don't have a lot of time and I have
even less patience." M'Briti tossed the knife with one hand
as she talked, staring into the man's gray, angry eyes.

"They're on to me. Two agents from Home came for me
last night. I might not be lucky enough to get away next
time."

"So what am I supposed to do about it?" Sandor asked
with a sneer. "I'm not your bodyguard."

"Shut up and listen." M'Briti slashed quickly with the
knife and the sneer vanished. The man clutched his bleeding
wrist and listened.

"I want to talk to the people in charge, not a middleman
or a flunky. Someone with enough pull to get me out of
here, to some place where Home won't find me. And they
have to guarantee me a steady supply of Purple."

"Why not ask for Yakimu while you're at it?"

M'Briti jabbed him in the thigh with the knife, just
enough to make him wince. "In return, I can give them the
undercover agent who identified me."

Sandor frowned worriedly. "I don't know if—"

M'Briti slammed him against the wall again. "I'll be
waiting at Cradoger's Ravine tomorrow night, midnight. If
nobody shows up, I'll give Home everything I know, and
maybe cause some trouble on my own."

She let the bearded man go and walked back to the
courtyard's crude entrance, then turned to look back at him.
"I know you won't follow me. You'll be too busy passing
my message on to someone with better connections. After
all, if this falls through, who do you think I'll come looking
for first?"

With that, she raised the knife and tossed it in a swift
overhand throw. It struck the wall point-first next to
Sandor's left knee. The blade shattered.

M'Briti shook her head. "You'll need better weapons
than that if you're going to play this game." She turned,
slipped through the rubble-strewn hole, and was gone. She

took precautions for several blocks to make sure that she was not followed.

I can only hope that Darrin and I have enough weapons, she thought, trying with only partial success to maintain the aggressive attitude she'd adopted for Sandor's benefit.

— 23 —

"Another meeting," Niala grumbled to herself. "I'm being meetinged to death." It was a nice evening for a stroll, clear and warm, with no wind, but the prospect of a second Executors' meeting in two days was not a happy one. She glanced up. On her right, the top of the Executors' Hall was just visible above the surrounding low trees.

The Executors' Hall was not a large building. A flattened dome, it was perhaps twenty-five meters in diameter and nine or ten high. It had been built during the Founding, but apart from the other buildings of Oldtown, on a small hill in what was now the southern section of Home.

The Hall was surrounded by a large park that covered most of the hill. The park was surrounded by a low white stone wall. The wall was primarily for decoration.

The real protection for the Executors' Hall was a neuronal barrier that would let anything pass except a human being, or something with an equally developed central nervous system. The exceptions were those whose identidisc codes were entered into the barrier's monitors.

Niala met Marguerite Venebles near the western gate in the wall. She had the impression that Venebles wanted their meeting to appear accidental, but that she'd intended it to happen.

Venebles greeted her with a too-quick smile. "At least the weather's back to normal." To Niala's ears, the pleasantry sounded even more pro forma than usual for such statements.

She gave a laugh. "It is a relief to have something going right." *Play the game, see what she wants.*

They turned and walked through the gate. Inside, one path wound around the south side of the hill and to the eastern gate. A second path did the same on the north side of the hill. The third path led up, with only a few curves, directly to the western arch of the Executors' Hall. They took the third path.

"I wonder if Executor Senyan has solved the Purple problem for us since yesterday." Venebles walked with jerky energy, her steps short and quick.

So that's it, Niala thought. "Probably not. If he has, he certainly hasn't told me."

Venebles stopped for a moment and looked directly at Niala. "Has he said anything? All this secrecy bothers me."

Niala shook her head. "No, not a word." *What's really bothering her?* Niala wondered. This seemed like more than the predictable Senyan-Venebles suspicion.

"Oh, well, maybe we'll find out more at this meeting." Venebles sounded as if she were still carrying around the tension of the previous meeting.

As they walked on, the setting sun's rays lighted Venebles's hair, turning it into a stream of orange and silver fire. None of the light reached the tall Executor's face. She seemed unaware of the beauty around her.

"We can only hope," Niala agreed. Senyan had not explained his current summons—just that an emergency meeting of the Executors was necessary, and that it should take place immediately "or sooner." Niala couldn't decide whether the last phase was a bad attempt at humor, or whether Senyan was just awkwardly expressing the meeting's urgency.

In truth, Niala was intensely curious about the reason for the meeting. As far as she knew, the Matrix failure was being handled well. Services to Home were being restored, backup copies of destroyed files were being assimilated into a new data system, and no security threats loomed on the horizon.

Other than Senyan's odd announcement the other day about solving the Purple Heaven problem, she could think of nothing that would justify this meeting.

She and Venebles reached the Hall, and Venebles seemed to hesitate ever so slightly before entering. The only thing stranger than Senyan's behavior over the last day and a half, she decided, was Venebles's.

Niala stepped boldly through the archway into the hall as if it were the normal thing to do, which it was. Inside, she saw no gang of Drath assassins waiting to do in Home's Executors, nor did she find the room filled with confiscated Purple Heaven. All she saw was Masanaru Senyan seated at the white table, hunched over and studying something on his tabletop screen.

"We're here," Niala announced in a cheery voice, hoping to fend off some of the gloom she read into Senyan's posture and facial expression. When he responded, it was clear her ploy had been less than successful.

"About time." It was more of a growl than usual for him. "Does either of you believe in fate?"

Niala and Venebles exchanged a glance. The question was puzzling to both of them. *What now?* Niala asked herself with a hint of panic.

Senyan shrugged and gestured at the two to be seated. "Whatever, we finally got the main hyperwave receivers functional this morning, and this afternoon a Priority message came through. That's why I called you here on such short notice."

A Priority message could only be deciphered in the presence of all three Executors. Their meeting table and its three individualized interface surfaces served as the decoding device. They were used rarely, and a hyperwave Priority message was likely to have come from only one place.

"One of our agents?" Niala asked.

Senyan shook his head. "We can't be sure. Without the Matrix, our directional capabilities through hyperspace are limited. We do know that it came from the general direction of the Interstellar Union." He paused as if to let that fact sink in, then said, "We won't know for certain until we decode it. I suggest we do so at once."

The three set their left hands on the table before them, where their data screens were, and leaned forward so their heads were over the table. Then Senyan pressed a series of commands into his control panel. The sensors in the table read their hand prints and the codes in their identidiscs, compared those to the ones currently listed for the Executors, then used that information as the key to decode the message they'd received.

The entire process was over in a second, and a tone sounded indicating that the message was ready for viewing.

They all sat back, and Senyan pressed a few more commands into his terminal. A gray haze formed in each of the room's two archways. It thickened and darkened until each arch was blocked by a solid black wall. An unnatural stillness settled into the room, the stillness of a privacy field in operation.

Niala looked over to Venebles and smiled. "Services are being restored quite well, it seems. Congratulations."

Venebles acknowledged the compliment with a brief nod. "The best people I can find have been giving it their best efforts."

Senyan cleared his throat. "Now, then. Are we ready?"

Two nods.

"Very well. Here goes." He pressed in another command.

The room's lights dimmed and a glow formed above the center of the table. It brightened, became more dense, took on a definite shape. A medium-sized man with a pale complexion looked down at Niala. His eyes were pale green, his hair jet-black. He had a strong, square face. He wore what looked like a soiled laborer's uniform. He was unshaven, and he looked worried.

"Greetings, Executors." He spoke directly to Niala, but she knew that the projection was addressing the other two directly as well. She recognized the man as Keena Rythmun, one of Home's agents in the Union.

Rythmun was stationed on Drinan Four, capital planet of Sector Seven. He operated out of Brinktown, as disreputable a city as Niala had ever had the pleasure to visit.

Events had proceeded rapidly on Drinan Four over the past several days, and in Home's favor. Aldon Rizlov had been removed as Senior Adjudicator, replaced by Umberto Phillips, whom Niala had met during the incident when her son had been killed. Lanya Selius, a Planetary Overseer accused of treason, had been acquitted with the help of Jarnice Chou, another Home agent.

Phillips and Selius were both in favor of moderating the Union's militaristic expansion, and both could be counted on to protect Seelzar's independence to the extent that they were able.

Yes, things had been going well indeed on Drinan Four, Niala reflected, but now Rythmun was calling, and worried.

"There has been a complication," he said. "Agent Chou missed her departure rendezvous." His voice had the calm, controlled tone of an experienced agent in a tight spot. Niala recognized the tone immediately; she had used it more than once herself, years ago.

"I have reason to believe she has been apprehended by agents of the Central Council. From what I was able to learn at the scene, there was no struggle. What this means, I have yet to determine." Rythmun paused, frowning slightly. He seemed to be listening for something off to his right.

What could be distracting him? Niala asked herself.

He continued, "Pending further instructions, I will continue to investigate her whereabouts."

Now Niala thought that she too could hear noises coming from off-projection.

Rythmun pulled a weapon from inside his jacket. It looked like a military-issue energy pistol of Union design. Niala wondered what power he had it set on.

"You can contact me at—"

A loud crash came from the right, as of something large and heavy going through a door. Rythmun turned and fired two blasts in that direction and yelled, "Contingency One!" Then there was a flash of light and the image vanished.

Only when Niala let out her breath did she realize she'd been holding it, caught up in the drama she'd just witnessed. Rythmun had seemed so close, so real, that she could have reached out and touched him, or leapt into the scene to help him face whatever had come after him.

Senyan brought the room's lights up to normal, but kept the archway blocks and the privacy field in place.

Venebles spoke first. "What do we do now?" She brushed a strand of long white hair back from her face and looked at Senyan.

"Obviously nothing," Senyan stated with impatience. "That is what 'Contingency One' means—we must wait for the agent to reestablish contact."

"What? The Central Council has just captured one of our agents, and probably two, and you propose to do nothing?" Venebles turned to Niala, and her outrage seemed genuine. "He can't mean that, can he?"

It was with considerable reluctance that Niala replied, "According to established procedures, that is the proper response. It's what agent Rythmun will expect us to do."

"It's what he *told* us to do," Senyan added.

Venebles waved her arms in exasperation. "But only because he didn't have time for anything else. If he escapes, maybe he'll be able to contact us. And maybe he'll be able to rescue Chou. But if not, we'll sit out here until the Union's fleet is overhead!"

Senyan frowned. "Hysterics will hardly help the situation, Executor. What would you have us do?"

"Rescue them, of course, before they're made to reveal Seelzar's location."

It was Senyan's turn to appeal to Niala. "How likely is that?"

"That they'd reveal our location?" The rescue option was certainly one Senyan would not care to pursue. "Our agents' psychblocks are very strong. From what we know of the Union's techniques, I'd say Chou and Rythmun could hold out for a long time, perhaps indefinitely."

She didn't add that it would be an agonizing ordeal for the agents, and probably end in their deaths. Even if they came to *want* to reveal their secrets, their blocks might keep them from doing so. Niala shuddered at the thought.

Venebles stood up and leaned forward with her palms on the tabletop. "But we don't know how long they'll hold, and we can't know that. Is that a chance we should take? Three or four of our largest ships could slip in and hit Drinan Four. We'd either rescue our agents or give them a chance to escape in the confusion. If necessary.'' Here she paused. ''If it were the only way, we could at least neutralize the agents.'' She looked at Niala apologetically. ''It would save them the interrogation.''

''What's the difference between that proposal and all-out war?'' Senyan remained seated. He was still and unyielding, a statue carved from sheenwood. ''To be sure we succeeded, we'd have to send more than three or four ships. Otherwise, we'd risk losing the ships with no guarantee of success.''

''It's going to be war sooner or later anyway. You know that. Unless you'd prefer surrender?''

''Surrender's not the only alternative, especially not yet. *You* know *that*. It's impossible to reason with you, Executor.'' Senyan glared up at Venebles, who returned the look.

''There is some truth in what each of you says.'' Niala spoke quietly into the charged silence. ''Three or four of our ships probably would be a sufficient force to use in attacking Drinan Four. But it is a sector capital, heavily protected, so we'd certainly lose a ship or two.'' That was for Senyan's benefit.

To Venebles, she added, ''And because it is well-protected, we'd almost certainly have to forget about rescues. Such a raid would only succeed with maximum firepower applied immediately. Chou and Rythmun would die, as would millions of others.''

Senyan and Venebles responded as Niala had hoped they would. They took turns pressing her to explain and defend her reservations about their own points of view. The discussion focused on questions of military hardware and tactics. She was on her own ground and was able to keep her two colleagues from each other's throats.

The holojector and the tabletop screens filled with schematics and technical specs for Home's ships and the Union's armament, as much as was known. Interspersed with the explanations of hardware came descriptions of the possible situations the ships would encounter on Drinan Four, especially emphasizing the problems inherent in locating two people being held covertly by unidentified parties.

By the time all the schematics had been run through, all the speed and shielding and firepower factors compared, all the attack strategies analyzed, and all the prisoner detention options explained, both Senyan and Venebles were looking glassy-eyed.

Her colleagues agreed with Niala's suggestion that waiting for a day or so would be for the best, to give Rythmun some chance to contact Home before taking further action.

The Executors' next meeting was scheduled for two days hence. That was as long as Venebles would wait and was the soonest Senyan was willing to meet with an eye toward deciding on a course of action.

With that decision made, the meeting adjourned. The privacy field was shut down, and the archway blocks dissolved. Senyan left by the eastern arch, Venebles by the one facing west.

Niala lingered for a time in the empty room. She turned the lighting down, then off. Quiet night sounds came in from the outside—a light breeze rustling through the trees in the park, a night bird whistling its territorial declaration, insects chirruping and clicking and buzzing their mating calls.

Human sounds were minimal. Somewhere in the distance the faint whine of some construction work rose above the natural background noises, then the breeze shifted and the sound faded away.

Niala's eyes gradually adjusted to the dark. The archways became bright openings in the heavily shadowed hall. She stood and walked out through the eastern archway and down to the gate in the low wall. There she took the path that meandered along the south side of the hill back to the western gate.

Rythmun's message was a decidedly mixed blessing, she realized, but mostly bad. It had deflected Senyan and Venebles from arguing about the Purple Heaven problem, but only by giving them something even more pressing to disagree about.

What bothered her, what made her feel a little guilty, was that she found herself focusing on the new problem too, and not just as something that demanded attention.

She had to admit that a part of her welcomed it. Rythmun's message gave her the opportunity to become an agent again, in a sense, not just a manager or administrator.

"If I were there, what would I do?" was one question that kept running through her mind. The other was, "As an Executor, what can I do to help Rythmun and Chou?"

There was also an idea, lurking in the back of her mind, that she was not yet ready to verbalize to anybody. She had a feeling that it was an idea neither Senyan nor Venebles would approve. She wasn't sure yet how much their approval would matter.

— 24 —

Bashir sat up in the cart and looked out and down. Below him, the city of Ebel spread out for several kilometers. It was a sprawling city of low buildings and narrow streets laid out according to no discernible pattern. A low wall marked the edge of its growth in all directions.

Bulbulian and Alyssa dismounted from their hexoxen and came back to join him. Their small party was atop one of the worn-down hills that formed a semicircle to the south of Ebel. The bulk of traffic entered the city from the east or the west, where the main trade route of Toria skirted the hills.

Bashir turned to Alyssa. "Quite a sight, eh?" He could tell that she was impressed, and she had every reason to be.

"It's so . . . It's huge," she said without taking her eyes off the city.

He nodded. "Largest man-made structure on Seelzar. Not as many people as Home, but several times the area." And it was a structure, of sorts. Bashir recalled wandering

through the narrow alleys and courtyards where every building was connected haphazardly to at least one of its fellows.

The sun was low in the sky. Long shadows reached from
the westernmost hills toward the city. The buildings below
glowed orange and rust-brown and red in the dying light.
Their shadows grew darker by the minute.

"It is getting late in the day. The city will soon be
closed," Bulbulian commented.

"That's all right," Bashir replied "I'd planned on entering in the morning anyway." In the morning, he knew, the
traders who'd arrived late in the day and overnight would be
gathered around two main gates, one east and one west,
awaiting sunrise and the official start of a new day. That was
where he wanted to be. One old man on foot would attract
no notice at all in such a throng. He'd entered the city that
way many times before with no difficulty. This time should
be no different.

"Will we be taking the cart and hexoxen in too?" Alyssa
asked.

"That's something we can discuss after we've settled in
for the night." *Walk softly on this, Bashir, old boy*, he
warned himself. Alyssa and Bulbulian would certainly
expect to accompany him into the city, and he wasn't sure
whether they'd be better or worse off by doing so.

"Should we stay up here and away from the others?"
Bulbulian pointed to the plain below them, where camps
were being set up near the two main gates and by some of
the smaller gates scattered around the city wall.

Bashir nodded. "That would be for the best. Less chance
of giving ourselves away to some prying or perceptive
traveler."

He was fairly certain that he and Bulbulian would have no
trouble passing such informal inspections, but he was much
less confident of Alyssa's ability to do so. True, she was
bright enough and had more at stake than anyone else, but
she had no experience at all in this setting. Better not to risk
it. Besides, if they were to camp out here in the foothills,
he'd have a better chance of slipping away during the night,
if he chose to—fewer people to notice his departure.

"That hollow we just passed would be a good place to camp," Alyssa suggested, "if we want to keep from being seen."

Bashir nodded his agreement. "I think it would do. It's close and we're nearly out of daylight." He knew the area fairly well, but this path was one he hadn't taken in several decades. He didn't want to wander around looking for a suitable spot farther on that might not even be there.

The path was narrow, flanked by thin but sturdy trees. Turning the cart around took some time. Bulbulian went ahead to lead the hexoxen on foot while Alyssa walked beside the cart and helped it around and between the trees.

Bashir stayed in the cart until they reached the hollow, then he climbed out and walked around the site. He wanted to be sure they arranged themselves for maximum concealment without being too obvious about it—they didn't want to arouse the suspicions of anyone who might come upon them by accident.

The hollow was twenty meters or so across. It was shallow, but set into the hillside against a vertical rock face seamed with large cracks and covered with moss. A few chunks had fallen from the rock face so long ago that they were now large mossy lumps crowned with hopeful saplings.

Knee-high undergrowth of broad-bladed grasses filled the hollow, and a patch of shoulder-high bushes separated it from the path.

Someone walking along the path would not notice the hollow. Someone riding might, if he were attentive, but probably not after dark.

Bashir walked around the boulders, through the dark green grasses, breathing in the sweet evening air. The day had been a warm one, made warmer by the fast pace Bashir and his companions had set. Now, with the sun behind the hills, shadows were deep and cool in the hollow. Only the tallest trees still caught a few of its rays with their highest branches.

He felt revived at last, mentally and physically. Not that he believed he was fully recovered—all his years had taught him the difference between desires and reality. He'd also learned how to turn the one into the other more often than not. That's what had brought him here, on the outskirts of Ebel, one more time.

He wasn't sure that what he had in mind would work, or even that it would be for the best if it did work. But uncertainty was something he'd come to accept as part of life. Resolving uncertainties, taking the risk, was something he'd come to relish.

That realization made him pause. Going into the Matrix could have killed him, but that had not deterred him. If anything, the possibility of overcoming such a risk had drawn him on. Being discovered entering Ebel could get himself and Alyssa executed by the Draths. If Bulbulian were caught helping them, he would probably share that fate. The execution would be especially unpleasant if they were all found inside the Drath temple. It never occurred to him not to make the attempt.

Bashir looked up through the leafy canopy. The last traces of sunlight had fled from the treetops. The sky was a deepening blue, unmarried by clouds. A few early stars shone bright and clear.

Somewhere from deeper in the hills, a shade hawk called, its lilting cry echoing through the trees. From the camps surrounding Ebel, Bashir thought he could hear the thin, sustained notes of a ten-stringed psaltry.

He'd sat around such campfires before, with traders and herdsmen and travelers of varied sorts, sharing stories and songs and drinks until the small hours of morning. He'd felt the instant closeness there of strangers with no responsibilities or obligations to one another, who could reveal their deepest fears or their wildest hopes without worrying about explaining, the next day or the next year, how they could say such things.

"Bashir?" Alyssa had come over to him, touched his arm. "Would over there be okay for our fire?" She pointed to a spot between the rock face and one of the mossy boulders.

He smiled apologetically. "Oh, yes. That's precisely where I was going to suggest." *Maybe I'm not as recovered as I thought, letting my mind wander like that.* He winced at the thought and its implications.

Alyssa nodded and squeezed his arm. "Good. We'll have it going in no time." She turned and went back to where the cart and the animals stood in the center of the hollow. She and Bulbulian began unloading the supplies they'd acquired along the way.

Bashir watched them bustling about, efficient and competent. He shook his head and couldn't find the words for how he was feeling at that moment.

Here were two people who were dear to him, and for whom he felt an enormous responsibility. He wanted to protect them, but they deserved to decide for themselves the path they would take. He walked slowly around the hollow one more time, then stepped over to where the campfire was beginning to push back night's shadows.

Alyssa sat with her back resting against the rock wall. The rock was more or less flat, and the moss softened it enough to make it almost comfortable. She stared into the dying embers of the campfire and let her mind wander.

In a little over two days' time, she'd gone from the odd alien tunnels beneath Bashir's shop, through the Borderlands, and well into Toria itself. Now she was waiting for dawn to come so she could go into Ebel—the capital of Toria and a place strictly off-limits to the Wellborn, a prohibition supported by both Home and the Drath leaders of Toria.

It had been an anxious, exciting, tiring trip. She marveled at how Bashir seemed to be getting stronger in the midst of all of it. He might have done better if he'd stayed in the rehab cylinder back in the tunnels, but she had her doubts. She could swear that some of the energy she saw returning to his face grew out of their illicit quest, and that he was feeding on the danger and hardship.

She raised her eyes to look over at the cart, where he was sleeping at her and Bulbulian's insistence. "You dear, dear old man," she whispered. "I do hope you don't regret getting involved in this. If anything more were to happen to you . . ."

Alyssa didn't finish the sentence because she couldn't imagine what she would do without Bashir Arak. The world would seem incomplete without the spry old man. If only he would tell her what he was after, he could stay here in relative safety and she could go into Ebel and take the risks.

The fire popped and Alyssa jerked, then smiled at her reaction. She'd been edgy for so long, ever since the Matrix failure five days before, and really for several days leading up to that. At some point, she thought, she should start getting used to the tension, the risks, the uncertainty. But she'd seen no sign of such an adjustment.

If it weren't for the fact that Bashir was doing this for Darrin, and that Bashir needed her, she might seriously have considered abandoning the adventure and returning to her research and her music.

A faint rustle, barely audible, sounded from behind the boulder on the other side of the nearly dead campfire. *Bulbulian*, she reminded herself. And there was another puzzle.

Who was Qatar Bulbulian, anyway? Certainly much more than a vendor of bozad pies. Beyond his association with Bashir, there was a quality about him that reminded her more of a Wellborn than a Normal. He'd hidden it quite well back in the Annex. Hawking his pies, he'd seemed like an ordinary Torian baker, but several times since then, since the night the Matrix failed, Alyssa had seen glimpses of another person entirely, one stronger and quicker and more self-assured than a Torian baker had any right to be.

He was out there now, seated on the other side of the boulder, keeping watch. He'd said nothing about being relieved. "I will keep watch," he'd declared after their meager supper, and Alyssa had sensed that he'd be offended if she or Bashir had offered to share the duty. Bashir had merely nodded his agreement, and Alyssa had seen no reason to argue.

One of the hexoxen snorted in its sleep, a deep *whuff* that sounded loud indeed in the still night. The two beasts had grazed eagerly on the hollow's tall thick grass, and then had folded their legs and settled to the ground, becoming two more boulders in the clearing.

Alyssa smiled at their large, lumpy shapes. The beasts had certainly earned their rest. For two days, with Bulbulian riding one and herself on the other, the hexoxen had pulled Bashir and his cart from dawn to dusk, at a pace little short of a gallop.

At first Alyssa had been leery of riding them, but the huge beasts were as gentle as they were ugly. And they were very ugly. Two meters tall at the shoulder, their bodies were knotted with muscle, as were their six legs. They had knobby skulls and broad mouths full of square teeth. There was nothing sleek about them, but they were strong and they were fast and they had staying power.

One of the animals *whuffed* again and shifted around so that its front hoof rested on top of its muzzle. Alyssa felt an urge to go over and give the beast's broad neck a hug and maybe scratch it behind the ear. Instead, she wrapped her cloak around her and lay down, using a pack filled with spare clothes as a pillow.

It was getting late. Bashir was planning an early start for tomorrow, and Alyssa wanted to be as fresh as possible. She was not going to be left behind, regardless of what Bashir had been saying about the dangers and risks. He was probably exaggerating for her benefit, but it didn't matter. She was going in any case.

She lay on her back and looked up through the black leaf shapes to the clear night sky. Stars shone down, bright and steady through the still air. She wondered whether Bashir was as recovered as he seemed. She wondered whether Bulbulian was really going to watch the entire night with no sleep. She wondered why she couldn't make herself relax, as those two apparently could.

Breathe in through your mouth and out through your nose.

She closed her eyes and started counting her breaths. At first, she saw the numbers appearing one after another behind her eyelids. Soon, the numbers began riding on the backs of hexoxen, in a long line. Eventually, the hexoxen started selling bozad pies to crowds of numbers milling about in great confusion. Then everything faded to black.

* * *

The dream came again. The observer part of Bashir recognized it as something experienced before. To the participant in him, that made no difference.

There was the dungeon and the beast and the dark man with the scepter in the field of Wells. But this time the dark man had a name, one known to every Wellborn—Achmar Z'areikh, one of the three Founders. And this time, Z'areikh freed Bashir before the beast caught him.

As he fled through the doorway, he found that Z'areikh had thrust the scepter into his hands. He turned back to see if the beast were still pursuing him, but the beast was gone, along with the doorway and the entire underground maze. In their place was a field of Wells stretching to the horizon. He looked around him, and it was the same everywhere, Wells glowing green as far as he could see.

Bashir began walking. He passed a Well, and its Glow faded and then vanished. He passed another Well, and it, too, died. He walked past a third Well, then a fourth and a fifth, leaving them all dead behind him.

In his hand, the scepter started to hum, an unheard vibration at first that grew as he walked until it was loud enough to hurt his ears. His arm ached with the effort of holding on, of keeping the scepter from flying away.

It began to glow like the Wells, the light increasing with the vibrations. Its marbled black surface was shot through with bright flashes of green light, blinding in their intensity.

Through slitted eyes, Bashir stared at the scepter. Where had he seen it before?

Its power continued to grow, as it absorbed more Wells' energies. His eyes watering, he saw the scepter begin to split along one side. A hairline fracture appeared and began to widen. Slowly, the fracture spread, and through it, Bashir could see into the scepter, into a seething chaos of energy, barely contained.

He gripped the scepter in both hands, trying to hold it together, but it was impossible. The pressure was too great. Soon it would burst out of its confinement, wreaking untold havoc on the Wellfield, and destroying Bashir in the process.

His grip began to weaken. Somewhere above the roaring of the green energy, Bashir heard a voice speaking—a woman's voice. She was trying to explain something. Bashir strained to hear the words, as if they were a lifeline he had to grasp.

The scepter split farther, and green fire began to eat at his hands. The woman was explaining the Glow ... and the Wells ... and the scepter itself! But it was too late. The scepter exploded in a ball of consuming energy.

The participant in the dream disappeared, and the observer saw nothing but an afterimage of the scepter glowing bright green in the blackness.

Bashir awoke from his dream with a feeling not of fear but of excitement. His memory had finally reassembled enough of the puzzle. He lay in his cart, eyes closed, and considered what he was planning to do.

A smile slowly curved his mouth as he thought about what Alyssa would say. Would she think he'd had a relapse, or that he was making up some outrageous story to keep her from coming along? Who could say?

He opened his eyes and looked up through the trees toward the sky. It was still dark, but from the positions of the stars, Bashir could tell that dawn would be coming soon. Before then, he wanted to be down on the plain, preparing to blend into the waiting crowd of traders and herdsmen.

"Bashir?"

He turned and saw Bulbulian standing beside the cart.

"It is time to be moving, is it not?"

Bashir nodded, then sat up. "Qatar, I haven't told you exactly what I'm planning to do."

"You will when you need to, my friend."

"But this is going to be extremely dangerous. You should know."

Bulbulian grasped Bashir's arm in a firm, warm way. "It does not matter. You will need my help, I think, and I will be there."

Bashir closed his hand over Bulbulian's. "And what about Alyssa? Does it matter for her?"

"I think not." Bulbulian looked into Bashir's eyes for a moment. "But I do think you need to tell her, and me."

"That, yes," Bashir agreed. *They may not need to know, but I need to tell them.* He hopped out of the cart with an energy that was not feigned.

Alyssa was already up, just starting a fire for a quick breakfast. Bashir sat down, and Bulbulian followed suit, facing in the direction of the path above the hollow.

Over hot cups of black naughtleaf tea and light bread with cumbra honey, Bashir told the others, in hushed tones, of what he'd learned in the Matrix, the memories that had come back to him in his dreams.

"There was a Builder artifact that could control the Wells, turn them on and off," he said. "The Founders discovered it, and Achmar Z'areikh for some reason used it to create the Dead Wells. Victoria Knebel Eldrath studied it extensively, attempting to learn its principles."

He paused for a drink of tea.

"When Eldrath left Home to establish the settlement that became Toria, the artifact disappeared."

Bashir looked up at Alyssa and Bulbulian. They said nothing, just sat watching him, waiting for him to finish. *Do they think I'm crazy?* He took another drink of tea and continued.

"The artifact was a rod, black with green veins, and it looked exactly like the Drath Hierarch's Ceremonial Scepter, housed at the temple in Ebel. I think they're one and the same."

This time when he looked up at his companions, it was with a challenging glint in his eye.

"The artifact could be of no use without the Wells, and the Draths could not possibly realize its true nature and value. I intend to bring it back to Home. If that isn't worth Darrin's reinstatement, I don't know what is."

When he finished, and the fire had been put out, Alyssa merely nodded and said, "We'd better be going then, hadn't we?" Bulbulian gave him a look that said *I told you so.*

Bashir stood slowly, turning back to look at Alyssa. "I just want to be sure that you understand—"

She held up a hand to interrupt him. "Are you going to stop me?"

"No."

"Then that's settled. Now let's go down and become a part of the mob." She spread the embers around with a stick and kicked dirt over them, then picked up her makeshift pillow and took it over to the cart.

Bashir watched her with mixed emotions. She looked so like her great-grandmother, it was almost painful for him. And it was more than appearance. Alyssa sounded the same, moved with the same energy, and even possessed the same strength of character.

As he helped finish the packing and started hitching the hexoxen up to the cart, Bashir realized that Alyssa could no more have stepped away from her perceived obligations than that other woman could have, so many years ago. He knew it would be futile to try to stop her.

It was with pride that he watched her climb atop one of the two beasts and, with Bulbulian, lead the way up to the path and along it down to the plain. Pride, and sadness, and a determination that in this particular case, what had happened before was not going to happen again.

— **25** —

M'Briti sat on a rock in the shade of the southern wall of Cradoger's Ravine. Darrin stood nearby. They had spent the night in the ravine. Since dawn they had been scouting the area and making what preparations they could. It was now midday.

"You should know what it's like," she said, looking up at him. "It's something that I can't control."

"Dear—" he began, but she kept talking. She needed to make him understand.

"I notice it first in my eyes. There's a brown fog, dark muddy brown, with a sense of motion to it, like eddies in a stream. Right now it's just at the edges, even in broad daylight.'' She blinked, then looked around experimentally, making sure. ''But it keeps getting worse. If I waited long enough, I think it would cover my entire field of vision.'' She paused for a moment. ''I start to hear things too, and I can't tell what's illusion and what's not.''

Darrin took a step toward her, but she waved him back. ''The worst of it is, I start feeling differently about things. I become jumpy, anxious, suspicious. I can't trust my own judgment, my own reactions. I might not be safe to be around.''

He sat on the ground, his back against the rock on which she sat. ''We're in this together, M'Briti.''

She reached down and lightly ran her fingers through his hair. ''Darrin, it's not too late to back out of this if you want to. It isn't really your fight, and there's plenty of daylight left.''

''You know better than that,'' he said with an edge to his voice. He reached up and grasped her hand for a moment, gave it a gentle squeeze, then let it go. He spoke more softly. ''I'm in this just as deeply as you are, and for just as long.''

M'Briti said nothing. They suddenly seemed so alone, they might have been the only people on the entire planet. What was the sense in arguing?

Cradoger's Ravine was a long, thin notch cut into the edge of a plateau about five kilometers into the Borderlands, east-northeast of the Trading Annex. The ravine's opening faced Home and the Annex, and it narrowed to a point aimed at Toria.

Few people ever saw the ravine. Almost no one went there. First, it was not on an approved road between Home and Toria, and was therefore forbidden territory to Wellborn and Torians alike.

Second, the ravine was nearly inaccessible, surrounded by a patchwork of bramble-covered flats and steep, loose-rocked slopes.

But everybody had heard about Cradoger's Ravine and had heard the stories.

Above M'Briti, the sky was a bright cloudless blue. There was a light breeze from the south that picked up strength as it funneled up the ravine. It gave her the illusion of coolness.

The breeze moaned faintly but steadily as it pushed out of the narrow northeast end of the ravine. The only other sound was the occasional wavering whine of an insect.

M'Briti glanced down at Darrin and frowned, troubled by a jumble of feelings. She worried for him, she trusted him almost without reservation, she welcomed his help and needed his support.

The breeze blew, the rock shadows moved a fraction of a centimeter. She closed her eyes and let her mind wander.

Cradoger's Ravine . . .

Disston Cradoger had been a prospector a few centuries earlier. He'd searched for mineral deposits, veins of ore, and Builder artifacts—anything of potential value. He was also a Wellborn who had voluntarily given up his Wellstatus, something rarely done, and an act that always raised questions about the person's mental balance.

Further questions were raised in Cradoger's case when he started dropping hints, late at night in Annex bars, of lost treasures, of storehouses of Builder artifacts, of a vast system of underground tunnels. Nobody believed him, but some tried to follow him to prove him wrong. He was careful and clever, and he lost them. His pursuers trudged back to the Annex to await his return.

And they waited.

After a few months' waiting, they decided that Cradoger would never be back. People speculated about where he'd gone, and where his fictitious treasure hoard was. Somehow, rumors began to spread, based on a half-remembered comment, a half-forgotten map drawn on a dusty tabletop. They spoke of a ravine several kilometers east-northeast of the Annex.

Those who went to check the ravine found a well-stocked, fully equipped shelter. The door was closed but not locked, and nothing inside was disturbed or, so far as anyone could tell, missing. They left a note on the door and began searching, but Disston Cradoger was never found. The ravine was named in his honor.

The shelter was emptied of its valuables and anything at all usable, and over the decades it collapsed and moldered and disappeared.

Long after every sign of Cradoger had vanished, people would occasionally go out to the ravine, and sometimes they came back with tales of ghosts or strange nocturnal beasts. Sometimes they came back with nothing but sore feet, scratched hands, and aching backs. Sometimes they didn't come back at all.

As time went by and no one found anything of any value in the ravine, fewer people went out there. Some of those few brought back the stories, and some never came back. Eventually, Cradoger's Ravine became the nighttime haunt of that most fearsome of Seelzaran beasts, the hugglebear.

Three meters tall, six-legged, razor-clawed, the hugglebear gave adults pleasant shivers down the spine around a fire late at night, and sent children to bed incredulous or amused or frightened into promises of good behavior. It was as real as the ghosts that haunted the black guard towers around the Wellfield, and more thrilling because, unlike those ghosts, it could come to get you.

It was a hugglebear that had taken Disston Cradoger without a trace, and it was hugglebears who kept others away from Cradoger's Ravine—the believers out of a fear that they would seldom publicly admit, the skeptics out of a reluctance to validate the mythical beast by their very real efforts that could not, after all, disprove, but only fail to prove its existence.

So Cradoger's Ravine was well known in a general way, but hardly ever visited. A perfect place for a clandestine rendezvous, especially at midnight, when the hugglebear was supposed to prowl.

M'Briti opened her eyes with a start and realized that the shadows had lengthened considerably since she'd last looked. Darrin was lying on a blanket on the ground beside her, and her neck was stiff from having dozed while leaning against the rock wall at an awkward angle.

She did not believe in hugglebears, but she did believe in many other dangerous things, such as drug dealers and security agents and traps and guns and knives. So she hopped down from the rock she'd been sitting on and made a quick tour of the ravine, checking on the precautions she and Darrin had taken.

Their first precaution had been to come armed with the weapons of the agents who'd arrested M'Briti. Their second precaution had been to arrive a day early to check the layout of the ravine and to make sure no one was waiting for them.

Their third precaution, and the one M'Briti was checking, was a number of trip wires set in the most likely places for someone to try to sneak into the ravine.

The southwest opening was the ravine's widest entrance—twenty-five meters, with the walls fifteen to twenty meters high. That was where M'Briti would wait for whoever was going to show up. No trip wire there.

About one third of the way back, on the left, a narrow cut ran down into the ravine from the plateau above. Partway down the cut, Darrin had set a wire at knee height. The wire was thin, clear filament, very lightweight. It held open a switch on a small transmitter. If the filament were pulled loose, the switch closed and a single tone was sent by the transmitter to tiny receivers M'Briti and Darrin wore behind their right ears. The wire was attached lightly enough to come off without alerting the person who'd tripped it, unless they were looking for such a thing and were very good.

M'Briti went into the two-meter-wide cut and checked where she remembered the wire being. It was hard to see, but it was still in place, still holding the transmitter switch open.

A second side entrance to the ravine was on the right, thirty meters beyond the first. This was a broader opening in the ravine wall, but steeper. Three meters wide narrowing to two, it descended at an angle of thirty degrees or better. The wire here was in a spot where stopping would be especially difficult, where the stones were loose and the slope dipped at a steeper angle. Here, the transmitter would send a two-toned signal if set off. It, too, was all set.

The final likely spot for an unannounced arrival was at the very end of the ravine. The ravine started as a random finger-wide crack in the hard ground. It widened slowly but got deep quickly. Where it was four meters deep, it was still only two meters across. At that point, M'Briti found the third wire and transmitter, programmed to send a three-toned signal if anyone were to go past. Someone scrambling into the ravine from farther down would have to make enough noise to be heard anyway.

M'Briti walked along in the hot afternoon silence, keeping to the shadows as much as possible. She kept a wary eye on the tops of the rock walls to either side of her. Foolish to go to all this trouble, then give herself away on a last-minute inspection tour.

A stone fell from somewhere across the ravine and behind her. She whirled and dropped into a crouch, her gun pointed toward where the stone had come from. All she saw was the last flip of a rock squirrel's tail as it scuttled into a crevice far above.

"The reflexes aren't dead yet," she muttered to herself, and eased her finger off the gun's firing stud. She couldn't help worrying about that, about how Purple withdrawal would affect her ability to respond in a crisis. She was starting to feel the edginess, the anxiety with no specific cause. The peripheral hallucinations had become a distraction, minor but constant.

That's what she'd been telling Darrin, describing her symptoms to him, warning him. Because he was staying with her for tonight's confrontation, he deserved to know, he needed to know.

She and Darrin had taken what precautions they'd had time for. They would prevent any crude attempt by the Purple traffickers to double-cross M'Briti. If something more sophisticated were being planned, they'd have to trust to their reflexes and luck.

Even without Purple withdrawal, M'Briti would be feeling edgy. She didn't know who would show up, how many, and what their intentions would be. The one thing in her favor was that someone fairly high up in the organization would almost surely come, either to agree to M'Briti's terms or to make sure that she never left the Borderlands.

"Comforting thought, M'Briti," she mumbled. She frowned at the reddish brown rock walls and the blue sky. She'd been doing a lot of that lately—talking to herself.

"Have to watch that," she whispered. "People will think you're going crazy."

"Only if you answer back," she said.

"Oh, right."

"What was that?" Darrin asked, stepping out from a niche in the rock wall.

M'Briti nearly shot him before she realized who it was. "Don't do that!" Her voice was strained.

He smiled nervously. "Sorry. I didn't mean to startle you."

She wiped a shaky hand across her suddenly sweaty forehead. "No, no. That's all right. I just expected you to be back down there by the supplies, where I'd left you."

"Hot, isn't it?" Darrin pulled a cloth out of his pocket and handed it to her. "Here, these work better than hands."

"Thanks." Her hand was still shaking, but at least her breathing was easier.

"I woke up just as you started off on your inspection tour." Darrin shrugged. "I figured I'd better make myself useful too, so I've been looking for good places to lurk in. This one's not bad." He gestured behind himself. "It has a clear view down to the entrance and for quite a distance up the ravine. And there are enough large rocks scattered around here to let me move if I need to."

M'Briti nodded and took his hand. "This spot looks like it will work quite well. Let's just hope the evening doesn't become quite that active."

He gave her hand a squeeze. "I'll go along with that. And speaking of active . . ." He pulled her close and moved his hands from her waist to her hips. "We can't afford to sleep at this point, but is there any reason we couldn't get ourselves in a more relaxed frame of mind?"

M'Briti looked up at him and felt a pleasant glow somewhere in the middle of her. "Just how relaxed were you planning to get?"

"I'm not sure." He gave a gentle tug and they began walking down to where they had been napping earlier. "Why don't we pull one of our blankets into a more secluded spot and see what happens?"

"Well, okay. But don't think you can take advantage of me just because we're out here all alone."

He looked down at her. "I'd never take advantage of you, M'Briti."

There was something so earnest in the way he said it that she felt tears forming in the corners of her eyes. *Oh, Darrin,* she thought, *I hope I haven't gotten you involved in something I can't get you out of.*

26

The sun was just lighting the tops of the hills west of Ebel when Bashir's small party merged with the larger flow into the city's eastern gate. The throng was large, but not unusually so. He'd seen it much more crowded during the first weeks after winter, when demand in the city was at its peak. Later in the year, when harvest time came, the traffic rose again.

Now, in midsummer, supply and demand achieved a balance of moderation. The flow into and out of the city was steady and heavy, but unspectacular. As far as he could see, no one had yet been trampled to death in this morning's rush.

"Fellow merchants, fellow travelers!" Bashir called out in a voice falsely high and weak. "Can you not make room for one of my years?" He waved his arms in a pleading gesture. "Our small wagon will delay no one, and the Goddess graces the generous!"

His pleas were met mostly with jeers or disregard, but Bulbulian and Alyssa managed to worm their way ahead by small artful degrees. A nudge here, a bluff called there, a short burst of speed to squeeze between two converging parties. Soon the eastern gateway was before them, rising above the city's low perimeter wall.

Two thick columns rose fifteen meters above the dusty roadway. They were covered with intricately detailed carvings of plants and animals native to Seelzar—rakeclaws, hexoxen, sheenwood and cumbra trees, jaks, shadehawks, lurga vines, nocturnal barkorns, even wurgles and small furry bozads. The carvings wound up and around the pillars, and were topped by the carving of a nude man on the right and a nude woman on the left.

The pillars stood roughly ten meters apart. A single stone block rested atop them, a gigantic lintel two meters high and two deep and fourteen long. On the surface facing outward were four stylized representations of the Goddess as earth, water, air, and fire. In the middle of that foursome was a more realistic portrayal of the Goddess.

Bashir wondered how many Torians knew that their Goddess was based on and strongly resembled one of Seelzar's Founders—Victoria Knebel Eldrath.

Every time Bashir entered Ebel, he marveled at the skill and determination that had gone into carving the gateways, one east and one west. He also wondered what the Torians would do if the city ever grew so large that the gateways had to be widened or moved.

So far that decision had been postponed by expanding the city in other directions and by opening secondary gates to ease the traffic flow. His personal guess was that eventually the original gates would be swallowed by the city and become historic landmarks and tourist attractions.

Bashir and his companions were nearing the thick iron-bound wooden gate between the pillars. They had reached the point where the broad mass of traffic was funneled into a single file. He smiled at the idea of this as a meeting place for tourists. The Draths would have to moderate their attitudes considerably to accept such a change with good grace.

As if to emphasize that thought, a disturbance broke out next to the gate. A trader was shouting, half frightened and half imploring. "I meant nothing by it! I didn't even know it was there!"

Several black-robed guards were pulling him and his train of five jaks out of line. The jaks, shorter and sleeker than hexoxen, were jerking at their reins, whistling, and snapping at the guards.

"Quiet, man!" The chief gatekeeper clouted the trader on the back with his rockwood staff and the trader subsided.

Alyssa glanced back at Bashir. Her look clearly asked, "What in Founders' folly have we gotten into here?"

Bashir pointed toward Bulbulian and made a quieting gesture. To his satisfaction and relief, she leaned close to her round companion, prodded him, and gave him the same quizzical look. He replied briefly and she nodded.

It would not do for any of their party to appear completely naive about the laws and customs of Toria, and Alyssa's accent was likely to raise some eyebrows too. Bashir had enough experience to pass as a Torian with little effort. Bulbulian had even less reason to worry.

They had agreed, with some resistance from Alyssa, that she should pose as Bulbulian's deaf sister, who was extremely shy and poorly educated. Bashir was their aging father, come to pay perhaps his last visit to this queen of cities, the capital of Toria.

The line had advanced considerably with the removal of the trader and his five jaks. He was standing off to the side, watched alertly by two guards, while his cargo was being searched roughly but thoroughly. Bags were torn open and their contents lay scattered on the ground. Several items had been set aside from the rest, and Bashir knew that the fellow would be lucky if he were only banned from Ebel for life.

Bringing Wellborn technology into Toria was a serious offense against Drath religious strictures. The offense was compounded if the goods were actually being taken into the capital itself. And that's what the trader had been attempting, from what Bashir could see. It looked as if he'd been caught with the parts to a moderately sized generator, and some small solar panels.

Bashir shook his head in sympathy. The man was undoubtedly an amateur, perhaps recruited by the promise of a large payoff, perhaps tricked into carrying the parts. A professional would have broken them down further, so they were less recognizable, and would have spread the shipment out so it would not be an all-or-nothing gamble.

The jaks had been led away, and the contraband was being dragged off as evidence for the formal hearing. The trader, a thin man of middle years, looked as if he wanted to cry as he, too, was led away.

Bashir could think of nothing he could do that would help the man. He'd made a mistake, and the swift heavy wheel of Drath justice was about to roll over him. Bashir hoped that he and his companions would not have to face the same fate.

"Ho, there! Round one! What is the purpose of your visit?" The gate guard looked up at Bulbulian with the permanent frown of one whose job is to distrust people.

Bashir smiled. For as long as he'd known Bulbulian, his friend had not minded references to his size, but he did enjoy pretending annoyance.

Bulbulian drew himself erect and looked down his nose at the guard. "My purpose is to see that my honored father is not fleeced by the merchants who lurk beyond yon noble gate. My sister's purpose"—he gestured toward Alyssa— "to save you the trouble of pestering her, is to protect her purity amid this rabble of travelers around us."

The guard scowled theatrically. "And your father's purpose, you bulbous babbler?"

Bulbulian opened his eyes wide in mock astonishment. " 'Bulbous babbler'? Such alliteration! It is a rare treat to meet with such a skilled and subtle tongue in such a drab outfit."

He leaned slightly toward the guard and turned to point back to Bashir. "My father is back there, and would be best equipped to answer your query. Indeed, it would be a sore loss to him should he be deprived of the opportunity to make the acquaintance of so gifted a poet."

Bashir put a serious but helpful expression on his face as the guard glanced his way and began walking back to the cart. Bulbulian had taken a small chance in poking fun at the guard, but it was safer to seem a little irritable and indignant than to seem nervous and timid. The guards expected mild abuse.

"Old sir, may I inquire as to the reason for your visit to our city?"

Seated in the cart, his back supported by tasseled cushions, Bashir was at the same height as the guard. He turned with the careful slowness of an old man and pretended to be gathering his thoughts.

"My visit? Why ... Yes! I wish to see this magnificent city once more."

He beckoned the guard closer. "I am an old man, my boy. I may not see another summer. I could not greet the Goddess beyond without paying one last visit to her house in Ebel." He coughed into his hand and then swallowed audibly. "That is why I asked my only son and daughter to take me here, while I am still able to travel."

During all of this, the guard was sizing up Bashir and the cart. When Bashir's brief explanation was through, the man nodded and walked once around the cart, eyeing it from all angles, occasionally thumping on the sides with his knuckles.

When he had completed his inspection, the guard nodded at Bashir again. "Very well, old sir. You and your children may enter. But keep a rein on your son's tongue—its sharpness may cut him a slice of trouble."

"I will indeed," Bashir replied solemnly. "And thank you, good sir."

It was a charade, but a necessary one. Bashir knew that getting into Ebel without arousing suspicion was the most serious problem. After that, in the crowded and mazelike streets of the city, they could be reasonably safe from official scrutiny.

Only the temple itself was guarded with the diligence shown at the city's gates. And Bashir had no intention of meeting the temple guards.

They were waved toward the gate, and Bulbulian and Alyssa urged their mounts forward. Through the gate, under the imposing weight of the stone lintel far above, and they were in Ebel. Immediately there was a sense of breathing easier, of relaxing. It was still a far cry from the Trading Annex, but once inside Ebel, pedestrians and riders alike jostled one another without scowling, without the tension exhibited outside the gate. They were in. They'd passed the test.

It was midday. Bashir sat at a small table, sipping a lukewarm beer. Refrigeration wasn't a part of Torian life. One had to pay handsomely for the mugs drawn from the deep-stored kegs, and Bashir was not posing as someone rich enough to do so.

Alyssa sat across from him, obviously working hard to hide her intelligent curiosity beneath the role of shy, backward daughter. She held a cup of warm, sweetened jak's milk in both hands, drinking from it sparingly. Each sip was swallowed with difficulty. Torian tastes didn't all seem to agree with her.

Bashir had sent Bulbulian off on a brief tour of the nearby marketplace. There were items Bashir wished to buy, but he didn't want the entire party wandering around searching for them.

A tall young man with a heavy beard wandered over to their table and leaned down. He slopped some wine from the mug he was holding.

"Hello, my dear," he said to Alyssa. She glanced at his mug on the table, then looked down into her own cup.

"There's no reason to be afraid. You could at least look at me." The man's voice had a slight edge to it. Bashir could tell he'd had more than one mug of wine already.

"Young sir, you must excuse my daughter. She cannot hear you." He tried to make his voice placating, tried to ease the man away.

The bearded man turned toward Bashir. "Tell a better lie, old man. I saw you speaking together earlier." He returned his gaze to Alyssa. "If she can talk to you, she can talk to me."

It was possible, Bashir realized. They might have been careless. But they could not afford to admit the deception to anyone in Ebel. That would be too likely to draw the attention of the authorities. And he could not afford to deal with this obnoxious fellow physically himself—a Normal of Bashir's apparent age would be far too frail.

"It might have looked like that," he quavered, "but in truth she is quite deaf. I can talk with her by mouthing words and by gestures, and I can sometimes make sense of the sounds and gestures she makes." He spread his hands. "That is all."

Some doubt flickered in the other's eyes. He'd hoped to make quick contact with this lovely young woman, but things were becoming complicated. Bashir could almost hear the gears grinding slowly inside his head: *Do I press this any further, or not?*

Just then, Bulbulian appeared, having finished his survey of the shops nearby. He bustled over to the table, all eagerness and energy.

"I'm back, Father. And what a marvelous array of wares they have here!" Then he stopped, as if just noticing the bearded stranger. "Hello. Is this a friend of yours?"

Bashir did his best to signal disapproval to Bulbulian while saying in a vague, old voice, "Well, my son . . ." He squeezed his hands together in apparent consternation. "I mean, actually, he's . . ."

Bulbulian smiled and offered his hand to the young man. "Greetings. I'm always pleased to meet a friend of my father's." The man shook hands, and a brief look of pain swept across his face.

"Actually," the bearded man said, pulling his hand free, "I'm afraid it was my mistake. I thought your father was someone else. Sorry to intrude." With that, he hurried away, spilling more wine in his haste.

"Thank you, Qatar," Bashir said when the other had gone. "I didn't know if you'd pick up my cues. I'm glad your grip is as firm as ever."

Bulbulian nodded once and smiled slightly. "Your hints were quite clear." He sat down at the table. "I take it he was about to create a scene over Alyssa?"

"Probably. And I didn't want to summon a guard if it could be helped." Bashir leaned closer. "We'll have to be more careful. He saw Alyssa and me talking, and we can't let that part of our story unravel. She is striking enough to be remembered." He winked at Alyssa, who looked embarrassed. "And we can't take a chance on her talking. Her accent alone would give her away."

"Very well. I know shyness won't hold up long around here as an excuse for silence." He waved a hand around to indicate the whole market, perhaps the whole city. "Most of these people are extremely friendly and outgoing. You cannot judge by the strict Draths. It is part of our . . . part of their culture. Even the polite ones would feel it their duty to draw Alyssa out of her shell.''

Bashir reached over and patted Bulbulian's arm. ''I know that, my friend. All the more reason for care. And now, what have you found in the shops hereabouts?''

Bulbulian described briefly the area he'd covered, essentially the open marketplace they sat in and two blocks along the two busiest intersecting streets. It took only a few minutes. He concluded, ''There are three shops we can go to for religious souvenirs, and one for art materials. I recommend Madame Danika's Holy Shop for the souvenirs.''

''Does it have full-size replicas?''

''They all do. But it is the farthest from the art shop. Down that way''—he pointed—''and a block up Spring Street. And''—Bulbulian paused and squinted at Bashir—''Madame Danika is as blind as a barkorn. She'd never recognize us again if that became an issue.''

Bashir laughed. ''Well done, Qatar. Here.'' He tossed several coins onto the table. ''Have a warm beer while I go visit Madame Danika. Later on, we can visit the other shop.'' With that he got up and did his old-man shuffle in the direction Bulbulian had indicated.

Part of him knew that it was too late for Bulbulian and Alyssa to back out of this undertaking. They'd come too far and too many people by now would probably remember them as being with him. But another part of him was still trying to protect them, to involve them as little as possible.

So he would visit Madame Danika alone, to purchase a genuine full-size replica of the Scepter of the Drath Hierarch. Then he would visit the art shop alone. Maybe if he were caught alone later that night, Bulbulian and Alyssa could somehow make their way out of the city to safety.

Alyssa ground her teeth together while maintaining her shy demeanor. It was very difficult to do. She wanted to grab the bearded youth by the neck and throttle him. Instead, she let Bashir try to defuse the situation, then let Bulbulian send the man packing.

Again she wondered about the pie vendor. He didn't look all that strong, but he'd obviously squeezed the man's hand quite hard, without any visible effort or trick. And the young man had been fairly sturdy himself.

Now Bashir had gone off to make his purchases.

Where do I fit in in all of this? she asked herself. There had to be something more active she could do to help out. *Sure.* She sipped some of the warm milk and choked it down. *Sit here and try to carry on a quiet conversation with Qatar without either of us moving our lips.*

"Hey," she whispered. "He won't try to lose us and do it alone, will he?"

Bulbulian looked up surreptitiously from his beer. "What?" he hissed back.

Alyssa repeated her question, just as quietly but more slowly.

Bulbulian shook his head ever so slightly. "I don't think so. We've come too far with him now. If he'd wanted to, he would have left us before entering Ebel, and he wouldn't have told us his plan."

Alyssa nodded minutely and let her eyes wander around the marketplace. It reminded her of the Annex, as did the other parts of Ebel she'd seen. There was the same crowding, the same hectic activity, the same unplanned, haphazard quality to the low buildings and the narrow, twisting streets.

Along with the similarities, there were a few notable differences. Here there was no technology to compare with that of Home, or even the Annex, nothing at all involving electricity, for instance. Here there were no other Wellborn, unless they were disguised as she and Bashir were.

And here there was a tension beneath the bustle, a wariness, a caution that one did not see in the Annex. Here the Draths ruled, and if they didn't directly observe and experience everything that went on, they had the power to step in at any time, whenever something caught their attention.

Alyssa felt herself absorbing that tension, that sense of being watched. She glanced at Bulbulian, who looked completely relaxed, sipping his beer.

She gave up even pretending to drink her own cup of sweetened milk. It tasted as if the milk were on the verge of souring, which it probably was. She couldn't wait to get back to the cheap inn they had found, where their hexoxen were stabled and where, in the privacy of their rooms, she would prevail upon Bulbulian and Bashir to order enough beer for three rather than two.

It was a wonder to her that Torian women lived past their teens with such a foul beverage as their customary drink.

Right, Alyssa, she thought. *Blame it on the drinks.* She knew the problem was much more serious than that. What Bashir had in mind was extremely risky, went against the laws of the Draths and of Home, and was based on speculation.

Bashir had seen things in the Matrix's Forbidden Files, or so he said, which had been blanked from his memory but which he said he now remembered. He'd been in Ebel before, and even visited the temple during a feast-day celebration some years ago. What he'd found in the Matrix and what he remembered seeing in the temple were guiding him now. If his memory was faulty, or if he'd drawn the wrong inferences, their quest was doomed to fail.

Alyssa suddenly realized that the drinks were part of it too. They represented the Torian culture, which was alien to her. She was suffering from culture shock of sorts, barely able to speak the language, ignorant of many of the customs, and playing a role totally out of keeping with her true nature. The realization did nothing to ease her state of mind.

Bulbulian took another casual sip of beer, and Alyssa gnashed her teeth. She wanted to brain him with his own mug. What was taking Bashir so long, anyway?

— 27 —

The midday sun was warm on Niala's back as she stood on the soft white sand and stared into the depths of Sapphire Lake.

It was a long walk from Home around the western end of the lake to the southern shore, opposite the city. Niala had started out shortly after sunrise, before many people would be up and likely to see her. She'd worn a small backpack with dried fruit and a self-cooling bottle of pale yellow wine in it. The pack now lay on the ground, with half the fruit and most of the wine gone.

You can't bring Shardon back, you know. The fact prodded at her from inside her own brain, whispered in a voice that was hers and yet not hers. A voice from her past.

The lake's blue depths were silent.

Agents knew the risks going in. They were told what could go wrong; they were shown some of the things that could happen to them; they talked with those who'd been agents before them. It wasn't that the worst was likely to happen— quite the contrary. And because that was a known fact, complacency was the real danger. That was what the trainers and evaluators had to work on, to overcome, to weed out.

Was it possible that Rythmun had waited too long before contacting Home? That he'd made too many inquiries first, become even the slightest bit conspicuous?

Niala knew a little about Brinktown, where Rythmun had operated from. Trust was at a premium there, and curiosity could be a killer. If that was where Chou had disappeared, Rythmun could easily have aroused suspicions trying to find her. And if the people who'd taken Chou had some creds to offer, they could have found out about him.

A light breeze drifted in from the west, sending ruffles across the surface of the lake. The lake's surface broke into a patchwork of blues, light sky and dark water.

Behind Niala, the sheenwood leaves rustled ever so faintly. She turned to look at them. The trees were planted close together here, almost to the point of overcrowding.

They blocked her view of what was beyond them.

Their blossoms had all fallen several days ago, and now they stood in unadorned glory—deep green leaves as shiny as glass, dark brown trunks almost black, and as shiny as the leaves.

Niala had come out here often over the years, to get away from the many pressures of Home. If was a peaceful, restful place. It was, in a private, quiet way, one of the most beautiful places she'd ever seen. And in a small clearing far into the sheenwood grove was a simple white stone marker where she'd buried her son.

It wasn't the impressive underground vault where for centuries the Wellborn had placed the cremated remains of their loved ones. Shardon had not been the sort to appreciate the solemnity, the grandeur. He would have called it ostentatious.

He'd lived his life avoiding convention; he'd died on a partially tamed planet light-years away. It would have been a lie to place his ashes in an elaborately carved urn, and that urn among countless thousands of others in a place reserved for grieving the dead.

Shardon Kirowa had enjoyed life and open space and wild places. And he'd given his life for Home. In his clearing, he was near Home, surrounded by living things, and open to the starry sky. It was the best Niala could do for him.

Niala had yet to visit Shardon's grave today, even though she'd made the long walk in part to do just that. She didn't want to face him until she'd decided what to do. She wanted to be able to say to herself that his memory hadn't unduly influenced her decision.

That would have been easier to say if she'd stayed in her reztower, but she needed to be away from the distractions she couldn't escape from in the city. Out here, she was alone. The Wellborn were too busy recovering from the Matrix failure for any of them to take the time to wander this far from their duties.

She knelt in the sand, sitting back on her heels. She was still looking across Sapphire Lake. From this lower angle, she could see fragmentary reflections of Home intermingled with the lighter reflections of sky and darker patches where the lake itself shone through. She brushed her hand through the sand, drawing random, meaningless patterns with her fingers.

The sand felt warm. Niala picked some up and let it trickle out of her hand. All those grains, barely distinguishable from one another, making up a handful, a beach, a world. She watched the grains sifting down onto the ground, drifting slightly in the breeze, forming a small hill where they landed. Who was to say which grains mattered more, which less?

I couldn't have saved him, she told herself for the thousandth time, *not without losing Phillips.*

Out of the corner of her eye, she saw some movement. She turned and refocused her gaze from the very near to the very far. To the left of Home, west, a small white ball was rising slowly on a thin blue-white flame. The flame was nearly invisible against the sky.

Supply ship to Yakimu Base. Following the message from Rythmun, Niala had ordered that the base be reinforced as much as possible and as quickly as possible. The spaceport twelve kilometers to the west of Home had been busy since then, assembling supplies, loading ships, readying them for takeoff.

The white ball accelerated rapidly until it shot out of sight. As small as it looked, it was one of Home's larger ships, a seventy-meter sphere that was drive unit, small control deck, and mostly cargo space. Another its size would be departing around daybreak tomorrow.

Other, smaller ships had already been dispatched to service the automated defense stations orbiting Seelzar. All of Home's fighting ships were being readied for battle, and one fourth were to be kept in space at all times.

Of the rest, some would move out to Yakimu Base, some remain on alert at Home's spaceport, and some move out to small bases scattered around Seelzar. No one strike, however much a surprise, would wipe out all of Home's defenses.

Niala stood up, brushing the sand from her knees.

What is best for Home?

Among the Executors, she was the military expert. She had more friends than the others with military experience and training. With her resources, she was certain that she could get at least one of the other two Executors, and possibly both, to support nearly any plan of action she cared to suggest.

She had tried to come up with such a plan. She'd gotten to bed late last night and gotten to sleep even later, worrying at the problem like a rakeclaw with a hexoxen's thigh bone. Like the rakeclaw, she got almost nowhere for all her efforts. Unlike the rakeclaw, she hadn't even enjoyed the process.

She turned away from the lake and walked over to a white stone bench sitting on the grass about two meters from where the sand of the beach began. She reached under the bench and retrieved her backpack, with fruit and wine inside.

In the small hours of the morning, she had actually come up with a plan, but it was one she knew she couldn't sell to Venebles or to Senyan. More than that, she still had some doubts about it herself. It seemed to her to be the least bad of a number of questionable alternatives.

Will Rythmun and Chou make up for Shardon? The internal voice, the voice from her past, had taken on a skeptical tone.

Niala had not yet put the backpack on. Holding it by its strap, she swung it experimentally. It was a comfortable weight for her right arm.

Will they all be better off if you die? Will you?

Why don't you shut up? she thought savagely at the other voice inside her.

She looked out across Sapphire Lake, momentarily calmed. If she took a good couple of swings to build up momentum, how far, she wondered, could she throw her pack? Not all the way across the lake, certainly. Halfway? Perhaps, though the strap might break with such an effort.

Playing games with yourself, Niala? the voice taunted.

"No, damn it!" she shouted out loud. "You've done your job," she said more quietly, but fiercely. "Now leave me alone." She put the backpack on and turned away from the lake.

It was a habit, a trick she'd developed during her years as an off-planet agent, to have an unseen companion at all times, a personal devil's advocate whose job was to challenge every decision she made. If she couldn't answer its objections, she would rethink the problem, looking for alternate courses of action.

She had been an excellent agent. Her advocate had served her well. It was trying to do so again, her old companion revived by Rythmun's message. She was thinking like an agent again, about an agent's problems. And her advocate was telling her, in no uncertain terms, that an agent has to be realistic, has to be practical, can't afford to be unduly swayed by emotion.

She started walking toward the sheenwood trees.

Shardon is dead, Niala. Your son is dead.

Niala gritted her teeth and kept walking.

She did not resent being reminded of the fact as much as she resented the idea that she needed to be reminded. She prided herself on being a practical, level-headed person, and had sought to function that way as an Executor. She could see how their passions affected Senyan's and Venebles's judgments, and had thought herself immune to that sort of flaw. Now, her advocate was suggesting otherwise, and she had no answer.

Within the sheenwood grove, the light was diffuse and green, filtered through the thick canopy of leaves. The breeze stayed in the upper reaches of the trees. Below, where Niala walked, the air was still, hushed, and heavy with the dusty-sweet scent of the fallen blossoms and leaves carpeting the ground.

There was no formal path, but there were many pathways within the grove, trails where the branches were a little farther apart, the ground a little more level. Niala wandered along them, moving gradually closer to that special clearing that she had first visited some twenty years before.

Of course my feelings are involved in this, she thought at her companion/critic. *How can they not be? But that doesn't mean my decision is wrong.*

The primary goal, everyone agreed, was to keep the Interstellar Union from discovering Seelzar's location. Niala's plan, she felt, had the best chance of doing that with the smallest cost. That there was some personal risk to her didn't make the plan better or worse, more or less appealing. So she told herself. But she knew Senyan and Venebles would never agree with her.

Niala came upon the clearing suddenly. She climbed a small rise in the ground, skirted a pair of intertwined trees, and there it was. Open to the sky, it was hemmed in by a profusion of thick growth. Responding to the sunlight, the sheenwood branches grew to the ground. They divided and divided again into a mass of twigs and leaves, woven into a nearly solid wall of dark green.

Even though she knew where the clearing was, it always came as a mild surprise to her when she actually stepped into it.

The clearing was roughly circular, around ten meters across, and covered by short flowering grasses. The grasses were light green with blue and white flowers. A crowd of insects buzzed and hummed among the blossoms.

In the center of the clearing stood a solitary white stone, somewhat less than a meter tall. On it in simple block letters was carved a name: SHARDON MANSARD KIROWA. No dates, no other inscription. Niala had done this for herself and for her memory of Shardon. It was not a showplace nor a public monument. If others came upon the clearing, that was fine. They would either know who Shardon was or they would not. That didn't matter.

Niala stood at the edge of the clearing for a while, then slowly stepped toward the center, careful to disturb the grasses and flowers as little as possible. She looked down at the gravestone, remembering Shardon as a baby, a child, a youth, a young man. She addressed him as an adult, as the son who was a friend and a fellow agent.

"You know what I'm up to, don't you?" she whispered, no louder than the insect voices around her. "I know Keena Rythmun and Jarnice Chou aren't you." The sun was bright and warm. It shone on the stone at an angle. Each carved letter was defined by a dark shadow surrounded by brilliant white.

"I'm doing this for them and for Home," she said. She added, almost inaudibly, "Not for you."

She stood there for a few minutes more, thinking nothing in particular, then turned and left the way she had come. She walked quickly, wanting to get back to Home before sunset. She left the sheenwood grove and began walking westward along the beach.

All the way back, her inner voice, her devil's advocate, asked the same half-mocking question. "And not for yourself, too, Niala?"

28

At night, even in midsummer, Ebel was an empty city, or so it seemed. As Alyssa and her companions crept through the darkened streets, they kept to the deepest shadows. Alyssa knew that within the walls of the city, hundreds of thousands of people were eating, drinking, sleeping, and carrying on business, but there was no sign of them. They were behind locked doors and shuttered windows.

That did not surprise Alyssa. Bashir had told her about some of the laws of Ebel.

Curfew violation was punishable by fines, flogging, or death, depending on the circumstances, the status of the violator, and the mood of the magistrate. Alyssa had the feeling that their small band, if caught, would not be dealt with mercifully.

They had left their inn while it was still light, carrying only what they needed. When it became dark, shortly after the gongs were struck announcing the closing of the gates, Bashir found a deserted building, an old empty shop by the looks of it, and they had prepared themselves. Dark gray cloaks, blackened faces, and soft-soled boots were disguise enough, if they were careful. They wore nothing that could clank or jangle, and spoke in whispers.

Bashir led the way, Bulbulian followed, and Alyssa brought up the rear. She also carried the stunner, in a pouch belted to her waist. It would be found if she were searched, but if that happened, a charge of possessing forbidden technology would be the least of their worries. If their plan went wrong, she might have to use the weapon to help them escape. She was glad of its weight bouncing against her leg.

They came to the end of a narrow alley, and Bashir held up his hand to call a halt. She could hear, faintly, the click of boots on stone pavement. The sound was getting closer.

The three backed away several steps and huddled down behind a low set of steps leading to a scarred wooden door. If the guard (who else would walk so boldly after curfew?) looked carefully down the alley, he would see dark humps against one side of the narrow way, only partly hidden by the steps. If he had a torch, and took a step or two in their direction, he would realize that the humps were people.

Alyssa cautiously slipped her hand into her pouch and gripped the handle of her stunner. The sharp *snap* of its charge would be much less likely to attract attention than would a guard clanging his hand bell and shouting about thieves or infidels or whatever he would imagine the trio to be.

The footsteps drew closer. Alyssa kept her head down and pulled her hood back just far enough so that she could see the alley mouth. A tall dark figure stepped into the opening at the end of the alley. It stopped, as did the footsteps. It paused for the space of a heartbeat, then moved on, and the clicking of its boots went with it.

Alyssa breathed a very quiet but heartfelt sigh of relief. Bashir stood and motioned his companions onward. The guard had disappeared around a corner a block away. The trio hurried quickly across the relative openness of an average-width street and hustled into a narrow walkway between two buildings.

And so it went. Alyssa lost her sense of direction with all the twists and turns they took, all the odd winding back routes Bashir led them through.

Scuttle across an open courtyard here, scramble over a head-high fence there, edge cautiously along a wider street, keeping to doorways, alcoves, and any other small cover the building fronts offered.

She kept one eye on Bashir and Bulbulian, the other on everything else, looking for any other movement but their own. Her ears were tuned for the sound of more guards' footsteps, but the only ones she heard were far off, on other streets, heading in other directions.

Alyssa knew they were going deeper into the city, to the center of Ebel where the Drath temple stood. She had never seen the building before, but Bashir and Bulbulian seemed quite familiar with it. They had described its layout well enough so that if she had to she could probably make her way out alone. She hadn't even bothered telling them that that was the last thing she would do.

The night was clear. Yakimu had set shortly after the sun, and only starlight lessened the darkness. Alyssa had not seen so much as a crack of light escaping from any of the buildings she'd passed. Bashir had explained that even those who violated the spirit of the curfew by socializing or transacting business after dark were fully aware that discretion was essential. If they didn't advertise their offense and stayed indoors, the guards were likely to leave them alone.

The air was still in the silent streets. It was a warm night, and Alyssa was beginning to sweat in her dark cloak. *Would you rather be damp and cold in the Borderlands?* she asked herself with some scorn, and was surprised when the answer was not immediately and definitely *No.*

The narrow streets had a stifling, oppressive feel to them. It was as if the buildings themselves were casting a suspicious eye on the intruders, pondering whether and when to call the Drath guards down on the three figures skulking through Ebel, obviously up to no good.

Bashir led them down another dozen streets, alleys, and unnamed crawl spaces between rows of buildings. Alyssa was beginning to wonder if he, too, had lost his way. *It can't possibly be this far to the Drath temple*, she thought, glancing anxiously from side to side.

They were walking down the middle of a narrow street bordered on both sides by what looked like wide low hedges. No doors opened onto the street, and no windows faced it from any of the buildings, but Alyssa felt very exposed. If someone were to appear at either end of this two-block-long passage, there'd be no place to hide.

The far end of the street was completely blocked by a low stone wall. When they reached the wall, they huddled behind it and held a whispered conference.

"The temple," Bashir said in hushed tones, gesturing toward the other side of the wall. Alyssa had guessed as much.

Just before ducking behind it for cover, Alyssa had gotten a good look at what lay beyond the low wall. There was a large circular courtyard perhaps two hundred meters in diameter. In its center stood a massive three-story building. The building filled at least half the courtyard.

Bashir had said that the outer wall was two to three meters thick, and it looked all of that. There was something daunting about it, a feeling of density. The top of the wall was crenellated, and Alyssa had seen someone walking along it. She could hear the measured, steady pace of a sentry.

"This is where we cross," Bashir whispered. "The temple's rear wall. But we must wait to time the sentry above and see if there are other guards patrolling."

So they sat and waited, watching. Bulbulian checked his wristchron when the sentry made the turn away from them. He'd been wearing it all along, disguised as a heavy leather and metal bracelet.

Alyssa took another look over the low wall, examining their destination. There was little to see. The temple wall facing them was roughly one hundred meters long. It was built of large stones, plastered over. In places the plaster had cracked and fallen off. Some of the cracks had been repaired.

The entire length of wall was broken by only two small doors, one-third in from each end. There was no handle or keyhole to either door. Clearly, they were meant to be opened from the inside. There were no windows.

Twenty-five meters of paved courtyard separated Alyssa and her companions from the temple. The courtyard was featureless except for two low hedges. They continued from the street the trio was on, ran under the low wall and straight across the courtyard toward the middle of the temple wall. They seemed to disappear a few meters from the temple.

The hedges weren't really hedges. They were the tops of plants that grew in the temple's drainage ditches. As Bashir had explained, the ditches were a reliable source of moisture even during the dry months.

The ditches were each less than two meters wide and a little over two meters deep. They ran beneath the temple's rear wall, and extended for some unknown distance under the temple itself. The openings were probably barred. That had been Bashir's guess, and it made sense, from what Alyssa had seen of the Draths.

It looked as if the courtyard paving covered the ditches for two or three meters out from the temple wall, to provide a walkway between the two small doors.

The drainage ditches were going to be their entrance to the temple, or so Bashir had said. Their dense undergrowth provided the best cover around for approaching the wall, and even if there were bars blocking them at the wall, that would be less of an obstacle than the wall itself, or the doors in it.

"Here comes the other guard," Bulbulian whispered. "Just over twenty minutes."

"That should be enough," Bashir whispered in return. "We'll have to wait for the sentry above to pass to be sure of their timing. When he does, we'll lower ourselves into the ditch and move along it to the temple." He pointed to the ditch on the right. Back at their inn, they'd picked that one by tossing a coin. Neither Bashir nor Bulbulian had given any reason to choose one ditch over the other.

If they couldn't get in through the first one, they'd try the second. If the second one failed them, they'd be in trouble.

They watched silently, peering just over the top of their low wall, as the courtyard sentry paced off the distance from one corner of the temple to the next. He did not look particularly alert to Alyssa. She noticed that he did not so much as glance down into the ditches as he walked over them.

Her robe was becoming hotter by the minute. If the two sentries' rounds were timed to minimize the gaps between them, they'd stay one-half round apart. If so, there'd be two twenty-minute gaps per hour when the ditches would not be under observation, one for every time either sentry completed his pass along the rear wall. But the huddled trio would have to wait to see whether or not that was the routine.

Time seemed to have slowed to a crawl. The lower sentry finally turned the corner and disappeared. His footsteps faded. Nothing moved anywhere. Alyssa felt for the stunner in its pouch, making sure it was still there and that she could reach it quickly. It was and she could. She wiped some sweat from her forehead and waited some more.

Finally, faint sounds of footsteps, getting louder. She stared up at the top left corner of the wall, and soon that sentry appeared.

Bulbulian whispered, softer than the footsteps, "Twenty minutes." Bashir made a small grunt of satisfaction, and Alyssa felt a measure of relief. Here, at least, was something orderly and predictable.

The upper sentry crept along his assigned route, as slow as his street-level companion. He glanced across the courtyard toward the low wall hiding Alyssa and her companions. She felt as if a glowing red sign, complete with arrow, were announcing their location. The sentry's glance passed their position. He continued walking without a pause.

As the sentry neared the far corner of the wall, Bashir whispered, "Ready. Alyssa first." When the sentry made the turn, Bashir gave the order. "Now."

Alyssa let herself down into the ditch. Immediately she was hit by the odor. How could she not have noticed it up above? It was a close, wet, overpowering odor of plants, living and dying and decaying. Her first breath of it caught in her throat. The air was so heavy, it was almost like drinking to breathe it in. She forced herself to gulp in one breath, then another. After that it became easier.

She stepped back to make room for Bulbulian and Bashir to come down.

Already her eyes had adjusted to the greater darkness, and she could vaguely see that the greenery protruding above the ditch was the leafy tops of otherwise bare stems. She felt one of the stems. It was hard, but covered by a thin film of slime.

Only then did she realize she was standing in thick water above her boot tops. The footing underneath her boots was slick and muddy. She wriggled her now-wet toes and grimaced. *Hurry up, Bashir. The temple can't be any worse than this.*

Bashir watched Bulbulian slip down into the drainage ditch, then lowered himself over the edge. He was careful with the bundle strapped to his back. If that were to break, there would be no point in going on.

He got his footing on the wet, slick channel bottom, then motioned the others to follow, Bulbulian then Alyssa.

He couldn't help feeling a little sorry for his companions. Bulbulian's girth made it more awkward for him to maneuver between the long plant stems without knocking them down. Alyssa's height made it necessary for her to hunch over to keep from disturbing the leafy upper growth.

Bashir was thin and short enough to pass along the channel with ease, walking between the stems and beneath the overgrowth with no special effort.

He set a quick pace. If the greenery were disturbed a little bit, that would probably go unnoticed. But if the sentries saw the greenery being disturbed, that would be a different matter entirely. With no wind at all, they would have to suspect a large animal or a human intruder. In either case, they would investigate, and discovery at this stage would be disastrous.

Slogging along the dim channel reminded Bashir of a journey he'd made many years ago to a swampy peninsula far to the south of Home. The area was poorly explored and so far labeled useless by everyone.

Somewhere he'd gotten the idea that there might be Builder relics in that remote territory. He hadn't found any, but he'd spent several days wading through murky water ankle-deep to waist-deep, fighting off clouds of stinging insects, and warily avoiding scaled amphibious carnivores larger than a hexox.

The drainage channel, with its stagnant water and grossly overgrown weeds, was that peninsula in miniature. The air here was worse, but the water was generally shallower. There were fewer insects in the ditch, and they weren't as vicious as their southern counterparts. The dangers in the swamps had all been natural. The dangers up here were all human.

Bashir wasn't sure which he preferred to face. A human being could certainly be every bit as deadly as any steel-jawed swamp creature.

Ahead of him, the channel was suddenly even darker. They must be nearing the temple wall. This was the first serious test. What sort of barrier would they find? Could they break through it? Could they break through it quietly enough so the sentries or someone inside the temple wouldn't hear them?

A portion of the courtyard paving covered the ditch before it reached the temple wall. The ditch became a tunnel.

As adapted as Bashir's eyes were to the dark, it was still difficult to see when even the starlight had to come in indirectly. He felt ahead of himself, moving slowly, and was finally brought up short by something hard and round.

"Stop," he whispered to his companions.

He moved his hands slowly in front of him, stepping sideways from one edge of the ditch to the other. Six metal bars blocked their way, running from floor to ceiling. The bars were about four centimeters in diameter. Bashir could not quite squeeze between them. Alyssa probably couldn't either, and he knew there was no chance that Bulbulian could do so.

The bars felt rough, corroded. They'd been in place for ages, soaking in the water and associated refuse from the temple. Bashir gave one an experimental tug and felt the slightest give in it.

"Time, Qatar?" he asked.

Bulbulian flipped over one of the metal circles on his bracelet. His chron glowed dimly beneath it. "Seven minutes, Bashir."

"Good enough." They needed to work quickly, but also quietly. A loud splash might attract some attention regardless of where the sentries were.

"We're going to have to remove two of these, if we can. Alyssa, together I think you and I can do it. Qatar, stand directly behind us. If the bar gives way, you'll have to catch us, stop us from splashing in the water."

In truth, Bashir thought he or Alyssa alone could probably break one of the bars, but speed was important. Just as important, he wanted to give Alyssa something to do. He felt bad enough about letting her come along, exposed to the danger. It was that much worse when all he'd given her to do so far was to pretend she couldn't hear or speak.

"Ready, Bashir," Alyssa said.

Feet braced against adjoining bars, Bashir and Alyssa pulled with increasing pressure on one of the middle bars. Slowly, he felt it giving. He pulled harder, and he could sense the bar bending near the middle. Suddenly he and Alyssa fell backward as the bar slipped out of its hole in the stone ceiling. Bulbulian caught them both with a muffled grunt.

They quickly wrestled the bar out of its bottom hole and set it aside, then repeated the process with the bar next to it. They finished with nearly a minute to go before the ground-level sentry was to reach the corner of the back wall.

Bashir and Alyssa slipped through the opening easily, and even Bulbulian managed without any strain.

Now they were truly entering the temple. Bulbulian pulled a small electric light from somewhere within his robes and handed it to Bashir. Bashir switched the beam on to low power, then turned it off. They were still too close to the barred exit to risk keeping the light on. Ebel was a dark city at night.

Bashir had seen nothing unusual in the quick flash of light. The channel continued, now a tunnel, straight with no projections or barriers that he could see. The water was at about mid-shin depth and either still or moving very slowly. A thin film floated on top.

"Come along," Bashir whispered, and the trio moved farther beneath the temple, treading quietly through the scummy water. The air got worse as they proceeded. The plant-filled ditch had been a clear mountain stream by comparison.

Bashir found it necessary to breathe through his mouth to make the odor at least bearable.

He flicked the light on occasionally to make sure no surprises were awaiting them, and to check for some exit from the tunnel. They passed several outlet pipes a few centimeters to nearly half a meter wide, but they didn't bother stopping to investigate.

Somewhere, Bashir felt, there had to be an access hatch or doorway or opening of some kind. The temple's builders must have included some way for people to get into the tunnel, to clear it of obstructions or repair its walls. Mustn't they? The farther they walked, the larger that question loomed.

Faint poppings and splashes and high-pitched squeaks sounded from time to time, but Bashir never saw what was causing them. Once or twice he thought he saw eyes glowing at him, from just beyond the edge of his light beam. When he swung the light in their direction, nothing was there.

They had walked perhaps one third of the temple's width when Bashir began to sense a change. Another several meters and he was sure—the tunnel was shrinking. The walls were getting closer together and the floor was rising.

Of course, he told himself. *It must end beneath the temple. There are no drainage ditches except on that one side.*

Knowing that the tunnel shrinkage was real and explainable didn't make him feel any better. They needed to find an exit soon or they'd have to turn back.

It was Alyssa who found what they were looking for. Bashir heard a dull *thud* and a stifled oath behind him. He whirled and flicked on the light, to see his young companion holding her head and looking as if she wanted to hit somebody.

He looked up, and there it was—the bottom rung of a ladder protruding from a hole in the ceiling. The hole was somewhat over a meter wide. When Bashir shone his light up into it, he saw that it ended a few meters up, at a round metal door.

Bashir reached over to Alyssa. "Are you all right?" He saw no blood, and she didn't seem to be dazed, but that didn't mean the blow had done no damage.

Alyssa nodded. "I'm fine, just a bump."

"Good." Her words, though whispered, were clear and concise. Bashir relaxed and returned his attention to the business at hand. "I'm going up there. I'll let you know if everything's clear."

He reached up, grasped the lowest rung, and pulled himself up without waiting for offers of help. To his surprise, he found it no strain at all. *I really must be recovered from the fire*, he thought with a smile no one could see.

When he was all the way up, standing with his feet on the second rung from the bottom, his head nearly touched the round door at the top. He felt around for a latch. There it was.

He listened intently, but heard nothing on the other side of the door. No light crept through around its edges. Slowly, he began to pull on the latch, twisting it clockwise. It moved a fraction of a centimeter and stopped.

They wouldn't lock this, would they?

He tried turning the latch counterclockwise. After some initial resistance, it gave. It felt as if the mechanism was rusted, but it kept moving, roughly, through nearly a full turn. The latch stopped moving and Bashir pushed against the door.

Carefully, scarcely breathing, he opened the lid on his access tube.

Fresh air sifted in around the door's edges, but no light or sound. He opened the door farther and stepped up another rung on the ladder. Now he could look out over the edge of the opening. There was nothing to see.

It was as dark as the tunnel below. He climbed up so that his shoulders were out of the opening. He held the door open with one hand, pulled his light out of a jacket pocket with the other.

Bashir was in a room the size of a large closet. It was empty, and a thin layer of dust covered the floor. In one wall was an opening covered by a tattered piece of woven fabric.

He lowered the metal door so that it rested on the floor, then climbed out of the access shaft. With his light off, he pulled the cloth door hanging aside and peered out. Again, nothing. The air was clean compared to the tunnel below, but it was still dusty and stale.

A brief flick of the light showed him a long corridor, perpendicular to the drainage tunnel below, with many doors along both sides. Some of the doors were simple squares of cloth, others solid wood. At either end, there was a flight of stairs going up.

He returned to the access shaft. "Alyssa. Bulbulian."

A pair of voices answered as one. "Yes?"

"Come on up. There's nobody up here." That was what he'd hoped for, of course. But he hadn't been prepared for the place to seem so empty, so deserted. Bashir had expected to have to dodge guards and priests and servants on his way through the temple.

Don't question your luck, Bashir. Accept it. The thought was a reasonable one, but it couldn't banish a mild feeling of unease.

— 29 —

A warm light wind blew into the mouth of Cradoger's Ravine. It wasn't strong enough to carry much dirt and dust with it, but it was strong enough to whisper softly over the ground and whistle softer still through a crevice far up in the rock wall to M'Briti's left.

The wind was strong enough to make the stars above waver and twinkle as their light was jostled by busy air molecules, and strong enough to make the dry sunmiser bushes around her wave their spiny branches ever so slightly.

M'Briti shivered, despite the warmth. The wind was just strong enough to cover the sounds someone might make trying to sneak up on her.

She knew that her anxiety was at least in part due to her body's craving for Purple. That did not comfort her.

If Purple withdrawal was affecting her feelings about the situation, perhaps her judgment and reactions would be affected as well. And if something unexpected came up and she needed to act quickly, what were her chances of making a mistake?

The edges of her vision were blurred, foggy. Had someone just made a sudden move across the ravine, or was it a branch nudged by the wind? Was it a Purple-spawned shadow?

"Stop it, for Founders' sakes!" she hissed at herself. She had to get her imagination under control. She hadn't gone to all the trouble to set this up just to let her own nerves ruin everything.

According to her wristchron, it was five minutes to midnight. Soon she would know whether her message had gotten through, whether Sandor had passed it on to someone who could pass it on to someone who could answer her questions.

She was sitting on a flat rock about fifteen meters in from the mouth of the ravine, behind a pair of waist-high boulders, closer to the north side of the ravine than to the south.

Darrin was in his niche in the south wall, another ten meters behind her. Where she sat, the ravine was perhaps twenty meters wide.

A stand of sunmiser bushes grew around and behind the two boulders, giving M'Briti some additional cover.

Behind her, in the upper reaches of the ravine, the trip-wire filaments were all in place. Before her, the field of view was cleared of significant obstacles. Beside her, the stunner Darrin had taken from Home's agent was set at moderate range and dispersion. At twenty meters, it would stop a person cold. Closer, it might permanently burn out some neural circuits.

Darrin had signaled that he was ready. M'Briti was as ready as she was ever likely to be. It was midnight.

A minute passed, then another. The sunmiser branches around M'Briti rasped against one another. Their dry rattling was sinister, conspiratorial. She glanced behind her. No one was there, despite the chill finger that had touched her neck.

Damned Purple, she thought with a mental snarl.

She turned back to watch the ravine's mouth, and the finger ran down her spine. Someone was out there, standing well within the range of visibility. M'Briti wondered how anyone could have gotten so close so quickly without making more noise.

The figure wore a hooded jacket and wide pants that were of a material light enough to billow in the wind. The jacket's hood was pulled up and hung over far enough to hide the person's face.

"M'Briti Ubu!" The newcomer's voice was loud enough to carry to where M'Briti hid and, she was certain, to where Darrin hid farther up the ravine. It was a woman's voice, sharp and commanding.

"M'Briti Ubu!" the woman called again, and began walking into the ravine.

M'Briti let her get a few steps inside the ravine, too far for her to escape the ravine before M'Briti could stun her. Then she responded.

"Stop. Don't move," she ordered. She stayed low, looking at the woman through the gap between the two concealing boulders.

The woman stopped and moved her head back and forth slowly, finally stopping in a position that had her facing M'Briti's shelter. "We need to talk," the woman said, seemingly directly to M'Briti.

"I know. Remember, I sent for you," M'Briti replied.

"It's a little awkward, shouting at each other from this far apart, isn't it?" The woman's voice sounded confident, as if she were in control. It also sounded like a voice M'Briti had heard before, though not often and not recently.

The woman was tall and seemed rather thin, but her clothes made such a judgment difficult.

M'Briti needed to know more before she could choose the best course of action. "How do I know you're a person I can deal with?" she asked.

The woman took a step closer. "If we could discuss this in a more reasonable way . . ."

"Pretend that I'm extremely nervous," M'Briti said quickly. "And that I have a gun pointed at you. If I were to shoot, the discussion could become a lot more awkward."

The woman spread her hands. In her right ear, M'Briti heard a single sharp tone. She smiled thinly. So someone was coming in the back way. That would be for Darrin to deal with.

The woman was speaking. "How could I be here now, looking for you, if I weren't in a position to make certain, ah, assurances?"

Plausible, M'Briti admitted to herself. *But I need more.* Aloud, she asked, "What else can you tell me?"

"That's a two-way street," the woman said with a laugh. "How can I be sure you're M'Briti Ubu?" Again, that sense of familiarity and of control. Whoever the woman was, M'Briti realized, she was not a person to take lightly.

Slowly, keeping her stunner leveled on the woman, M'Briti rose from her hiding place. The woman's challenge could be a trick to get M'Briti to reveal her location, so the woman's confederate could shoot her from behind. *Keep your eyes open, Darrin, and don't be squeamish about shooting first.*

In the dark, M'Briti could still not see the woman's face, but the hood bobbed once as if the woman were nodding. "Very well, it's you. As far as my proof is concerned, let me tell you the junkies you've hooked over the last year. That's not something I'd know if I were just another dealer, is it?"

M'Briti shook her head. "No, I imagine that would take higher level connections, unless you'd just been following me all that time."

The woman laughed. "That would hardly be a productive use of my time, would it? Here are the names." She recited without pause a list of fifteen names, the last of which was Sanders.

M'Briti blinked. The names were all correct. And each one, as she'd heard it, had brought a person along with it, a person she'd seen and talked to and whittled away at, until that person had asked if they could try Purple, and would she know where they could get some?

"Oh, by the way. Number seven, Farouk Nguyen, passed away last week." The woman said it casually, pleasantly, as if she were mentioning a weather forecast or a new place to eat. "It seems he stepped off the top of one of the reztowers. Sixty-five stories, I believe." She laughed again, lightly. "Made quite an impression on the sidewalk below."

Founders' damn! That's how M'Taba... M'Briti swallowed. Her throat felt very dry.

"But not to worry," the woman continued. "There are always more to take up the slack, aren't there? Weaklings who can't face life without a crutch, who aren't even satisfied with the Glow. We'll never want for customers as long as Home turns out such an abundance of dependent fools."

She enjoys this. M'Briti struggled to get her feelings under control. Suggestions of shadowy movement surrounded her, just at the edges of her vision. *Has Darrin spotted our interloper yet?* She wanted to look behind and up to where Darrin was, she hoped, still keeping watch.

Sixty-five stories. She shuddered. *That's how M'Taba died.*

The woman was saying something. M'Briti forced herself to concentrate. "What was that?" She hoped she didn't sound as confused as she felt.

"I asked where we go from here. Don't you think you can put your gun away?"

M'Briti looked down at the stunner. It was heavy, shiny, efficient. It didn't fade in and out, it didn't taunt her. It made a comforting weight in her hand.

"No!" The word came out louder than she'd wanted it to. "You know who I am. We can't possibly deal until I know who you are."

Again the woman laughed, this time with nothing but mockery. "Oh, my dear, dear girl. So you want to know who I am?"

Girl? M'Briti thought it hardly a fitting term for someone sixty years old. *Surely she knows I'm Wellborn.* She didn't seem like a person to be deceived by appearances.

"I don't think it would be such a good idea to tell you."

Snap. The sound of a stunner firing behind M'Briti made her jump. She heard another *snap* and a man's brief groan, then something heavy tumbling down a small slope. The woman stiffened but otherwise did not move.

"Darrin?" M'Briti risked a quick glance back and up to where he had been stationed.

"I'm fine. Watch her!"

M'Briti whirled around to see a movement that might have been the woman leaping into the cover of some rocks, several meters from where she'd been standing.

"She's over to the left, behind that pile of rocks," he called down to her.

M'Briti crouched down and looked toward where she'd seen the movement. She kept her head low, peering around the corner of her sheltering rocks at nearly ground level.

Sssst! She heard the thin hissing sound and a loud *crack!* almost simultaneously. The top of the rock she'd been standing behind exploded, showering her with small sharp fragments.

She heard Darrin fire two or three shots at the woman as he scrambled out of his hiding place. The woman fired at him once. Bits of rock flew off the ravine wall near where he'd been. That was no stunner the woman had. It was a full-powered energy pistol!

M'Briti wormed her way backward, away from the two rocks she'd been using as cover. As she inched her way slowly beneath and through the sunmiser bushes, she made no more noise than the wind was already making. She hoped.

Energy pistols were strictly military weapons. Not even Home's domestic security agents used them. M'Briti wondered how on Seelzar a drug dealer could have gotten hold of one.

"That wouldn't be Darrin Montoya, would it?" The woman's voice echoed within the ravine. It was hard to tell where she was. M'Briti had not seen or heard any movement since the initial flurry. "If you were going to turn him over to me, dear, you should have disarmed him first."

Two more shots blew away pieces of M'Briti's initial hiding place.

M'Briti slipped behind a larger group of rocks, closer to the ravine wall. Darrin fired again, and the woman returned the favor. M'Briti could just make out a faint trail, here and gone in an eyeblink, of ionized molecules along the path the woman's shot had taken. She seemed to have moved forward from her original position.

"Executor Senyan's going to be disappointed when his two little agents don't report back to him," the woman called out. She fired two more shots at where M'Briti had been and another in Darrin's direction.

M'Briti saw some movement and fired toward it, but the woman was behind new cover before M'Briti's shots could reach her.

She's Wellborn. The realization chilled M'Briti. This woman was moving too quickly to be anything else. Again the sense of familiarity prodded at her mind. *I have heard her before.*

M'Briti fired a few shots into the jumble of stones behind which the woman had disappeared. Wellborn or not, she had to show herself to fire her own weapon, and if either of the stunners hit her, the fight would be over. M'Briti ducked. There was a loud *crack* and bits of rock flew up from her left.

They were two to her one, and the stunners didn't leave a trail, so the woman would have a more difficult time spotting them when they fired. *Right,* M'Briti told herself. *But that isn't slowing her down. And her shots pack a lot more punch than ours do.*

She heard some stealthy noises farther back in the ravine toward the opposite wall. Someone fumbling around, shifting something slightly.

"Forget it, Montoya. I didn't give Sandor a blaster." Two quick hissing shots followed the taunt.

Poor Sandor, M'Briti thought. *Still without the right weapon.* She wondered how this woman could possibly have known about Darrin's connection to Senyan. From what Darrin had told her, only a very few trusted security people knew Darrin was involved in security work of any sort, and no one but Darrin and Senyan had known exactly what he would be working on.

"For what it's worth, dear, you had me fooled." The woman's voice came from close to the middle of the ravine. "I really thought your brother's death had messed you up. And I actually bought that stupid crime you tried to pull."

Darrin snapped a couple of shots. The woman continued after a pause.

"The Wellborn in general aren't nearly as special as they think they are, but sometimes one of them surprises me."

Why does she talk like that? M'Briti wondered. *I'm sure she's Wellborn too.* M'Briti slipped along to her right, closer to the ravine's mouth. Their best chance lay in keeping the woman between them. She adjusted her stunner to wider dispersion.

"Senyan's more typical, however. It's too bad he got you mixed up in one of his petty little schemes. Founders' folly, but my Purple epidemic is eating away at that man!" There was a bark of spiteful laughter. M'Briti raised herself just above her new cover and fired three times in the direction the laugh had come from.

At that same instant, the woman rose, firing at Darrin and starting to move to a new location. Two of M'Briti's shots caught her and she flopped down behind a thicket of bushes.

It could be a trick, M'Briti warned herself. She stayed under cover, waiting to see what would happen. Even with their weaker intensity, her shots should have immobilized the woman. She heard some rustling, sliding sound coming from the thicket, but it could have been the wind.

A raspy voice, gasping and strained, spoke from the darkness. "You're not going to take me. *He's* not going to."

"No, wait!" M'Briti stood up, shouting, and aimed her stunner at the voice, but it was too late. A muted hiss and a dull, sickening noise like a wet half-smothered explosion froze her for a moment. Then she was racing toward the thicket, heedless of the potential danger, ignoring the spiny branches that ripped at her.

She got there at the same time Darrin did. They stood silently, looking down at Marguerite Venebles, the person behind Purple Heaven. She was a familiar enough figure in Home. There could be no mistaking her, despite what she'd just done.

Venebles had somehow been able, even after being shot with a stunner, to bring her energy pistol to bear on herself. A gaping hole was blown in her torso.

With what must have been a truly superhuman effort, she opened her eyes and looked at M'Briti. "Always so superior, the Wellborn," she gasped. "Parents accepted it, maybe for my sake." The light began to fade from her eyes.

"I couldn't. Always be grateful, thankful. Sick of smiling and bowing." The eyes closed. The voices faded to a barely audible whisper.

"No better than the rest of us. Worse. Too dependent on the . . ." Her voice died. Her face settled into an expression that was anything but peaceful.

M'Briti stared at what remained of the Executor. Now she remembered. Of all the people who'd been involved in her case a year ago, she'd always thought that Venebles was the most sympathetic, the most understanding. How right she had been, and how wrong.

Darrin reached out, put his arm around M'Briti's shoulders. She couldn't help thinking of Darrin breaking the news to Executor Senyan. How would the man take it?

"Is anyone going to believe this?" she asked, still finding it difficult to believe herself.

Darrin breathed out a loud sigh of pent-up tension. "We'll make them." He sounded as if he meant it. "Senyan would probably be glad to pin all of this on Venebles. I don't think they got along very well."

M'Briti shivered. "She certainly hated him. But still, an Executor—"

"That won't matter. Now that we know, we should be able to find enough evidence to prove it." He gave her shoulder a comforting squeeze. "This will certainly stir Home up, coming on top of the Matrix crash, but things will get resolved and settle down again. You've done what you set out to do. The rest is just sorting out the details."

Is that all? M'Briti asked herself. She shook her head slowly, sadly. So many deaths, so much misery from one extraordinary and twisted person.

She looked down at the woman lying amid the thorny branches. Even in death the strength was somehow there. Even with the horrible wound in the tall, thin body.

Venebles had lost, but she hadn't really been defeated. M'Briti watched the wind blowing some strands of long white hair that had come out from under Venebles's hood.

"Let's go home, dear," she whispered, and Darrin nodded silently.

There were other questions still hovering around her, like the shadows in the brown fog, threatening, taunting. Was avenging M'Taba worth all of this? Was there any future for her and Darrin? Could she ever be free from Purple, or was it going to kill her anyway?

In the warm night wind, the sunmiser branches rattled dryly.

M'Briti tried to ignore the questions, and she almost succeeded.

— 30 —

The road was two lanes wide in each direction and twelve kilometers long. It ran in a laser-straight line from Home to the spaceport west of the city. Light globes hung along both sides at forty-meter intervals.

Niala kept her gravscooter down to around one hundred kilometers per hour. Speed was less important than safety. She couldn't afford not to reach the spaceport tonight.

There were few others traveling the road, in either direction. That was what Niala had hoped for and expected. Midnight was the midpoint of the night shift, so the spaceport workers would be on the job or at home, not in transit.

Niala didn't expect to go completely unseen and unnoticed. She would arouse more suspicions trying to sneak out to the spaceport and being spotted than she would traveling openly.

She grinned as the dull gray road surface sped by beneath her scooter's levpads. There was no reason for anyone to be suspicious. After all, she was in charge of Home's security, and the spaceport was where most of the security preparations were actually being carried out. What was more natural than that she go out to inspect the work firsthand?

As long as she acted as if she had nothing to hide, she'd be fine. The only person who could cause her any real problems was herself. Senyan and Venebles might be able to, but there was little chance they'd be out at the spaceport at all, let alone so late. They still had their own duties to carry out.

The warm night air pushing against her face seemed to be rubbing decades off her age, sanding away cares and worries and complications. The rust and corrosion of the past several years were sloughing off. She was being honed down to a younger self, more energetic, more confident.

It felt inexpressibly good to be doing something she knew was right.

Part of her wished the ride could go on forever, but all too soon the sign appeared: SPACEPORT—.5 KM.

There were no separate entrances for passengers, cargo, and employees. Home's space travel was nearly all for scientific or security purposes, and the volume was usually quite small. Everyone went in through the same broad gate, and everyone exited through its identical twin.

Niala slowed her gravscooter until she coasted to a stop at the gatekeeper's office. Only then, with her own motion stopped, did she feel the natural breeze coming softly from the southwest, winding its way among the massive buildings and scattered ships. It seemed to her a gentle reminder of her new resolve, her new self.

She felt the hum of an identidisc scanner, reminding her she wasn't yet on her own.

"Greetings, Executor," the gate guard said. He glanced down at the screen in front of him and nodded. "Just a formality," he said apologetically, looking up at Niala again. "You have blanket clearance to come and go out here, of course."

"Thank you," she replied.

"Anything special I can do for you?" he asked, sounding as if he wanted to prolong their conversation.

"No, thank you. I know my way around." She smiled to remove the possible sting from her reply. Before he could say anything more, she started her scooter forward again, heading for the admin building.

Admin was one of the smaller buildings at the port. It took much less space to schedule flights and coordinate cargoes and work crews than it did to construct and service the ships.

Niala stopped beside the two-story building. It was all metal and glass, and shone brightly with reflections of the port's sprawling field of lights. She paused as the door sensors read her identidisc code, then stepped forward as the thick metal door rose upward into its second-story slot.

The building was full of people being almost frantically busy. The possibility that the Interstellar Union would break down Chou or Rythmun had to be considered and acted upon. As a precaution, Niala had ordered that all operations be shifted to maximum security mode, which meant that admin was physically moving into the bunker fifty meters below ground.

Niala moved through the bustle, exchanging a few salutes and greetings along the way. Most of the people there were too harried to notice her or to pay much attention.

She ignored the crowded lift tube and took the emergency stairway to the second floor. The Port Director's large office was as yet mostly unaffected by the transfer. The Director himself was still at work, and Niala noticed an adaptapod formed into a bed in one corner. The job was at the moment an around-the-clock responsibility.

Niala knew the man slightly, and what she knew was positive. He was a tall, heavyset man who looked pleasant and responsible, and whose appearance was not deceiving.

"Executor Kirowa, good to see you." He stood and, when she reached his desk, shook her hand. "To what do we owe the pleasure of your visit?"

Niala had known the question would be on his mind. Even during the emergency, she didn't have to come to the port to carry out her responsibilities. She had been able for the past several days to issue orders through the commnet, and had gotten progress reports the same way.

Niala smiled politely, then allowed the smile to disappear. "Business, I'm afraid. I need to go up to Yakimu Base to check on their preparations." She tried to sound as if it were a burden, but only a slight one.

"You know how it is—sometimes you have to be there in person to get things done right." She glanced pointedly at his adaptapod bed.

He nodded, at once agreeing with her statement and extending his sympathy. "That's true enough. Please, have a seat and tell me what you need."

She sat opposite him and reflected fleetingly on the advantage of authority, of having people do what you requested or ordered, eager to please. It was an advantage she was planning to forfeit tonight, and the Port Director would help her, in all sincerity and innocence.

"What do I need? Well, let's see what you have on line." Even before she'd experienced the advantages of authority, Niala had discovered that it is sometimes better to know the answers before you ask the questions. This was such a time. So now, knowing the answers, she asked the questions confidently.

Was there a ship being readied for Yakimu Base? The Director said there was. What class ship was it? Long-range scout. Its mission? Reassignment to Yakimu Base for the duration of the emergency. Would it be fully supplied, equipped, armed, and fueled at Home's spaceport? Yes. How soon would it be leaving? Within the hour.

The Director was cooperative, telling Niala everything she already knew. It didn't seem to occur to him to question why she hadn't found all this out before coming to the port in person.

Advantages of authority, she reminded herself.

The arrangements were made quickly. Niala would take the ship up in forty minutes. The assigned pilot and copilot would go up to the base on the next available cargo ship. Niala could return from the base whenever she completed her inspection.

"Thank you, Director. You've been most helpful." She stood and headed for the door. At the door, she paused and turned back to him, a slightly embarrassed smile on her face. "I have to admit, it'll feel good to be up in one of those things again, if only for a little while."

The Director nodded. "I know how you feel. If it weren't for all my other responsibilities, I'd take one up myself. It must be worse for you."

"At times," she agreed. "At times."

The ship was a good one, improved in nearly every way from the one she'd used in the Union twenty years before. It was faster, better armed, had a more effective detection-beam dissipator, and the navigation computer was both more sophisticated and easier to program.

Niala settled into the pilot's seat and ran her hands and eyes over the controls. She could operate the ship by voice, by manual controls, and by eye-scan integration helmet. The latter was best for quick-response situations such as close-in fighting and tight maneuvering.

Niala didn't like to use the helmet because it tended to make her lose track of the distinction between ship and self. Once that was gone, it took with it the awareness of limitations. She'd seen enough pilots try for turns they couldn't make. She didn't want to end up like them.

After a brief exchange of pleasantries with the control tower, and pro forma permission to lift off, she was on her way. The drive unit fired, and there was a momentary sensation of motion, quickly compensated for.

The lift-off brought back memories. That part hadn't changed. The ship she used to fly had had that same fleeting delay, when for just an instant she could feel the power of the ship's drive battling the gravity of the planet. Then the gravity generator would kick in, and the sensation of thrust would disappear.

So it was now, in this new ship. But that brief sensation of struggling forces had changed her, nudged her further along the road she'd set out upon. She was less than ever Executor Kirowa.

The ship rose with increasing speed until it burst Seelzar's bonds and shot up into the dark night. The spaceport shrank away, along with Home. They dwindled to lighted dots and then to nothing on the black night side of the planet.

The assigned crew had already set the navigation computer for Yakimu Base, and Niala let that order stand as the ship rose higher and higher.

Soon she was above the atmosphere, then in the higher orbit that would let her swing out on her jump to Seelzar's small moon. Only then, when she was effectively out of the spaceport's control, did she cancel the computer's orders and tap in a new set.

Her ship started to move out in the widening spiral that would take it to Yakimu. The moon swung into view, above and ahead. It came closer, and soon it was time to maneuver her ship into orbit around the small white moon. The moment came, and went.

Instead of slowing into moon orbit, Niala's ship accelerated, putting Yakimu and Seelzar farther behind. She ignored the red light that started flashing on her communication board.

She didn't bother to watch for pursuit ships. Instead, she fastened herself in and punched yet another command into the ship's navigation computer.

For a timeless instant she felt twisted and stretched in impossible directions. It was an instant during which down and up, left and right, front and back had no meaning. Inside and outside were indistinguishable from each other. She was at once a part of the ship and a billion kilometers away.

The disorientation passed as quickly as it had come. Niala's ship had slipped into hyperspace.

It was just conceivable that Home could track the ship, but without the Matrix to help, that was a long shot. More likely, Senyan and Venebles would guess what she'd done. That didn't matter. The important thing was that they couldn't catch her or stop her now.

She was on her way.

Though it had been over twenty years, she had still remembered the coordinates. A check with the navigation computer confirmed what she already knew. Her next stop was Drinan Four.

She had all the weapons and all the supplies she would need. She knew the Union quite well and was reasonably familiar with Drinan Four. Rythmun's and Chou's reports had kept her up-to-date on developments there, in Drinan City and Brinktown.

Her job was simple and straightforward. All she had to do was land on Drinan Four without being detected, rescue Chou and Rythmun, and leave again without being traced. That was all.

Niala leaned back in the pilot's chair and grinned up at her image in the silvered-over viewscreen on the ceiling. She could have cleared the screen, but h-space images never made any sense to her. Far better, far more satisfying, to check out her new self, so unlike the Executor, so much more like the off-planet agent of twenty years ago.

Let Senyan and Venebles take care of things on Seelzar. They could manage without her. Chou and Rythmun needed her more. They were fellow agents. She wouldn't let them down.

— 31 —

"Stay close together," Bashir had said. "Make no noise," he'd added. The advice struck Alyssa as being very sound. As in the city streets, Bashir led the way, Bulbulian came next, and Alyssa brought up the rear.

They had removed their cloaks in the closetlike entryway leading to the drainage channel. They had also taken care to wipe off their boots so they would leave no obvious tracks in the temple.

Alyssa carried the stunner in her right hand, prepared to fire at the slightest provocation. She had it set on wide dispersion. The setting was strong enough to knock out any Normal at the distances the building was likely to allow, and she didn't have to aim carefully to hit her target.

They walked along the main ground-floor corridor, seeing no sign of life. Bashir kept his light on but adjusted down so that it was just sufficient to keep them from bumping into things.

Not that there was anything to bump into. All Alyssa could see was a long empty corridor with several doorways on each side of it. Unless her sense of directions had become completely unreliable, the corridor ran from one side of the temple to the other, rather than front to back. As far as she could tell, it stretched the entire width of the building, and there seemed to be no cross-corridor intersecting it.

A bizarre setup, she thought. *Especially for the ground floor.*

Bashir and Bulbulian had explained that the altar room was on the second floor. The public approach to it was up a wide stairway from the temple's entrance. Two anterooms, one after the other, separated the altar room from the top of the stairway. The rooms had large, metal-bound wooden doors that were probably closed except when services were being held.

Her companions had both thought that the altar room had to have at least one other entrance, hidden from the public. Alyssa was in no position to argue. She hoped they were right.

The trio reached the far right end of the corridor. There, a flight of stone stairs led up and around in a tight spiral. The corridor's other end had seemed to be the same, from what they could tell with their small light. The right end had just been a few meters closer.

Bashir started up the stairs, carefully, one step at a time. Bulbulian followed, staying to the inside curve.

Alyssa stayed a few steps behind, but took the outside of the spiral curve, to give her a clearer field of fire if anyone should come upon them from above or below. It also made her more vulnerable, she realized, but that was unavoidable. Besides, there shouldn't be anything or anyone in the temple that the three of them couldn't handle. After all, she and Bashir were both Wellborn, and Bulbulian was considerably more capable than most Normals.

Alyssa went up the stairs sideways, with her back to the outer wall of the stairwell. She held the stunner away from her body, so she could move it freely. She kept it aimed slightly ahead and up. Her left hand trailed against the stones of the wall. The stones were cool and dry.

She had to keep fighting an urge to look back down the stairwell, to see if someone or something was coming up after her.

The only sound was the occasional barely audible scrape of boot on stairs as the three advanced. The temple was so silent, its air so stale, that it could have been abandoned for a thousand years for all the life that could be felt in it.

Alyssa scarcely breathed, afraid to create a disturbance, however small.

When Bashir had explained what he planned to do, less than a day earlier, Alyssa had wondered at first about his state of mind. It seemed highly unlikely that the Drath ceremonial Scepter in Ebel had anything at all to do with the Wells. To claim that it was a Builder artifact that could turn the Wells on and off was crazy.

That had been Alyssa's initial reaction. But she'd known Bashir for a long time. All her life, in fact. He didn't seem crazy. He didn't act or sound as if he were in any way impaired.

He described the images he'd absorbed from the Matrix's Forbidden Files, and he described the temple and altar and Scepter in Ebel, so thoroughly and in such detail, that Alyssa had to give him the benefit of the doubt. It could be. He might be right. And if he were right, bringing the Scepter back to Home might well be enough to reinstate Darrin.

How much worth would the Assembly and Executors put on a Builder artifact that could be the key to the Wells, an alien rod that could reactivate the Dead Wells? Surely one Transgressor wouldn't be too much to ask.

In their small camp in the hills outside the city, the idea had been difficult to accept. It had seemed unreal in the clear air under the open skies of Seelzar. Alyssa had agreed, but largely because Bashir had seemed so intent on going anyway, with or without her.

Now, in the unnaturally still temple, Alyssa found it easier to believe in Builder artifacts with strange powers.

Something in the atmosphere of the place made such speculations seem more reasonable, opened the mind to odd possibilities. The stones beneath her hand were more than stone. They hummed with repressed energy, waiting to be released and directed.

Alyssa's foot caught the edge of a step and she nearly fell. Only an instinctive twist of her body and a lucky reach with her other leg saved her.

Pay attention, idiot! she berated herself. Bashir needed her. Whether or not he was right, he needed her. And he deserved every bit of help she could give him.

And so it went, step by agonizing step. It seemed to Alyssa that they had walked farther than a single story.

Just nerves. She wondered, but she couldn't afford to give the question too much attention. The wavering dim shadows from Bashir's muted light didn't help matters any.

At last they reached the top. A small landing a few meters square faced a door of sheenwood bound in iron. There was no lock, merely a thick wooden bar dropped into two U-shaped metal brackets mounted on the wall at either side of the door.

Bashir turned off his light and the darkness became complete. Alyssa could see nothing at all.

The three stood on the landing for a while, letting their eyes adjust to the darkness, but there was still nothing to see. No light seeped around the edges of the door, no dim glow shone up the stairwell.

The silence was nearly as complete as the darkness. The only sounds were the faintest whisperings of air that Bashir, Bulbulian, and herself made as they breathed. She doubted that a Normal could have heard even that much. The sounds were near the limits of her own Wellborn senses.

"All right," Bashir whispered. Alyssa gave a small involuntary jerk at the unexpected noise. Her grip on the stunner tightened. "I'm going to remove the bar from the door. Don't move until I say to."

She heard him step closer to the door, then a slight scraping noise as he lifted the bar. A cautious step and a quiet *bump* told her he'd set the bar on the floor against the wall.

"Now I'm going to ease the door open. Let's hope the hinges are oiled."

Yes, let's, Alyssa thought fervently.

Bashir added, "Alyssa, you should have the stunner ready, just in case. Don't worry about hitting me and Qatar."

"Right." The word came out a hoarse, hushed croak. Alyssa tried to remember how long it had been since she'd spoken in her normal voice. She raised the weapon, pointing it at where she knew the door must be. Bashir needn't have reminded her about the gun. Her fingers were wrapped tightly around its grip.

She felt steady, but tense. Anything unexpected, any movement seen or heard, was likely to get shot at. She could apologize later if it turned out to be a mistake. Failing to fire when she should was a mistake that would be much harder to overcome.

She heard Bashir step up to the door and then she heard the soft rasp of his fingers sliding along the door, searching for the handle.

A sharp, very small *creak* announced his first tug, then a metallic rubbing sound, light and steady, told her that the door was swinging slowly open on its hinges.

Though she had not thought it possible, her grip on the stunner became even tighter. She imagined any number of unpleasant surprises waiting on the other side of the door, but she could see nothing. The darkness was total. If anything were lying in wait for them, it waited without light and made not a sound.

Bashir pulled the door open as slowly as he could. Except for an initial squeal, the hinges were as quiet as he'd hoped, and quieter than he'd expected them to be.

From what he could remember of the temple's arrangement, they had to be close to the altar room, since it occupied a good portion of the second story and part of the third. It seemed that the stairway had taken them somewhat higher than floor level for the second story, but the door he was opening had to be the way to go.

Bashir was vaguely worried. There had been absolutely no signs of life so far in the temple. There'd been no near escapes from wandering priests, no dodging from servants on nightly rounds. He'd heard and seen no evidence that anyone else was in the building. That was too much of a good thing.

The bundle strapped to his back was not heavy, but it was beginning to make itself felt, exerting more pressure with every step he took, with each moment he spent in the temple.

All in your head, old man, he told himself sternly. *Just stick to the business at hand.*

The door continued to swing open with little resistance. Bashir knew where the door's opening was, but he could see nothing to indicate its presence. The darkness was complete all around him, unrelieved by areas of light or of greater darkness.

When he'd opened the door all the way, he whispered to his companions, "I'm stepping into the doorway. Don't follow until I give you the word."

Bashir put one foot cautiously in front of the other, shifted his weight, repeated the process. Arms in front, moving slowly to feel for odd obstructions, he moved into the gap of the doorway.

He noticed a change, then, or a difference. The air was a little less stuffy than in the stairwell, and there was the slightest suggestion of movement to it.

Bashir stood just on the other side of the doorway, trying to get some impression of the area around and in front of him. There was a feeling of space, some quality of openness impossible to define. Perhaps in the stairwell he'd heard echoes he wasn't aware of, returning quickly, and now they were delayed or absent. Perhaps it was the fresher scent of the air, suggesting more open areas.

The barely noticeable air movement seemed to come from ahead and to his right. That would be toward the front of the temple. If this were the altar room, that's what he would expect, some fresh air slipping in through the sets of doors in front, wandering through the temple and funneling down the stairwell.

The next temple services are in two days, Bashir reminded himself. *You could just stand here until then, so you'd know for sure.*

His lips curved in a smile of self-derision, and he pulled the light from his jacket pocket. Aiming it down and in front of himself, he nudged the light's switch enough to turn it on, very dimly.

He saw a short flight of stone steps a few meters in front of where he stood. They rose to a walkway with an ornamental stone railing along it. Beyond, there was darkness.

He moved slowly to the steps, listening for sounds of any sort. He heard nothing. He walked up the steps and shone his light across the walkway. The beam was largely swallowed up by the space beyond, but Bashir could make out enough to realize that he'd found the altar room.

A stealthy sound came from behind him, a furtive step, the rustle of cloth on cloth. Bashir whirled and turned the light on bright, using it as a weapon to temporarily blind whoever it was.

"Bashir, it is I! Turn the light down." Bulbulian somehow managed to put an urgent appeal in his voice while still speaking quietly.

"Sorry." Bashir dimmed the light. "But I did tell you to wait."

"I know." Bulbulian was blinking his eyes.

"But we could see it was safe," Alyssa added, "and you were wandering too far away." She sounded cross, as if she were scolding him. "We didn't want to be left behind."

Bashir nodded. Alyssa was right. He had briefly forgotten them, and their need to be involved. And now, so close to the end, he couldn't afford such lapses. They would all share the same fate, the same success or failure, and they would all have to share the responsibility.

"We've found it," he told the others. He gestured with his light. "This walkway nearly circles the room. Recognize it, Qatar?"

"Yes," Bulbulian replied. "It's about three meters above the floor."

"Uh-huh, with the front doors to our right, and the altar to our left." Bashir pictured the room in his mind, as he had last seen it during a Drath ceremony.

The altar itself was a huge block of fleckstone, covered with intricate carvings similar to the ones on the city's gates. During the ceremony, the walls were lined with lighted oil lamps, filling the room with a warm yellowish orange glow.

Almost as if he were there again, Bashir could see the fleckstone of the altar sparkling brilliantly with reflected lamplight. Atop the altar was the Scepter of the Hierarch.

Supported by two carved fleckstone stands, it, too, glittered and gleamed, but with a greenish tint.

Bashir had always thought that it was simply reflecting the lamplight, like the fleckstone, but now he thought otherwise.

"I remember a flight of steps coming down from the walkway directly behind the altar. This way, quickly." Alyssa and Bulbulian joined him on the walkway and they headed left.

It's a Builder artifact, Bashir thought, moving as quickly as he could without making more noise.

The Hierarch's Scepter was what he'd seen Z'areikh carrying and Eldrath explaining in the Matrix's Forbidden Files and in his dreams. It was, he was sure, a key to the Wells, and Eldrath had taken it with her over a thousand years ago, when she'd left Home with her followers.

Since then, the Draths had forgotten what they had. It held only symbolic significance for them now.

They might not even miss it, Bashir reassured himself, *if it's replacement is similar enough.*

They reached the steps leading down to the altar. Beyond the small circle covered by Bashir's electric light, the altar was a dim shape within the darkness. He could not see the Scepter on top of it, nor even the green scintillations he'd expected.

Was it not here after all? A sinking feeling settled inside him. They didn't have time to search the entire temple, no matter how few people were in it.

Bashir raised the power in his light so that its circle of illumination touched the altar.

Atop the altar was a heavy black cloth. The center of the cloth was raised, as if it were covering a thin object somewhat less than a meter long.

Relief replaced Bashir's anxiety.

"There it is," he whispered.

The fleckstone altar sparkled brightly, even in the dim light, but no light could penetrate the Scepter's covering.

Bashir had to force himself to walk slowly down the stairs. He had to remind himself not to celebrate success before the fact. With trembling hands, he removed the leather satchel he had strapped to his back. He set the satchel down next to the altar and untied its top. From it he pulled out a cloth-wrapped bundle, thin and somewhat less than one meter long.

"Keep an eye out," he cautioned Bulbulian and Alyssa. "We're not out of here yet."

He unwrapped the cloth bundle. Within the folds of soft Torian wool lay a replica of the Hierarch's Scepter. He and Bulbulian had added touches to the one he'd purchased to make it look more like the real thing.

It was mostly black, with a rough texture. Scattered around its surface were thin smooth veins of dark green, with green and silver glitter set into them. It was as close as they could come to the actual Scepter, as they remembered it.

Bashir smiled as he lifted the false scepter. They might have spared themselves the trouble. If the Draths kept the Scepter covered except during ceremonies, their switch wouldn't be noticed for nearly two days anyway.

Oh, well, he thought, *better too good a job than one not good enough.*

Bashir set the replica on an edge of the altar not covered by the black cloth. Slowly, he pulled the cloth back and reached for the real Scepter. He paused momentarily before touching it, remembering again the terrible power it had unleashed in his dream.

Then his fingers wrapped around it and he lifted it from its two small stands. He set the replica in its place and rearranged the black cloth, all the while clutching the real Scepter tightly in one hand.

He bent to set the Scepter on the wool wrap that had carried its counterpart. A frown slowly etched itself into his face. Something was wrong. The Scepter didn't feel like he'd expected it to. There was no sense of reined-in energies, or power waiting to be unleashed.

The Scepter felt absolutely unextraordinary, no different from the replica he'd brought along. Worse, it looked even more ordinary than the replica. There was no green scintillation from within the Scepter. There weren't even any sparkling reflections from its surface. It was dull, unrelieved black, very unlike the blinding Scepter of his dreams or the glittering Scepter that he remembered from his last visit to the temple.

Bashir's frown deepened. Was the Scepter he now had a replica as well? Did the Draths only bring out the real one for ceremonies? If so, why keep a replica on the altar, covered to protect it?

"Bashir!" Alyssa's voice was hushed but urgent.

He turned to look at her. "Yes?"

"I think someone's coming." She pointed toward the side where they'd entered the altar room, where the door was now hidden by the raised walkway.

Bashir heard something that could have been many people walking up the stairs quietly. It could also have been a peculiar echo of the breeze coming through the front doors and speeding up as it passed down the stairwell.

"We'd better head for the other doorway," he said, hurriedly wrapping up the Drath Scepter. "We can probably break down that door if we have to." His doubts about the Scepter were suddenly his second priority. Avoiding detection and capture were tied for number one.

He packed the Scepter into his leather satchel, flung it over his shoulder, and started up the steps to the walkway. He dimmed his electric light again, on the off chance that they wouldn't be noticed. Bulbulian and Alyssa followed close on his heels.

Bashir glanced back and saw a faint light coming through the door they'd entered by. It flickered and had a yellowish orange cast to it, like torches or oil lamps.

He began to jog toward the other door, the one presumably still barred. It looked as if they were going to lose the benefit of secrecy, but they could at least still escape.

Just then the door they were heading for opened, and several people stepped through it, carrying torches. Before Bashir could react, he heard the *snap* of Alyssa's stunner and the figures all collapsed, their torches falling haphazardly around them.

A shout went up from the direction of the other door.

Bashir glanced back to see a small crowd heading their way. "Run for it!" he yelled, all thoughts of caution gone.

He turned, but before he could take a step, two things happened. His light went out with a sizzle and a faint *pop*, and a voice, clear and sharp, cut through the air with the force of an energy beam.

"Stop!" It was a woman's voice and held a power beyond mere volume.

The woman was standing in the doorway he'd been headed for. She was illuminated in part by the torches lying on the floor and in part by something else.

She wore a long, hooded robe, the hood pulled back to reveal her face. Her arms were crossed, her hands concealed beneath her robe.

The flickering torchlight shining up from the floor cast confusing shadows, but still her features were clear, and seemed to glow with a greenish phosphorescence.

Bashir's eyes narrowed as he studied her. *Who did she—*

He heard a sharp *crack* behind him. He turned to see Alyssa holding her right hand protectively in her left. Her stunner lay on the walkway, its casing split and glowing a dull red.

Far behind her, the Draths who'd been coming through the other door had all stopped and were kneeling, heads bowed.

"Your weapons will not work here," the woman declared, and began coming toward them. She pulled her left hand out of her robe and raised her arm high above her. "The Scepter protects us." In her hand was the Drath Scepter, glowing and flashing with green veins on black.

"It is the Hierarch," Bulbulian said, his voice a mixture of surprise and awe.

"More than that, Qatar," Bashir replied as the woman came nearer. His chest felt constricted. A chill breeze seemed to touch his skin. Her features were so clear and so distinctive, he couldn't be mistaken.

"That's the Goddess herself." The Scepter spread a green glow all around the woman. Bashir had seen her in the Matrix, in his dreams, and in the Archives' image files.

"That's Victoria Knebel Eldrath."

The woman stopped within a few meters of Bashir. She lowered the Scepter, holding it across her body in both hands.

Bashir could feel the Glow from it suffusing his body, strengthening him, sharpening his senses and his mind. His tension began to ease.

Eldrath stared intently at him for a time, a puzzled frown on her face. When she spoke, she sounded less commanding than she had at first, and more uncertain. She drew in her breath sharply.

"Achmar? Achmar Z'areikh? Is it really you?"

What? Bashir barely kept from speaking out loud. She thought he was Z'areikh, one of the Founders? His mind could barely conceive of the possibility.

"Why have you come, after so long a time?" Her voice was softer, more intimate.

Do I really look that much like him? He strained to remember Z'areikh's features and had to admit that there was more than a passing resemblance. Had the two been allies, friends, lovers? What was the best approach for him to take?

He glanced beyond Eldrath and noticed that the torches on the floor seemed to be flickering in slow motion. Had the Scepter's Glow speeded him up that much?

"Why don't you say something?" A note of impatience had crept into her voice.

"I, uh, I know it's been a long time, Victoria." *Think fast, Bashir!* "And I've wanted to come sooner, but my duties have kept me tied to Home."

She nodded. "And now?" Her expression was unreadable.

"Now," Bashir said, trying to sound just a little desperate but not at all afraid, "I need your advice and your help, Victoria. Home needs you and I need you." Bashir held his breath, not daring to think he could pull off this impersonation for more than a few minutes.

"You need me?" Eldrath's mouth curved in a slight smile. "That is good to hear. Come." She reached out her hand to him. "Let us find some rooms for you and your friends to rest up in. Then we can talk."

Her smile widened and she gave his arm a squeeze as she turned toward the door she'd come through only a few minutes before. Her fingers felt as if they could crush his arm if she willed them to.

Bashir turned his head to glance at Alyssa and Bulbulian. Both looked as startled as he felt, but both were responding quickly, no doubt benefiting from the Scepter's Glow as he had.

"It is so good of you to come, Achmar, even if it has taken you far too long." Eldrath was smiling, and her voice was pleasant and friendly, but Bashir returned her smile with difficulty. He looked into her eyes and saw something not quite human in them, something not quite sane.

It was going to be a challenge indeed to get out of this alive, let alone with the Scepter.